I0549600

The Surprise Party

THE
SURPRISE
PARTY

ROWEN CHAMBERS

JOFFE BOOKS

Revised edition 2025
Joffe Books, London
www.joffebooks.com

First published as *She Didn't Fall* in the United States
of America in 2023

© Rowen Chambers 2023, 2025

This book is a work of fiction. Names, characters, businesses, organizations, places and events are either the product of the author's imagination or are used fictitiously. Any resemblance to actual persons, living or dead, events or locales is entirely coincidental. The spelling used is American English except where fidelity to the author's rendering of accent or dialect supersedes this. The right of Rowen Chambers to be identified as author of this work has been asserted in accordance with the Copyright, Designs and Patents Act 1988.

No part of this book may be used or reproduced in any manner for the purpose of training artificial intelligence technologies or systems. In accordance with Article 4(3) of the Digital Single Market Directive 2019/790, Joffe Books expressly reserves this work from the text and data mining exception.

Cover art by Nebojša Zorić

ISBN: 978-1-80573-156-6

PROLOGUE

"Oh, honey, this house is absolutely beautiful!" Alexis says to her husband, Mark, as she gazes at the open living area just off the foyer.

"What kind of wood is this?" Mark asks, pointing to the floors.

"Walnut," I tell him. "It's extremely durable. Perfect for families. It can easily stand up to the wear and tear of children and pets."

I always tailor my answers to the buyer. Mark is very practical. I could immediately see the concern on his face when he saw the shiny wood floors, worried they wouldn't hold up to his three young boys and two dogs.

"Mark, look at this fireplace!" Alexis gushes, racing over to it. "Imagine us all here on Christmas Eve, sitting in front of the fire, singing carols."

"That'll never happen," Mark mutters.

"Honey, come over here," Alexis says, sounding annoyed with her husband. He's not nearly as enthusiastic as she is in the home-buying process.

"The stonework was done by hand," I say as Mark and I join Alexis. "They used fieldstone collected in the area."

"It's absolutely gorgeous," Alexis says.

Mark looks around the empty room. "How big did you say this place was?"

"Just over four thousand square feet," I say. "And the lot is almost an acre. It's rare to find a yard that big with new construction."

"The kids will love it," Alexis says to Mark.

"Will?" His brows rise. "Honey, we're just looking. We haven't decided anything."

"I know, but doesn't it seem perfect? The location? The size? And it's new, so you don't have to worry about things breaking down."

"We've only seen one room," Mark says. "It's too soon to be making a decision."

"Let me show you the kitchen," I say, leading them down the short hallway to the back of the house.

"Oh, Mark, it's just what I wanted!" Alexis says, her eyes growing wide as she walks around the room. "Double ovens. An oversized refrigerator. This massive island." She runs her hand over it. "I can already see the kids sitting here doing their homework while I make dinner."

"When has that ever happened?" Mark says.

She shoots him an irritated look. "It would, if we had an island like this."

He rolls his eyes, but Alexis doesn't notice, her gaze moving to the window that looks out at the backyard.

"The yard is perfect for three little boys," I say. "They can be out there running around while you keep an eye on them from the kitchen. And the yard's fully fenced, so the dogs can be out there too."

Mark walks up behind his wife and looks out the window. "It *is* a good size. But that's a lot of lawn to mow."

"You can hire that out," I tell him, knowing he can easily afford it after just making partner at one of the top law firms in Greenwich. "Let me show you the upstairs."

2

We go upstairs and I show them the luxurious master suite that includes a sitting area with a fireplace, his and hers walk-in closets, and a bathroom with a deep soaking tub.

"It's like my own private spa!" Alexis squeals, racing over to the tub. She turns and her eyes land on the shower. "Mark, look at this shower! It's huge and has multiple shower heads."

"Yeah, it's nice," Mark says, not sounding at all impressed by the shower. "Let's go see the rest of the house."

The three remaining upstairs bedrooms are large, but basic. There's not much to see, so after a quick look, we return downstairs. I show them the dining room, the additional bedroom, the laundry area, and the three-car garage, then return to the kitchen.

Alexis walks up to Mark. "I really love this house."

He sighs. "It's over our budget."

"Not that much over. And our budget never made sense given what we wanted. This house has everything we were hoping for."

"We wanted a house in a neighborhood. There's nothing out here but woods."

"It won't be that way for long," I say. "The developer will begin preparing the other lots in the coming weeks. A year from now, this street will look much different. You'll have the neighborhood feel you're looking for."

"That's wonderful!" Alexis says.

"You won't be saying that when we're having to listen to construction noise for a year," Mark gripes.

Even though they can easily afford the house, Mark doesn't want to pay more for it than the number he had in his head. He's looking for flaws that'll convince his wife it's not the right house for them. I've seen this played out so many times, I can predict what comes next. After twenty years in real estate, you start to see patterns in people. It only takes a few minutes of meeting someone and I've got them figured out. It's why I'm such a good agent.

"What about the basement?" Mark asks me. "Can we see it?"

"Yes, of course." I clear my throat, my smile still there but harder to maintain at his mention of the basement. "Right this way." I walk them over to the door that's just off the kitchen, my heart racing as I turn the handle. As I open the door, I notice my hand is shaking. "Go ahead and have a look. I'll be in the kitchen. I just need to check on something."

Mark and Alexis go down to the basement. After what happened, I can't make myself go down there. Whenever I show the house and someone asks about the basement, I have them go by themselves.

A few minutes later, Mark and Alexis return to the kitchen.

I look up from my phone and smile at them. "Well? What do you think?"

"The house is absolutely gorgeous," Alexis says, her face beaming. She has that look, the one that says she's completely fallen in love with the house.

"It's more than we wanted to spend," Mark says to me. "I think we need to keep looking."

"Mark, no," Alexis says, her eyes pleading with him to reconsider. "We've looked at so many houses and none of them were as perfect as this one. Stop thinking about the money. Our home is a place where we'll make wonderful memories for our children. You can't put a price on that."

Not all memories are wonderful, especially the ones in this house.

"It wouldn't hurt to look at some others," Mark says in a last attempt to change his wife's mind.

"I don't need to keep looking. This is the house. I just know it. It has everything we could ever want."

Mark lets out a heavy sigh and looks over at me. "I guess we found our house."

"Wonderful!" I smile at them. "I know it's a tad over your budget, but this house seemed so perfect for your family, I just had to show it to you."

4

"You were right," Alexis says. "It's perfect for us. Absolutely perfect!"

I knew she'd want it the moment she saw it. And I knew Mark would give in and buy it for her. I'm an excellent agent. I know my buyers. I know what they want. And I know just what to say to persuade them to buy a house, even one that exceeds their budget.

Sales is about creating a story, a fantasy, that draws the buyer in and lets them imagine how much better their life would be if only they had whatever you're selling. In terms of houses, you focus on the good. The benefits they'll receive. The memories they'll create.

You leave out the bad stuff. Like the fact that just a few weeks ago, in this beautiful new home, there was a dead body in the basement.

CHAPTER 1

Two Months Earlier

"I can't thank you enough for doing all this," I say to Valerie as we stand in the kitchen, sipping our champagne. I've probably had a whole bottle by now. People keep refilling my glass, and given what this champagne costs, I'd be silly to turn it down.

"It wasn't just me," Valerie says, leaning against the granite-topped island as we gaze out the kitchen window at the guests scattered around the backyard. "Marcus did most of the planning. I just helped with the guest list and decorations."

"I'm still shocked you were able to hide this from me." I sip my champagne.

"It would've been harder if we'd had it at your house. Having it here, I could take my time setting everything up." She nudges me. "But you almost ruined it when you said you were going to stop by here last week."

"You know I can't go a whole week without checking on one of my projects. Contractors are notorious for not following through on what they say they'll do." I glance at her, smiling. "You really had me fooled. I couldn't figure out why you kept offering to come check on this place for me until Adam surprised me with that last-minute trip."

"Which was his idea, by the way." She sips her champagne. "You're lucky to have a husband who's still crazy about you after all these years."

I reach behind me to the tray of appetizers and pick up a stuffed mushroom, popping it in my mouth so I don't accidentally tell Valerie the truth about my marriage. I've had a lot to drink and my inhibitions are down. I need to sober up so I don't say something I shouldn't.

"So how was the trip?" Valerie turns to me and my eyes go to her champagne flute, noticing the way her fingers elegantly hold the stem, just the tips of them touching it. I glance at my own glass and notice my hand wrapped around it. Even after all these years, I sometimes slip into old behaviors, remnants of the old me. It tends to happen when I've been drinking a lot.

Hoping Valerie doesn't notice, I adjust my hold on the glass to match hers, then smile and say, "The trip was wonderful. Adam booked a hotel that overlooked Central Park, then after dinner, he surprised me with a carriage ride."

"How romantic," she gushes. "What about dinner? Where did he take you?"

"Really, Valerie?" I stare at her, waiting for her to fess up.

"What?" she asks, feigning innocence. "You're not suggesting—"

"I know you helped him. There's no way Adam would do that on his own. He's terrible at planning things, especially a trip to a city he doesn't know well."

"Okay, you caught me," she says with a shrug. "But in his defense, he asked for my help, which just shows how much he loves you and wants to make you happy. Most men don't bother even trying to please their wives, especially after being married as long as you two have."

Adam's surprise trip to New York wasn't done to please me. Or perhaps it was, but only in the hopes it would get him what he wanted. The real reason he took me there was to revive our physical relationship.

Fortunately for him, it worked, but it wasn't what I wanted. I gave in because I felt I had to, as part of my "wifely duties" as my mother called it when she spoke to me about sex the day before I got married. She assumed Adam and I hadn't done it yet, despite dating all through high school. Did she really think we dated for three years and didn't have sex? Adam and I were at it all the time. We'd even sneak out of school during lunch and do it under the bleachers. We couldn't get enough of each other.

Now I dread being intimate with him, which is why it only happens once a month, at the most. It's not that I don't love Adam. I'm just no longer excited by him. I'm aroused by a man with ambition and drive, and unfortunately, that's not Adam. Getting him to move up in his career has been like pulling teeth. He's fought me every step of the way, saying he'd be happy working in a garage the rest of his life, fixing cars like his father did.

But I didn't work this hard for this long to be married to a grease monkey. If I wanted that life, I would've stayed in Pittsburgh, bought a house in the run-down neighborhood where I grew up, and copied the life my parents have, where every day is a struggle.

Adam would've been fine with that, but not me. I wanted more for my life, and since Adam married me, I assumed he wanted that too. He did at first, or he pretended to, but as my success grew, he reverted back to the old Adam, saying he wanted a simpler life. Recently, he's even suggested moving back to Pittsburgh. If that's really what he wants, he'll have to go without me. There's no way I'm moving back there.

"There you are," Adam says, coming into the kitchen, a bottle of beer in his hand. I wish he'd drink wine, but he refuses, saying it gives him a headache. He won't drink champagne either so when he gave my birthday toast a few minutes ago, I had to clink my glass with his beer bottle. This was in front of all my guests, people I'm trying to impress. It was horribly embarrassing, but I plastered on a smile and quickly moved on with a short speech about how appreciative I was to have so many people show up to celebrate with me.

"We were just talking about you," Valerie says to Adam as he comes up beside me.

"I hope it was good." He puts his arm around my waist and I feel him staring at me, waiting for a kiss.

"Of course it was good." I look up at him long enough for him to give me a quick peck on the lips, then I take a long sip of my champagne.

"I had to fess up," Valerie says to Adam. "About your trip."

"I thought you already knew." He tugs on my waist, bringing me closer to him. "You didn't think I did all that on my own? You know how much I suck at planning shit."

That's another thing he does that I find to be a turnoff. Cursing in front of people. This is a very wealthy and exclusive area of Connecticut. The people around here don't curse in public. It's crude and not socially acceptable. I told Adam that when we moved here from Pennsylvania, and yet, more than twenty years later, he's still doing it.

"I'm glad you're not upset," Valerie says to Adam as she refills her glass of champagne. "I know you wanted to keep it a secret, but Blaire knows you far too well. She could tell I was lying."

I turn to Adam, my lips forming a tight smile. "What other secrets are you hiding?"

"That was it." He swigs his beer. "You know me, babe. I'm an open book."

Why must he call me babe? He knows I despise it. It was fine in high school, but we're adults now, and around here, men don't call their spouses babe. It's either honey or sweetheart or men will just use their wife's name.

"I'll let you two lovebirds be alone," Valerie says.

"Val, no," I say. "You don't have to go."

But she's already heading back outside, leaving me alone with Adam.

I should want that. I should want a moment alone with my husband. Just the two of us having a private moment while the party goes on outside. So why don't I? Why do I dread being alone with the man I claim to love?

CHAPTER 2

Adam sets his beer down and steps in front of me, his arms circling my waist. "You look really hot in that dress."

"Thank you," I say, noticing the desire in his eyes. I hope it doesn't mean what I think it does. We just had sex two days ago. I don't owe him that for at least another month. I might even stretch it to two.

"Everyone's outside," he says, leaning down to kiss my neck. "We could go upstairs. Have a little fun."

"Adam, no. We're not leaving the party." I push him away and walk past him to the window, looking out at my guests, a mix of friends, neighbors, and co-workers. Valerie also invited a few of my clients, the ones who've given me repeat business and numerous referrals. Over the years, I've made more than a million in commissions with these particular clients, enough to pay for my house, a large two-story brick colonial with a pool in the back, situated on a corner lot in a very desirable neighborhood.

"It was just an idea," Adam says, sounding offended. "It's your birthday, the one day you should be able to loosen up."

I turn to him. "And by that you mean I should spend it pleasing you physically?" I shake my head. "I swear, Adam, that's all you ever think about. It's all about you. And *your* needs."

"It's about our marriage. You used to want me all the time. Now you don't even want to kiss me, and I'm getting really fucking tired of it."

"Watch your language," I say in a hushed tone. "This is not the time to talk about this." I return to the island where I left my champagne and gulp down what remains of it.

"When's the right time?" Adam asks, coming up beside me. "All you do is work. You're almost never home, and when you are, you're on your phone or your laptop."

"And because of that, we have a great life. A beautiful home."

"Yeah, and that's all because of you," he says, sarcastically. "I've just been sitting around doing nothing."

"I didn't say that."

"You didn't have to." He shakes his head. "Just forget it, Blaire. I don't know why I even bother trying to talk to you. You never listen." He walks away, then turns back. "I'm not going to keep living this way. You either make some changes or this isn't going to end well."

"What's that supposed to mean?"

Instead of answering me, he leaves out the sliding glass door to the patio.

I pick up the bottle of champagne and refill my glass. I shouldn't keep drinking, but I need to after that little spat with Adam. I'm so tired of him constantly demanding more of me and more of my time. Even if I gave in, what does he think we would do? We have different interests, different goals. It's sad to admit this, but I feel like Adam and I have outgrown each other.

"Mom, I'm leaving," Caitlyn says, flying past the kitchen so fast all I see is a flash of her red dress and her long, dark hair flowing behind her.

"Caitlyn, wait!" I chase after her, catching her just before she reaches the front door. "Where do you think you're going?"

"To my friend's house. He's picking me up." She opens the door.

I grab the door from her and slam it shut. "You are not leaving. It's my birthday and we're in the middle of a party."

"Yeah, with all old people." She folds her arms tightly over her chest. "I don't want to be here."

"Too bad. You're not leaving on my birthday, especially with some boy." I glance down at the tight red dress she's wearing that barely covers her. "Where did you get that?"

She shrugs. "I bought it with my allowance."

"The money I give you is for school supplies or going out to eat with your friends. It is not for dresses that make you look like a—" I stop before saying something I shouldn't.

"A hooker?" she snaps. "Is that what you were going to say? Real nice, Mom. I can't wait to tell people at school that my own mother called me a prostitute."

"I didn't say that." I take a breath, trying to remain calm. "But I will say that the dress you're wearing is not appropriate for someone your age."

"I'm fifteen!" She throws her hands up. "I'm practically an adult!"

"You're not an adult, and you are not leaving my party and going out with some boy. You know the rule. No dating until you're sixteen."

"That's not fair!" she says, raising her voice. "You and Dad dated when you were fifteen."

"That's different. Your father and I had been friends for years, and we ended up getting married." I put my hands on my hips. "Are you planning to marry this boy who's picking you up?"

"No." She scrunches up her face. "I'm never getting married. All married people do is fight."

She thinks that because of Adam and me. We didn't use to fight, or when we did, we'd hide it from Caitlyn. But for the past year or so, our fights have become more frequent and

13

we've been arguing in front of her. I feel bad about that. I know it causes her stress to see her parents fight.

"He's here," Caitlyn says as a car honks in the driveway. "I have to go."

"Caitlyn, you are not leaving. Text the boy and tell him you can't go out tonight."

"Are you serious?" She points to the driveway. "He's here. Waiting for me. I can't just tell him to leave."

"You can. And you will. Or I'll go out there and do it myself."

She narrows her eyes at me. "You can't do this. You can't make me stay here."

"I'm not changing my mind. This isn't just any birthday. It's my fortieth. It's a big deal. And I want my daughter here to celebrate with me."

"No, you don't," she spits out. "You're gonna go back outside with your rich, snobby friends and ignore me. You want to keep me hostage here because you hate me and don't want me having a life!"

"Honey, don't be like this," I say, putting my hand on her shoulder. "You know I love you. Let's go back to the party."

"I'm not going to your stupid party!" She yanks away from me. "I hate you!"

She storms off, nearly knocking over Marcus on her way to the stairs.

Marcus watches her, then turns back to me. "I remember that stage. The teenage years were a nightmare."

"Yes. They're not fun."

Marcus is in his fifties and has twin girls who are twenty-five. One of them works in finance and is engaged to be married to a lawyer who comes from a very wealthy and influential family. His other daughter is in graduate school, getting her PhD. They're both smart and successful and have very bright futures. I can't say the same for my own daughter. Caitlyn is smart, but her grades are poor because she doesn't want to put effort into her schoolwork. I blame Adam for that, telling her she should be having fun in her teen years instead of planning for her future.

Marcus walks over to me. "Don't take it personally. My girls used to fight like that with their mother. They eventually grew out of it."

"I don't know if Caitlyn will. I think she really does hate me."

Opening the door, I see a guy in a black Porsche backing out of the driveway. He looks old enough to be in college. Where did Caitlyn meet him? I hope it wasn't online. Adam and I keep warning her about the dangers of meeting people in online chat rooms.

I sigh as I shut the door. "I think I need more champagne."

Marcus smiles. "You're in luck. We have plenty. And it's the good stuff."

"Thank you again for throwing me this party. You certainly didn't have to."

"You deserve it. You work hard, Blaire. Harder than anyone I know."

It's the best compliment he could give me. Marcus is one of the few people who acknowledges how hard I work and praises me for it. But I suppose that makes sense since he profits off all the work I put in.

Marcus is my broker at the Rockingham Group, the real estate agency where I've worked for the past twenty years. He's technically my boss, but knowing him all these years, I see him more like a friend. He gave me a job when I was just twenty years old, when nobody else would hire me because they thought I was too young. I'd passed the real estate exam and was eager to start my career, so when Marcus said he'd hire me if I brought in two listings in a month, I happily accepted the challenge, not realizing that was a lot, especially for a new agent.

But I did it. In that first month, I acquired two listings and also sold a house listed by someone else. It was a cheap house, so the commission wasn't much, but it was enough that Adam and I could finally pay our rent on time and have money left over for groceries.

After that successful month, Marcus officially hired me. The Rockingham Group, based in Manhattan, was known for buying and selling very high-end, multimillion-dollar properties. The office I work at is in Greenwich, Connecticut, which is close enough to Manhattan that a lot of people live here but work in the city. Some don't work at all, having enough money to spend their days in more leisurely pursuits, like golfing or enjoying long lunches at the country club.

Living here, I'm surrounded by wealth, which is why I moved here and why I wanted to work at the Rockingham Group. If you want to make money, you need to surround yourself with people who have it. I wanted to be one of those people and I was determined to make that happen.

When I started at the Rockingham Group, Adam and I had been married for two years, and I was tired of living in a dilapidated apartment and driving a rusty car that was always breaking down. So I studied the market and went to every social event in town that would connect me with the right people. Wealthy, well-connected people who would help pave my way to success. It paid off, and I'm now one of the top-selling real estate agents in the area.

"You should go back out to the party," Marcus says. "Everyone's waiting for you to cut the cake."

"It looks wonderful. Thank you for getting it. And for letting us use the house for the party."

The house we're in is one of my listings. It's new construction and isn't yet finished. The house itself is done, but the basement is delayed. The workers haven't even started on it.

"The builder owes me," Marcus says. "He promised me this place would be ready to sell a month ago and now he's saying he needs three more months."

"Three? He told me two."

"He's just throwing out numbers. I'm guessing three is more accurate."

16

The house is going to be priced at three million. I'll get a substantial commission from the sale, which is why Marcus and I keep pressuring the builder to finish it. A house like this will sell quickly. It's rare to find new construction around here and the property is absolutely gorgeous and on nearly an acre lot. There's a large patio out back, complete with an outdoor kitchen, making the house perfect for entertaining.

"What are you two doing in here?" Valerie says, smiling as she comes toward us. "Having a secret meeting without me?"

Valerie is also a real estate agent. Marcus hired her a few months before hiring me. She was twenty-two and had just graduated from college with a business degree. She didn't need a degree to sell real estate, but her parents, who are wealthy and very concerned about appearances, insisted their daughter go to college.

"Marcus was trying to console me," I say, "after hearing Caitlyn tell me she hates me."

"I'm sure she didn't mean it," Valerie says. "You know how teenagers are, always creating drama. She'll get over it." Valerie loops her arm around mine. "C'mon, Birthday Girl. Your guests are waiting."

When Valerie and I met, we were both working long hours, trying to learn the business. We didn't have time for other friends, so we became friends with each other. It's nice to have someone who understands real estate and how it consumes your life. Adam doesn't get it. Most people don't. They assume you can just work whenever you want. They don't realize that our clients demand a lot from us, calling all hours of the day and night, expecting us to be there for them the moment they need us. Like just last week, I had a woman call me at midnight to say her soon-to-be ex-husband was staying at the house they'd put up for sale, even though they both agreed to vacate it. It was an issue for the police or her attorney, but instead she called me. I calmed her down, then advised her to call her lawyer in the morning. I felt more like

17

her therapist than her real estate agent, which just shows how many roles I'm forced to play just to sell a house.

Marcus, Valerie, and I go back to the patio to where the cake is set up. It's a gorgeous cake with three tiers covered in dark chocolate ganache. Thick stripes of light pink frosting are piped along the perimeter and the top is coated with pink and silver sprinkles. It's from a very expensive bakery and probably cost close to a thousand dollars. I'm a little surprised Marcus would get me such an expensive cake after already picking up the tab for the caterers, but I know he can afford it. The business I bring in alone has made him a very wealthy man, not that he needs the money. His wife, Lydia, is from one of the richest families in the area.

Marcus gets everyone's attention and makes a short speech before I cut into the cake. It's simply a symbolic gesture, then the caterers take over, making neat, even slices. I'm given a slice with a candle on top, and as I blow it out, Marcus leads everyone in singing "Happy Birthday."

I put on a smile and pretend to be happy. The day started out well. I woke up feeling hopeful about starting a new decade. After a quick stop at the office, I went for a massage, met a friend for a leisurely lunch, and held a showing in the afternoon that I'm certain will lead to a sale. Around four, Marcus called and asked me to stop by here at the house to check if any work had begun on the basement.

When I drove up to the house, people were gathered outside, waiting to surprise me. I was completely shocked. I assumed Adam and Caitlyn would take me to dinner and that'd be it. A simple birthday dinner and then we'd go home. So I was thrilled to find out I was having a party. I don't usually make a fuss about my birthday, but turning forty is a milestone, one that deserves to be recognized.

But now, three hours later, I just want it to be over. That fight with Adam put me in a bad mood, which only got worse when my daughter told me she hates me.

So much for a happy birthday.

CHAPTER 3

"Blaire," Alice says, stopping me as I walk by. "This cake is amazing."

"I'm glad you're enjoying it." I force out a smile as I watch her shove cake in her mouth. "It was so nice of you to come."

I'm lying. Alice is the absolute last person I'd want at my party. We've been cordial to each other since becoming neighbors two years ago, but it's all fake. I've never liked her, and her feelings for me go beyond dislike. The woman hates me. She hates that I'm ambitious and successful and won't leave the house without looking my absolute best.

Alice spends her days lounging on the couch, watching soap operas and eating delivered meals. She has no ambition. No desire to do anything with her life. She comes from money and lives off a very large inheritance from her parents. It's why Rob married her. He won't admit that, of course, but everyone knows it's true. Rob is a celebrity in the fitness world, known for his online diet and workout programs. He also owns several gyms. He's forty-one but has a better body than most twenty-year-olds. And yet he's married to a woman ten years older than him who's at least two hundred pounds overweight and whose only exercise is walking from the couch to the kitchen.

"How's it feel being forty?" Alice asks in a snide tone, loving that today marks my entry into a new decade.

"It feels great!" I say. "In fact, I feel better now than when I was younger."

"If that's what you need to tell yourself," she says, her mouth full of cake. "You might change your mind in a few years. Just wait until menopause hits." She stuffs more cake into her mouth. "Hot flashes. Night sweats. Weight gain. And that nice skin of yours will get all blotchy and dry." She shrugs. "There's nothing you can do. It's just part of being a woman."

"I'm not worried about it," I say, looking around for someone to talk to, an excuse to get away from her.

"You should be." Her gaze moves up and down my body. "You won't be skinny for much longer."

Alice is always making comments like that. She does it with everyone, mostly other women. She's always spreading gossip about women in the neighborhood, making catty comments about their looks or how they act. I can only imagine the things she's said about me. I'm sure she thinks I'm a terrible wife and mother for working all the time. And because I keep myself fit and trim, she assumes I'm obsessed with my appearance. Just last week, she saw me leaving for a run when she was out getting the mail and said, "Hoping to fit into an even smaller bikini?"

She winked as she said it, as if she was joking, but it wasn't a joke. I caught her looking at me in my bikini last week when I was sunbathing by the pool. Her lips were pursed, and she was eyeing me with disapproval and probably a good dose of hate. She's a very unhappy person. In a way, I feel sorry for her. She has all that money and yet she's miserable.

Rob, Alice's husband, walks up to us, holding a bottle of sparkling water. "Happy birthday." He smiles at me.

"Thank you," I say, trying to ignore the way my heart sped up when I saw him. "I was just telling Alice how nice it was for you two to come. It's a bit of a drive."

"Only a half hour," Rob says. "Not bad."

"It was worth it for the food," Alice says, licking frosting off her fork. "Who did the catering?"

"I'm not sure. Marcus did the arrangements. You'd have to ask him."

Alice turns to Rob, shoving a forkful of cake in front of his face. "You have to try this. It's amazing."

"I don't want it. You know I don't eat sugar."

"One bite won't hurt you. Come on." She puts the fork closer to his mouth.

"No." He pushes the fork away. "I don't want it."

She frowns, looking ashamed and insulted.

"More for you," I say in a cheery tone, hoping to lighten the mood. I may not like Alice, but I don't want her feeling bad for enjoying some cake.

I honestly can't believe these two have stayed married for so long. They have nothing in common, and Rob, with his perfect physique, is disgusted by Alice's body, which seems to get bigger every year.

"You're right," Alice says to me, her smile back and even bigger than before. "I'm going to get another piece."

"Of course. Go ahead." I step aside as she waddles past me to the cake table.

"She's going to eat herself to death," Rob says, watching her.

"Maybe she should see someone. A therapist. Sometimes overeating is caused by emotional pain."

"She already tried it. It didn't help." His gaze goes from his wife to me, a slight smile sliding up his handsome face. "You look gorgeous. I love the dress."

"Rob," I mutter under my breath. "Stop it."

"What? I can't say you look nice?" He glances at the people around us having their own conversations, seemingly unaware of us, and yet I feel like everyone's watching us.

"We shouldn't even be talking," I say in a hushed tone as I search the crowd for Adam. I don't see him. Maybe he went inside.

"We're neighbors. It'd look odd if we didn't talk."

"Okay, fine. We've talked. And now we're done." I turn to leave and feel him grasp my arm, then his warm breath by my ear.

"Stop fighting this and let yourself be happy," he whispers.

I pull my arm from his grasp and turn to him, smiling. "Thanks again for coming. I should go mingle with the other guests."

"What's the big secret?" Adam says, coming up behind me.

"What do you mean?" I ask innocently.

"I saw Rob whispering something to you." Adam laughs, looking from me to Rob and back again. It's an uncomfortable laugh. "Anything I should know?"

"I was telling Blaire what I'm thinking of getting Alice for her birthday," Rob says. "You know how it is, trying to figure out the perfect gift for your wife. It seems like no matter what we do, we always get it wrong. I needed a woman's opinion, so I asked Blaire."

I turn to Adam, hoping my smile looks real and not forced. "He's getting her diamond earrings. I told him you can never go wrong with diamonds."

Adam glances at Rob, then back at me again. "It's good you helped him out."

"I should go find Alice," Rob says. "We need to head home soon. I've got an early morning."

"Thanks again for coming," I say.

Adam watches as Rob leaves. "Why is Rob here?"

"Because he's our neighbor."

"Yeah, but we're not exactly friends with him. And you can't stand his wife."

"I never said that."

"You didn't have to. I can tell whenever you're around her that you hate her. Is it because of how she looks?"

"No! Of course not." I look back and see Alice helping herself to more appetizers. Rob isn't with her. He said they were leaving, but I don't know where he went. "And I don't hate her. I just have nothing in common with her."

"I can't believe he stays with her," Adam says, glancing at Alice at the buffet table. "I mean, shit, the guy's got zero body fat and makes a living selling diet programs and his wife keeps gaining weight."

"Looks aren't everything. I'm sure they have other things in common."

They don't, but I'm not telling Adam that. I want him to think their marriage is strong.

"I bet he cheats," Adam says. "There's no way a guy who looks like that isn't fooling around on his wife."

My pulse races and I feel my face getting hot. "We shouldn't gossip about the neighbors." I wrap my arm around Adam's. "Let's go get a drink."

"Are you sure? You've had a lot to drink tonight. You're going to have a headache later."

"I'm not going to worry about that. It's my birthday. I should be able to have all the champagne I want."

And I desperately need a drink after having Adam catch Rob whispering in my ear. What the hell was Rob thinking, doing that in front of everyone? Luckily, Adam didn't suspect anything and bought that lie about the earrings.

As Adam and I walk to the bar, he stops suddenly and kisses me. It's not a quick peck on the lips but a deep kiss that should be done in private, not at a party with people staring at us. I try to pull away, but he puts his hand on the back of my head, keeping me locked in the kiss until finally, he lets me go.

"Happy birthday." He smiles at me, then looks to the right of us.

Following his gaze, I see Rob standing just a few feet away. Did Adam know he was there? Was that why he kissed me? To show Rob that I'm his? But that would mean Adam knows what I did with Rob.

That's not possible. How could he know? It was only one time and Rob and I were alone. There's no chance anyone saw us.

I'm not even sure it happened. I'm taking Rob's word that it did. I remember us kissing, but the act itself was a blur. I'd had far too much to drink and don't remember much past the kiss.

"Okay, I'm ready," Alice says, going up to Rob. She notices him looking at Adam and me and grabs Rob's hand, dragging him over to us. "Thanks again for the invite," she says to me, even though I had nothing to do with the guest list. "The food was absolutely wonderful." She looks at Rob. "I got the catering company's business card. Maybe we could hire them for my birthday next month."

"Of course." He smiles at her. "Whatever you'd like."

"Enjoy the rest of your party," Alice says. She winks at me. "And welcome to your forties!"

They walk off as Adam and I continue to the bar.

"Maybe I was wrong," Adam says.

"About what?"

"Maybe *she's* the one who hates *you*." He laughs a little. "That comment she made about your age? She was trying to make you feel like shit for being old."

"First of all, I'm not old." We stop at the bar. "And as for Alice, that's just how she is. She's a very unhappy woman." I turn to the bartender. "Champagne, please."

He pours me a glass and hands it to me.

"Same as last time," Adam says. The bartender hands him a bottle of beer.

"We're lucky to have such nice weather," I say, noticing the warm breeze as we step away from the bar. "You never know what you'll get this time of year. Remember last September? We were wearing winter coats."

"Yeah, I guess," Adam says, before gulping down his beer.

I sip my champagne. "Marcus did a wonderful job planning all this. Valerie said she offered to help, but he insisted on doing it all himself."

"He really likes you," Adam says, almost like he thinks there's something going on with Marcus and me. He couldn't be further from the truth.

"He's definitely been good to me over the years," I say. "Oh! I caught Caitlyn trying to sneak off with a boy. I stopped her before she left, and now she's mad at me. She ran upstairs. She's probably in one of the bedrooms, talking on the phone to him."

"Who's the boy? Do we know him?"

"I've never seen him before. He looked older — too old to be with our daughter." I glance up at the house. "I should go talk to her. I hope she's still in there and didn't try to sneak off again." I gulp down the rest of my champagne and hand Adam the glass. "Wish me luck."

"Good luck," he says as I leave.

Adam doesn't offer to go with me or to talk to Caitlyn himself. He says he doesn't understand teenage girls. As soon as Caitlyn turned thirteen and started becoming rebellious and moody, Adam stepped back from his parenting duties. Sometimes I think he's scared of her. Not scared as in she'd physically harm him, but scared of her rapidly changing moods and over-the-top emotions. I assure him it's just her hormones and that she'll grow out of it, but he'd rather just avoid her until this phase of her life has passed.

That's Adam. Avoiding the hard stuff and leaving me to deal with it. It's another reason my attraction to him has waned over the years.

"Caitlyn," I call out as I go into the house. She doesn't answer, but I didn't expect her to. She'll make me search for her until I find her. "Caitlyn, please come out to the party," I say as I go up the stairs. "You should at least try the cake. You'd love it."

I search all the bedrooms, but can't find her. Going back to the main level, I look in every room and find they're all empty. She better not have left with that boy. If she did, she'll be grounded for a month and I'll cut off her allowance.

"Caitlyn?" I call out, but again, there's no answer.

The only other place she could be is the basement, but I can't imagine her going down there. It's cold and dark and littered with construction equipment left by the workers who keep saying they'll show up to work but then don't.

I open the door to the basement and turn the light on. It's just a lightbulb in the ceiling for now until the actual lights are installed.

"Caitlyn!" I call out. "Are you down there?"

I hear footsteps behind me, and just as I'm about to turn around, someone shoves me. Hard. I fall forward, tumbling down the stairs. It happens so fast I can't stop myself. My body lands with a thud on the concrete floor, my head banging against it.

The light above me goes out, leaving the basement dark except for the light coming from upstairs. My vision is blurred, but I can see the outline of someone standing at the top of the stairs.

"Help!" I yell, but it comes out more like a whisper.

I try to breathe through the intense pain coursing through my body. My head is throbbing, and I feel blood running down my face.

"Help!" I say, louder this time. "Please, help me!"

The shadowy figure at the top of the stairs slowly closes the door, leaving me in complete darkness.

"No! Wait!" I cry out. I try to sit up, but feel like I'm going to pass out. I collapse back down onto the cold concrete floor.

The pain in my head becomes more intense, a splitting pain shooting through my skull.

"Please," I whisper. "Someone help."

But nobody can hear me. Everyone's outside at the party. Everyone except whoever did this to me. The person who shoved me, watched me fall, then left me here, bleeding and in pain.

Who would do that to me? At my own party? The people here are my friends, neighbors, colleagues.

As my eyes fall shut and I feel myself losing consciousness, I wonder if this is it. If this is how my life will end. Alone in a dark basement.

Dead on my fortieth birthday.

CHAPTER 4

"Dad, I think she's up," I hear Caitlyn say.

My eyes flutter open and I see Caitlyn sitting next to me on the bed.

A hospital bed.

Why am I in the hospital?

"Mom?" Caitlyn says. "Can you hear me?"

"Yes, honey," I say, my voice weak and scratchy.

"Dad, she's up!" Caitlyn leans down and hugs me.

"Honey, be careful," Adam says, standing behind her. "The doctor said she's still healing."

"Oh, sorry." She backs away but remains seated beside me.

"It's okay." I reach for her hand. "It's my head that hurts the most." I look up at Adam. "What happened? Why am I in the hospital?"

"You don't remember?" Adam says.

I pause to think, but my mind's blank.

"Was it a car accident?" I ask, assuming that's the most likely cause.

"Caitlyn, why don't you go get a soda from the machine?" Adam takes a couple dollars from his wallet and hands them to her.

"I don't want a soda."

"Then get a snack."

"I'm not hungry."

He lets out a frustrated sigh. "Just go wait in the hall. I need to talk to your mom."

She rolls her eyes but does as he says and walks out of the room.

"What's wrong?" I ask, panicking. "Why'd you make her leave? Is it that bad? Am I dying?"

"No." He sits beside me. "I just didn't want her in here when we talked about this. I don't want her worrying more than she already is."

"Tell me what happened. Why am I here?"

"You fell down the stairs. At that house where we had your birthday party. It was the stairs that go to the basement. You landed at the bottom and hit your head on the concrete. You have a bad concussion and some pretty big bruises, but the doctor said it could've been a lot worse. You could've had serious brain damage or ended up paralyzed. Or if you'd snapped your neck you'd be—" Adam stops suddenly and holds my hand, looking down at it. "I could've lost you, babe." He blows out a breath. "I know we've had our issues, but I don't know what I would've done without you. You're my everything, Barb."

"Barb," I mutter, knowing that's not my name, or not the one I use now.

"Sorry," Adam says. "I was looking at old pictures last night. Of us in high school. Back when you went by your first name." He pauses. "You remember that, right? That you changed your name?"

"I didn't change it." I stare at the wall across from me. "I just use my middle name now."

"Yeah. That's right," Adam says, sounding hopeful. "You go by Blaire now."

Barbara was my grandmother's name. I never liked it. My middle name is Blaire, a name that's much more sophisticated and youthful than Barbara. I always wished my parents had made Blaire my first name instead of Barbara, so when I moved here, I decided to go by Blaire. That's all anyone here knows me by. It took Adam a while to get used to calling me Blaire. He hasn't called me Barb in years.

"I guess your memory isn't as bad as we thought."

I look at Adam. "What do you mean?"

"You keep waking up but can't remember what happened. The doctor said you might have some memory loss from the concussion, but he wasn't sure how far it'd go back or how long it would last."

"Were you here when I woke up before?"

"Yeah. I've been here almost the whole time since you got here. I only went home once to shower and change clothes. One of the reasons I told Caitlyn to leave is that I didn't want her asking you about something she told you earlier and having you not remember."

"She doesn't know about my memory loss?"

"She does. I talked to her about it. But it scares her, especially when you can't remember what she told you a few hours ago. She's never seen you hurt like this before. She's freaking out. I kind of am too. The doctors say you'll be fine, but I still hate seeing you here. The only time I've seen you in a hospital bed was when you had Caitlyn." He rubs my hand. "And you didn't even spend the night. You made the doctor release you." He softly smiles. "You're the strongest person I know, which makes seeing you like this so much harder."

It wasn't my strength that made me convince the doctor to release me soon after Caitlyn's birth. It was concerns about money. I knew spending the night at the hospital would increase our bill and that our insurance would stick us with most of the cost. Adam and I were still struggling back then, barely able to pay our bills. I was twenty-five and making good money as a real estate agent, but I was also spending a lot. My belief that you have to look successful to be successful drove me to buy designer clothes and a luxury car that cost far more than our earnings could cover. But it paid off. By appearing to be rich, I attracted better buyers. The kind who can pay cash for multimillion-dollar homes.

"How long have I been here?" I ask Adam.

"Three days. The doctors want to make sure you don't have any swelling of the brain before they send you home."

"And other than my head, the rest of me is fine?"

"You've got some pretty bad bruises." He holds out my arm, pushing up the sleeve of my hospital gown, showing me the dark bluish-purple marks. "It's the same on your other arm and both of your legs. Your back looks the worst. It's really beat up from hitting the stairs. The doctor has you on painkillers, but he said you'll be sore for a few weeks."

"I'm surprised I didn't break anything."

"We all are. Like I said, the doctor was shocked your injuries weren't more serious. He said a fall like that, and your head hitting the concrete floor, could have killed you, or caused enough brain damage that you'd have to be put on life support." He wipes his eyes.

"Adam, I'm fine." I squeeze his hand. "Or I will be after I've had some time to heal."

He nods. "I know. I've just never come this close to losing you, or thinking I might." His eyes rise to mine. "I think I'll feel better once you're home."

"When can I leave? Did they say?"

"Maybe tomorrow. They'll do some more tests and if all looks good, they'll let you out of here."

The door opens and Caitlyn pokes her head into the room. "Can I come in now?"

"Just give us another minute," Adam says.

She sighs and goes back out into the hall.

"Why can't she come in?" I ask.

"I want to talk about what happened. When you fell." He looks down, then back up at me. "Do you remember anything about that night? About your party?"

I take a moment to think. "No. The last thing I remember was showing a couple the house on Baker Street."

"I don't know when that was, but I could call Valerie and see if she knows. You remember Val, right?"

"Yes, of course. I feel like my memory ends more recently, like within the last few days."

"The doctor said that's normal. He said sometimes the trauma of the accident can wipe out the memory of it." Adam gets up from the bed and takes his phone out. "I'm gonna call Valerie. See if she knows when you took people to see that house."

"Put her on speaker," I say as he calls her.

"Adam," she answers in an urgent tone. "How's Blaire? Any news?"

"She just woke up. I'm here with her. You're on speaker."

"Blaire, how are you feeling?"

Adam brings the phone over to me. "I'm tired, and my head really hurts, but other than that, I'm okay."

She lets out an audible sigh of relief. "I've been worried sick. You know how many wrinkles I'm going to have from all this stress? When you're better, you owe me a Botox treatment."

I smile. "I'm sorry I worried you. I honestly don't know what happened."

"That's why we're calling," Adam says. "Blaire says the last thing she remembers is showing a house on Baker Street. Do you know when that was?"

"You've shown that house at least a dozen times, Blaire. Do you remember anything else? Anything about the people you showed it to?"

"It was a couple. The wife was a lawyer. Oh, and the owners had just dropped the price of the house."

"That happened last week," Valerie says. "It's possible that's the house you showed the day of the party. Actually, yes, it was. I remember Marcus saying you were going there that afternoon and that he'd call you after that to get you to come to the party."

"So it's just that night I can't remember," I say, looking at Adam. "The night of the party, and everything that happened after that."

Adam talks into the phone. "Thanks for your help, Val. We'll talk to you later."

"Wait! Is it okay if I stop by? I just showed a house and was heading back to the office. I'm only a few miles from the hospital."

"It's up to Blaire," Adam says, looking at me.

"Sure," I tell her. "But I may not be great company. I'm really tired."

"Why don't you wait until she's home?" Adam says to Valerie. "She needs her rest."

"Okay, but keep me updated. We all miss you, Blaire. We hope you get better soon."

"Thanks," I say as Adam ends the call.

"Oh, I should've asked her about my clients."

"Forget about work." Adam puts his phone away. "You need to focus on getting better." He sits beside me. "So going back to when this happened, you don't remember anything about it?"

"No. I don't know how it's possible. Why would I fall down the stairs? And why the basement? Why was I going down there?"

"Before it happened, you were out back, telling me Caitlyn was fighting with you about some boy. You said you were going inside to talk to her. Maybe you thought she was in the basement."

"She wouldn't go in the basement. It's not finished. It's a mess. The construction crew left all their equipment and supplies down there."

"Valerie thought maybe you were going down there to check if any more work had been done."

"I wouldn't do that during the party."

"Yeah, I didn't think so either," he says, rubbing his jaw. "Who found me?"

"I did. I hadn't seen you for almost an hour and people were leaving. They wanted to tell you goodbye, so I went looking for you. I searched the whole house, but couldn't find you. I found Caitlyn out back and asked if she'd seen you and she said she hadn't. That's when I got worried. I knew you wouldn't just leave your own party, at least not without telling me."

"You searched the house but not the basement?"

"Not at first. I didn't even think to check down there. Like you said, you wouldn't go to the basement during your party."

"But the door was open. You didn't see that and think I might be down there?"

He shakes his head. "The door wasn't open. It was shut when I came inside to look for you."

"How is that possible? There's no way I could close the door as I was falling down the stairs."

"I'm thinking the wind blew it shut. We had the slider door open and all the windows. It was a breezy night. The wind must've blown through the house and caused the door to shut."

"I suppose that's possible. What about the light? Was it on?"

"No. You must not have turned it on before you fell."

"I wouldn't have gone down there without the light on. I don't understand how this happened. How could I have fallen down the stairs?"

Adam looks away.

"What?" I sense he's holding something back. "What are you not telling me?"

He shrugs. "It's just that you had a lot to drink that night. More than you normally do."

"You're saying I fell because I was drunk?"

"Maybe." He looks back at me. "I'm not judging you. I mean, shit, I was drunk too. Most everyone there was. I'm just saying it's possible you got dizzy and fell."

"Is that what people are saying? That I fell because I was drunk?"

"Yeah," he mutters.

"Wonderful," I say, gazing up at the ceiling. "I've ruined my reputation because of some silly party. People are going to think I'm some out-of-control drunk and no one's going to hire me."

"Babe, no." Adam takes my hand. "Everyone knows you're the best in the business. Nobody gives a shit if you got drunk. We all do it. We've all gone over the limit and done shit we regret. And it was your birthday. You deserved to drink a little extra that night."

My eyes go to his and I softly smile.

"What?" He smiles back. "Why are you looking at me like that?"

"Sometimes you know just the right thing to say to make me feel better. I've always loved that about you."

"I love you too, babe." He leans down and kisses my forehead. "Should I go get our girl?"

"Yes. Please. Before I fall asleep."

As he goes out to get Caitlyn, my mind goes back to what he said about that night. Why was I going to the basement? Did I really fall because I was drunk? And how did the door close? Was it really the wind or perhaps someone saw it was open and closed it, not realizing I was down there?

I have so many questions. I wish I could remember that night.

CHAPTER 5

"Finally," Caitlyn says as she comes into my room, rolling her eyes, a habit that developed at the start of her moody teenage years. I find it annoying, but telling her that will only make her do it more.

"It was only a few minutes," Adam says to her.

"Dad, there were people bleeding out there!" she says dramatically. "It was gross."

"Go talk to your mom. We have to leave soon so your mom can rest."

Caitlyn comes over to me and sits on the bed. "Do they know when you can go home?"

I glance at Adam. "It sounds like tomorrow's a possibility."

"Really?" she says, sounding more excited than she has in years. Since becoming a teenager, nothing excites her, or she pretends it doesn't.

"We don't know for sure yet," Adam says. "They have to run some tests before they decide."

Caitlyn looks back at Adam. "Can I have some time with Mom? Alone?"

"Why?" He laughs a little. "Is there some secret you two have that I'm not allowed to know about?"

"No. I just want to talk to her alone. You got time with her. Why can't I?"

I give Adam a look to go along with it.

"Okay, fine," he says with a sigh. "I'll be out in the hall." He smiles a little. "With all the bleeding people."

Caitlyn rolls her eyes as he leaves.

"What did you want to talk about?" I ask.

She looks down and chews on her bottom lip.

"Honey, what's wrong?" I hold her hand, expecting her to pull away, but she doesn't.

"It's my fault," she mutters.

"What's your fault?"

"What happened to you."

I don't know what she means. I try once again to remember the night of the party, but my mind comes up blank.

"You went in the house to look for me." She swallows. "I'm the reason you fell."

"Caitlyn, no. This wasn't your fault. I just slipped. It was an accident."

Her eyes rise to mine. "But you never would've gone in the house if it weren't for me. We'd been fighting, and I was mad at you for not letting me leave and—"

"Caitlyn, stop." I look her in the eye. "Listen to me. This was not your fault. Whatever happened was an accident."

She pulls her hand from mine and stands up. "I should've just gone back to the party with you. If I had, this never would have happened. You wouldn't be in the hospital with your brain messed up."

"My brain is fine, or it will be. It just needs time to heal."

"Mom, you can't even remember Dad and me being here this morning. That's not normal."

"I remember," I say, thinking about what Adam said about not wanting to scare her.

"You asked Dad how long you've been here. You've already asked him that like five times. You ask him that every time you wake up."

"Yes, well, the memory loss is only temporary."

"What if it's not? What if you keep forgetting things? What if you never get better?"

"I will." I smile a little. "I promise."

She looks down, shaking her head.

"What is it, honey?"

"You always promise me stuff and it never happens."

"Like what?"

"Like saying you'll show up for school events and then canceling because of work."

"Honey, it's not that I don't want to be there. It's just that sometimes things come up. But I always make sure your dad can be there."

"Maybe I don't want Dad there. Maybe I want *you* there, or both of you." She sits down on the bed. "I want you to stop working so much. Maybe that's why you fell. Because you were tired from always working."

"I don't think so, but I'll try to cut back on my hours. I have to if I want to get better."

"And when you're better, you'll go back to working all the time?"

"Caitlyn, we've talked about this. Real estate isn't like a normal job where you work a set number of hours a week. It's all the time."

"Then get another job. One where you don't have to work so much."

I had no idea Caitlyn wanted me around more. She's always telling me to go away, but maybe that's just the teenager in her, trying to gain independence while fighting the side of her that still needs me.

"I'll think about it," I tell her. "It's too soon to say what's going to happen."

"Can you at least get rid of that guy?"

"What guy?"

"That one that fixes stuff for you."

"Troy? The handyman?"

38

"Yeah." She shudders. "He's creepy."

"How do you know Troy? I don't remember you ever meeting him."

"He was at the house. Not ours. The house where you had your party. He was there that night."

"Troy was at the party? That can't be right. Marcus wouldn't invite the handyman to the party."

"He wasn't there for the party. He was there to fix the sink in the upstairs bathroom. He said you told him it'd been leaking and asked him to fix it."

"I did?" I wonder why I didn't ask the builder to fix it. But knowing how long it takes him to get things done, it makes sense that I called Troy to do it.

Troy was hired last year to do maintenance jobs for us. A lot of homes need minor repairs done before we list them for sale, and instead of making the homeowner deal with it, we offer to take care of the repairs for them, to get the house on the market faster. Troy gets a monthly retainer to be on call for us whenever we need him. He can fix most anything and he's fast. It was my idea to hire a handyman, and so far, it's worked out great. And our homeowners love it since it saves them from having to find someone to fix something minor like a leaky sink or cracked bathroom tile.

"Why do you think Troy is creepy?" I ask Caitlyn.

She shrugs. "Just the way he looked at me. And he didn't say anything. He came upstairs and saw me in the bedroom and didn't say anything. That's creepy. Why wouldn't he say something?"

"You were upstairs during the party?"

"I didn't know where else to go. After we had our fight and you told me I couldn't leave, I ran upstairs to one of the bedrooms to be alone."

"But there's nothing up there. No furniture."

"I sat on the floor and looked at my phone. Then I got this weird feeling that someone was watching me, and I looked up and there was that guy. Troy, or whatever."

"And he didn't say anything?"

"Not until I asked him what he wanted. He said something about fixing a sink. He asked where you were, and I told him you were outside. He finally left, and that's when I ran downstairs and went outside."

"He left? Like he left the house?"

"No, he went down the hall. I don't know if he went in the bathroom or one of the bedrooms. I didn't stick around to see. I just wanted out of there. I didn't like him."

"Troy is awkward socially, but he's a very hard worker. He was probably just surprised to see you up there and didn't know what to say."

"No, I'm telling you, Mom, there's something wrong with that guy. Val said he used to be in prison."

"You talked to Valerie about this?"

"Yeah. At the party. I found her out back and told her some weird guy was in the house, claiming he had to fix something. She said it was probably the handyman and that she'd go inside and check."

"And did she?"

"I don't know. I'm guessing she did. After I talked to her, my friend called and I went to the front of the house so I could hear her and get some privacy. So, is it true? Was that guy really in prison?"

"Yes, but only for a short time. He had some issues when he was a teenager that got him into trouble, but he's learned from his mistakes and is trying to get a fresh start. He's very good at his job and a hard worker."

"Why was he in prison? What'd he do?"

"Honey, we don't need to get into this. Let's talk about something else. Tell me what's new at school."

"Mom, I want to know what he did." She pauses. "Did he . . . kill someone?"

"No, it was nothing like that. He held up a gas station with a friend of his and the two of them were caught."

"So he stole stuff?"

"Some money, and I believe some alcohol."

"And they put him in prison for that?"

"He had a gun. It was armed robbery, which is a serious crime."

"But he didn't hurt anyone?"

"No," I say, deciding not to tell her about his history of violence. His arrest record includes several incidents of assault, but they were all fights he got into as a teenager. A lot of young men have short fuses and get into fights at that age. He's older now, and I really do think he's learned from his mistakes. I've never had an issue with him losing his temper. He's always been very polite and agreeable.

The door swings open and Adam walks in, followed by a man in a white coat. He must be my doctor, although I don't remember seeing him before.

"Mrs. Banks," the doctor says, smiling as he comes up to me. "Your husband tells me you're hoping to get out of here tomorrow."

"Yes," I say as Caitlyn gets up and goes over by Adam. "I'd really like to go home."

"We'll run some tests first thing in the morning and make a decision after that." He extends his hand to me. "I'm Dr. Abrams. We've met before, but you probably don't remember me."

I shake his hand. "No, sorry, I don't."

"No need to be sorry. It's normal. Your brain is still recovering from the trauma of what happened."

"Will it get better? I mean, how long before I stop forgetting things?"

"I can't say for sure. We'll just have to wait and see. It's your short-term memory that's affected. That usually comes back after your brain has had time to heal."

"Meaning she'll remember what happened that night?" Adam asks the doctor. "Before she fell?"

"Every case is different, but it's quite common for memories to return after some time has passed."

Adam clears his throat. "How much time are we talking about? Weeks? Months?"

Why does Adam care when my memory returns, or if it even does? I only lost a few days, and if those memories never return, I'm okay with that. I just don't want this to continue. I don't want to keep forgetting things, like meeting the doctor. I wonder how many times I've met him before now.

"It could be as soon as a week," the doctor says to Adam. "It really varies by patient. Some people don't get their memory back for months, or even a year."

"But Blaire's concussion was pretty bad," Adam says. "Wouldn't that mean it'd take longer for her memories to come back?"

"Not necessarily," the doctor says. "Like I said, everyone's different, and so far, your wife has improved faster than I would've expected."

"But she shouldn't work, right?" Caitlyn says to the doctor. "She should take time off?"

"For now, yes," he says. "I'd recommend a good week of rest before going back to the office."

"A week?" Caitlyn says. "That's nothing."

"Caitlyn, we'll talk about this later," I tell her. "The doctor's on a schedule. He needs to see other patients."

"Not just yet," the doctor says to me. "I'm here to run some tests. If your husband and daughter wouldn't mind stepping out for a few minutes, we'll get started."

"Actually, we need to get going," Adam says. "Visiting hours are about to end." He comes over to me and kisses my forehead. "We'll see you later. Get some rest."

"Yes. I will." I smile at him.

"Bye, Mom." Caitlyn gives me a wave.

"That's it? I don't get a hug?"

"Dad said I couldn't."

"Get over here." I hold my arms out.

Caitlyn comes over and gives me a distant and gentle hug. She's worried she'll hurt me. It's sweet and not what I'm used to after years of her acting like she hates me. I feel terrible she thinks this is her fault. I hope after our talk today that she realizes she wasn't the reason I fell.

So what *was* the reason? Why did I fall?

I hope the doctor is right and my memory returns soon so I can finally figure this out. I'd also like to get back my memories of the party. It was a major birthday and the first time I've had a big party like that. It'd be nice to remember it.

CHAPTER 6

"Can I get you anything?" Valerie asks. "Maybe another pillow?"

"No," I say with a laugh. "And if you keep asking me, I'm going to have to ask you to leave."

It's Saturday and I've been home for a few days now. I'm feeling much better and my energy is starting to return. I still can't remember anything from last weekend, but I've been able to remember the past few days. I remember Valerie stopping by several times, bringing meals so Adam wouldn't have to cook. And Marcus came over yesterday with flowers. He was on his way to a meeting so didn't stay long, but it was good to see him.

It's only been a week, but I already miss being at the office. I've always been someone who has a hard time relaxing. Even on vacations, I want to stay busy. Lying on a beach for hours is torture for me. Adam doesn't get it. He could sit on a beach all day and be perfectly content.

"You're a horrible patient," Valerie kids. "I see what Adam was talking about."

"Why? What did Adam say?"

"That you won't sit still. He says he goes to get you something and when he comes back, you're gone, usually down the hall to your office, doing work you shouldn't be doing."

"He's exaggerating. I only did that twice."

"Still, you're not supposed to be working at all this week, or next week. I told you I'd cover for you. Don't you trust me?"

"Of course I do, but it doesn't feel right to make you do both your job and mine."

"Blaire, you know I don't mind. What else do I have to do? I'm not married. I don't have kids. I have plenty of time to help you out."

"Speaking of that, I do have a favor to ask."

"Sure, what is it?"

"Would you mind getting Caitlyn from school next week? Adam can drop her off in the morning, but he'd have to leave work to pick her up and he already took a lot of time off after my accident."

"I'd be happy to get her."

"It doesn't have to be every day. I could talk to Adam and see if he could—"

"Blaire, would you stop? It's not a big deal. I'll pick her up. Adam doesn't need to take time off." She smiles. "It'll be fun! Maybe Caitlyn could get me caught up on all the lingo the kids are using these days."

I laugh. "Maybe, but as soon as you learn it, it changes. A few weeks ago, Adam tried using some word he thought was the latest thing and Caitlyn just rolled her eyes at him, which is her way of saying he didn't use it right or it's already outdated." I pause, thinking about Caitlyn. "I wish I could make her feel better. She's been so down lately."

"She's just worried about you."

"It's more than that." I look at Valerie. "Caitlyn blames herself for what happened. I told her it's not her fault. Adam tried telling her too, but she doesn't believe us."

"How could it possibly be her fault? It was an accident."

"Apparently, she was fighting with me before it happened and went upstairs to get away from me. I went looking for her later and that's when I fell. So now she thinks she's to blame.

She's been moping around the house all week, and every time she sees me, she gets this guilty look on her face."

"I'm sure she'll get over it once you're better and back to your routine. She's not used to seeing you like this, being on the couch all day or in bed. Once you're back at work and everything's back to normal, she'll be able to let go of whatever guilt she's holding onto."

"Yes, I suppose you're right."

"I could take her somewhere. Get her out of the house? Try to cheer her up?"

"If you have the time, I'm sure she'd love that."

"Tell her I'll take her shopping after I pick her up next week. Shopping always cheers me up. And then maybe we'll go to dinner."

"Actually, that'd be great. It'll give me some time alone with Adam."

Her brows rise. "Are you sure you're ready for that? Did you ask the doctor?"

I smile. "That's not why I want to be alone with him. And yes, it's too soon for that. The doctor didn't actually tell me that, but I'm not exactly in the mood after everything that's happened. What I meant is that I'd like to talk to Adam without Caitlyn around. He's been acting . . . off, I guess, is how I'd describe it."

"What do you mean?"

"He's been really quiet and kind of distant."

"I think he's just dealing with what happened. He's been through a lot the past week. When you were in the hospital, he was worried he might lose you. You just need to give him some time. You know how men are. They'd rather work their feelings out in their head than talk about them."

"Maybe you're right."

Her phone rings and she silences it.

"Did you need to get that?" I ask.

"I'll call them back."

"You don't have to stay here. I know you have a lot to do, especially now that you're doing my job as well as your own."

"Speaking of that, the Conleys want to see the house on Elmhurst again. I was going to set up a time for next week unless you want me to tell them to wait until you're able to take them there."

"No, don't wait. We'll risk losing the sale. If they're asking to see it again, there's a good chance they'll make an offer."

"Yes, it sounded like they might when I spoke to them earlier. I just didn't want to overstep."

"You're not. I asked you to cover for me, and if you didn't, Marcus would have someone else do it. I'd rather split the commission with you than with one of the other agents."

"Blaire, I'm not taking your commission. You've been working with these people for months."

"Yes, and you're the one closing the deal, assuming they buy the house. I already talked to Marcus and told him I'd split whatever commissions come in while you're covering for me."

"Half is too much. And if you return to the office in a week, you'll be the one doing the closing."

"Don't argue with me, Val," I say in a stern tone, but it's followed by a smile. "Consider it payment for getting Caitlyn from school next week."

"I'd do that anyway. Like any friend would." Her phone rings again and she sends it to voicemail. "Sorry, but I really should go." She gets up, slinging her purse over her shoulder. "I'm meeting a man for lunch who's interested in those new luxury condos being built off Hayward. I need to get in touch with the builder and see if he's got an agent assigned to the project. Or maybe Marcus knows. Actually, I should talk to him first."

Should I tell her? Maybe it'd be better coming from Marcus, but then she'll think I was hiding this from her, which could damage our friendship. It's tricky being friends with someone you compete with for sales. That's why Valerie and I have never been close. We go out a lot, for drinks or dinner, but we're not the type of friends who share all the intimate details of our lives. In fact, telling her about Adam acting distant and Caitlyn being depressed is more than I'd usually tell her.

"Call if you need anything," Valerie says as she turns to leave.

"Val, wait!" I get up from the couch. "I need to tell you something."

She walks back to me. "What is it?"

"About those condos. The ones being built?"

"What about them?"

"Marcus knows the builder. He met with him a few weeks ago and convinced him to sign with the agency to sell the condos. And he, um . . . already picked an agent to take the project."

"And?"

I don't answer. I don't need to. She already knows. I can tell by the uncomfortable look on her face.

"It's you," she says.

"Yes. I was going to tell you, but then the accident happened and—"

"Blaire, you don't have to explain." She smiles. "You're our top agent. Of course it would go to you. I'm not surprised."

"You're not mad?"

"I'm jealous," she says with a laugh. "But out of anyone at the agency, I'd rather have this go to you than someone else. I mean, sure I'd love to get a big project like that, but I haven't earned it. You have." She puts her hand on my arm. "You've worked hard to get to this level and I'm happy for you."

"Really?"

"Absolutely." Her phone rings again and she sighs. "I need to go, but I'll check in with you later." She answers her phone as she leaves.

Despite what she said, she's disappointed she didn't get the condo project. And I totally understand. If I were her, I'd be disappointed too. People are already showing interest in those condos so selling them will be easy, and given the price, I'll be making a fortune in commissions. But I don't feel guilty about that. Like Valerie said, I've earned this. I didn't give up weekends and time with my family for nothing. I've worked hard to get where I'm at, so I'm not going to feel bad that Marcus gave this project to me and not someone else.

I'm also not going to let myself believe it had anything to do with the dirt I have on Marcus. Has it helped me in the past? Sure, but I still had to do the work to make the sale. It wasn't just handed to me. And anything Marcus has done for me was his doing, not mine. I didn't use his secret to coerce him in any way. Did I think about it? Sure, but I like Marcus and don't want his life falling apart because of my need to get ahead.

Then again, it doesn't hurt to know a secret like this about your boss.

CHAPTER 7

"Mom, I'm fine," I assure her. "Really. I've been resting for over a week now and I'm feeling much better."

"Your father and I wish we could be there. It's just that with his eyesight being so bad and my fear of driving on the interstate, I don't know how we could manage it."

My parents haven't left Pittsburgh in over twenty years. They rarely even leave their neighborhood. They're very set in their ways, and the older they get, the more fearful they become. They won't even get on a plane anymore, which means if I want to see them, I have to go back to my hometown, back to my old neighborhood. I always dread going there. I like to pretend that was never my life, that I was never the girl who had to buy her prom dress at a thrift store and save up change to eat fast food. I'm not that person anymore. I'm Blaire Banks, successful real estate agent who lives in a two-million-dollar home and drives a luxury SUV. I will never be anything less.

My parents don't understand my lifestyle, so it's probably good they don't come here to visit. If they did, all I'd hear are comments about how I'm wasting my money buying things I don't need, and how I should save every penny to prepare for some unfortunate incident that may or may not occur. I love my parents, but everything is gloom and doom with them. Having them here while I'm recovering wouldn't comfort me in the least. Instead of telling me I'll get better, they'd be telling me stories of people whose brain injuries got worse and how I need to rest more so it doesn't happen to me. They think they're helping, but their negativity just adds to my stress.

"Mom, don't worry about it," I say. "Just having you call and check on me is all that I need."

"I really wish we could do more, but it sounds like you've been getting along okay."

"Yes, everyone's been wonderful. People have been coming by all week, bringing us meals, helping out with the house. And Valerie was kind enough to get Caitlyn from school this week."

"Why isn't Adam getting her?"

"He missed a lot of work when I was in the hospital. I didn't want him missing even more."

"You think he might lose his job? Your dad heard those luxury cars aren't selling like they used to."

There she goes with the gloom and doom. It seems like every time we talk, she has more bad news to share.

"It really depends on the region," I say. "Around here, luxury cars still sell well."

The doorbell rings.

"Mom, someone's at the door. I need to go."

"Okay, dear. We'll talk later."

I end the call and head to the door. Since the day I got home from the hospital, people have been stopping by non-stop. Adam said we should put a note on the door telling people I'm resting and not to ring the bell, but I don't like turning people away. And I'm done resting. I've been up and around for days now.

"Rob," I say, seeing him at the door. "What are you doing here?"

He smiles. "I came to see how you're feeling."

"You can't be here," I whisper. "Your wife is home. She'll know you're here. She's probably watching you from her window right now."

"She's not home. She's having a spa day. She'll be gone for hours."

My heart races as I look at Rob, like some teenage girl with a crush. I'm embarrassed to admit that, but I'm sure Rob has that effect on a lot of women. He's extremely handsome. Over six feet tall with thick dark hair and a golden-brown tan. His body is like a work of art, every muscle chiseled and lean, but not overly huge like those men who use steroids to make their muscles so big they look cartoonish.

Rob's dressed in basketball shorts and a tight-fitting T-shirt, like he's about to go for a run. I usually prefer a man dressed in a well-tailored suit, but I don't mind the gym clothes on Rob. They accentuate his perfect physique.

"You still shouldn't be here," I say, trying to ignore my attraction to him. "Someone might see us together."

"What's the big deal? We're neighbors. And if you're worried about people seeing us, maybe you should invite me inside."

"Hurry up." I open the door enough to let him into the house.

"Jesus, Blaire, you act like we committed a crime."

"According to you, we did," I mutter, walking to the living room.

Rob follows me, coming up behind me and wrapping his arms around my waist. "What we did wasn't a crime." He leans down and kisses the side of my neck.

"Rob, stop it!" I yank away from him. "Is that why you're here? Because you think something's going to happen?"

"I came to see how you're doing." He smiles. "But I wouldn't be opposed to something happening. If you were up for it."

"I'm not." I fold my arms over my chest. "I never was. What happened between us was a mistake. I was too drunk to even remember it."

"That's too bad, because that was something you'd definitely want to remember." He sits down in the leather chair next to the couch, making himself comfortable. "You and I have amazing chemistry, Blaire. You'd find that out if you gave us another chance."

"No. Absolutely not." I sit on the couch, on the end farthest away from Rob. "I'm not cheating on Adam."

"Even if he's cheating on you?" Rob casually asks.

"Adam is not cheating." I almost roll my eyes like Caitlyn does, but catch myself before I do.

"You sure about that?"

I look at Rob. "What's that supposed to mean?"

He shrugs. "I saw him out with some woman. At that sports bar by the car dealership he works at. But hey, maybe she was just a friend."

"When was this?" I sit up straighter. "When did you see him?"

"A few weeks ago. One of my old clients is managing the place now so I stopped by to say hello."

"At lunch? Or what time of day?"

"It was seven or eight at night. I can't remember the exact time."

Adam should've been home by then. He gets off work at six, then comes home and makes dinner or orders something in. I'm guessing I was showing a house that night. A lot of my showings are in the evenings, after people get home from work.

"She was probably a customer," I say. "Adam's taken customers out before, especially if he knows them well."

"Maybe, but he was sitting really close to her. Closer than you'd sit to a customer."

"I'm sure it was nothing. You're reading too much into it."

"Just letting you know what I saw." He leans forward, resting his forearms on his knees, looking very serious. "I've been worried about you. I wanted to come by sooner, but wasn't sure if I should. Or if you'd let me."

"Rob, I know you want this to be more than it is, but it's not going to happen. Adam and I have our issues, but I'm not ready to give up on us."

"That doesn't change how I feel about you." He sits back. "Just be honest, Blaire. I know you've at least thought about us being together. You and I are a way better match than we are with our spouses. We're driven. Ambitious. Always wanting more. Alice and Adam are stagnant. They're happy just sitting around doing nothing with their lives."

It's true, and it's one of the reasons Adam and I aren't as close as we once were, but I still love him. And I'm not giving up on my marriage.

"People can be different, but still in love. Maybe you should try harder with Alice. Put your energy toward fixing your marriage instead of looking elsewhere."

He shakes his head. "My marriage ended soon after it started. Alice pretended to be someone she wasn't, and by the time I found out what she's really like, we were already married and she was holding me hostage with her money."

Rob met Alice at the luxury fitness center where he used to work as a personal trainer. He was twenty-five and she was thirty-five. According to him, Alice was extremely thin back then and wanted to put on muscle so she hired Rob to be her trainer. Soon they were dating, and Alice used her money to help Rob buy his own gym. They got married, and Alice gave Rob the money to open three more gyms and start an online diet and fitness program. The online program took off and became the success that it is today.

"She's not holding you hostage," I say. "If you divorced her and she got half of everything, you'd still be a wealthy man."

"It's not that simple. When we drew up the contracts to form the company, Alice insisted on being involved, meaning I can't make changes without her approval. It made sense back then, when she was as into fitness as I am. We had the same goals. We were going to create a fitness empire together.

I never in a million years thought things would turn out like they are now."

"So what happened? How did she go from being fit to not wanting to move off the couch?"

"Honestly, I think she set me up. I think she wanted me to marry her, so she pretended to like what I like, then once she had what she wanted and had the paperwork to make sure I was chained to her for life, she became someone else. Someone who just wants to sit around doing nothing all day."

"Why haven't you ever told me that? All the times we've talked, you made it sound like Alice has always been this way."

"Why would I have married her if she was like how she is now?"

"I assumed you married her for her money."

"Really?" he says, sounding offended. "That's really what you think of me?"

"Rob, everyone thinks that. The whole neighborhood."

"Well, that's not what happened." He shrugs. "But whatever. It doesn't matter. I'm stuck with her."

"And you think that's an excuse to cheat on her?"

"Wouldn't you? What am I supposed to do? Never be with a woman again?"

"You and Alice don't . . ."

"No. We haven't in years. Neither one of us wants that."

"Then why are you two still married? I would think she'd want a divorce as much as you do."

"That's the last thing she wants. I'm like an expensive piece of jewelry to her, something other women want. Alice loves watching rich, skinny women look at us together and be jealous that she got a guy that looks like me. It's all about ego for her. Showing me off to other women, making them wish they had a husband that looks like this." He points to himself. "Instead of some fat, bald guy. Those guys may be rich, but they've let themselves go. Their wives aren't attracted to them anymore."

"And you're saying Alice isn't attracted to you? I find that hard to believe."

He cracks a smile. "I'll take that as a compliment."

"I never said you're not attractive. If we were single, perhaps things would be different between us. But that's not our situation. So going back to Alice, is she really not attracted to you?"

"I wouldn't know. I don't ask. When we're home, we don't talk. She stays on her side of the house, and I stay on mine. We live like roommates who don't like each other."

"I knew you two didn't get along, but I didn't think it was that bad. You put on a good show when you're out in public."

"Good enough, I guess."

"Does she know? About you being with other women?"

"I'm sure she does, but we don't talk about it. I don't think she cares as long as I'm discreet about it. She wants to keep up the illusion that I only want her. She did catch me once. It was a few years ago. I ran into a former client from my personal training days and we spent a night together. Then I found out later that Alice had gone to college with her and word somehow got back to her about what I'd done. Alice was so angry she got the woman fired. And Lexi had a really good job. CEO of a tech company in Boston."

"How did Alice get her fired? She doesn't have that kind of power."

"Lexi thinks Alice made up some story about her fooling around with one of her employees and reported it to the board of directors. I don't know if Alice really did that, but I wouldn't put it past her. The woman will do anything to get revenge."

"I had no idea things were so bad between you two."

"It's not something I tell people. I'm embarrassed to be in this situation. Here I am, a successful entrepreneur, telling people to take charge of their lives and make the changes needed to be their best, and I'm not even doing it myself."

"Maybe you could talk to a lawyer and just see what your options are, or if you even have any."

"Yeah, I've thought about that." He blows out a breath and stands up. "I'll leave you alone. I didn't mean to dump all my problems on you."

I get up and walk him to the door.

"You never answered my question," he says. "About how you're feeling."

"Better, but I still don't have my memory back."

"You took quite a fall. I'm glad you didn't get hurt worse than you did."

"Me too." I put my hand on his arm, trying to ignore the desire he stirs inside me, desire I wish I still felt for Adam. "You're a good guy, Rob. I hope things get better for you."

"Thanks." His eyes meet up with mine and he leans down, almost like he's about to kiss me, but then straightens up. "If you change your mind . . ."

"I won't. I'm committed to my marriage."

He nods and opens the door.

"What you said about Adam," I say. "Did you really see him at that sports bar?"

"Yeah. He was definitely there with a woman. But like you said, maybe she was just some woman who bought a car from him. Who knows?"

"Yes, I'm sure it was nothing. Bye, Rob."

He returns to his house while I'm left wondering why my husband is spending time with another woman. I never imagined Adam would cheat on me, but thinking about it now, I could see why he might. I'm never home. We rarely make love. And we've been together since we were fifteen. We were each other's first and only. Maybe Adam regrets getting married so young and not being with other women. Maybe he wants to see what it'd be like to be with someone else, someone different. Someone who isn't me.

CHAPTER 8

"Welcome back," Marcus says as I go into his office.

It's Friday morning. I'm still supposed to be at home recovering, but I couldn't take another day of sitting around the house. And it's not as though I'll be doing anything strenuous. I'll just be going through my listings, making some phone calls, and updating my files.

"I can't tell you how good it feels to be back," I say, sitting across from Marcus at his desk. "I was losing my mind being at home."

He smiles. "Come on, Blaire. It couldn't be that bad. All that time off with nothing to do? It's like a vacation."

"Yes, and you know how I feel about vacations," I say, knowing he's teasing me. After working with me for years, he knows sitting around doing nothing is my absolute nightmare.

"Well, you'll be plenty busy the next few months. You may find yourself wishing for a day off."

"Trust me, I won't. I won't need another day off for years." I move to the edge of my chair. "So tell me about the condo project. You said on the phone that we've already had a couple people asking to be put on the reserve list?"

"More than a couple." He wakes his computer up and looks at the screen. "It looks like we have four so far, maybe five. I'll send you their contact information."

"I'll call them today and set up a time to meet."

"I'll let the builder know. He's been asking when you'd be able to start." Marcus leans back in his chair. "One of the potential buyers is Valerie's client. I'm not sure how you want to handle that."

"Like I would any other agent. She'll get a percentage of the commission on the sale. Or were you thinking something else?"

He glances to the side, and I get the sense there's something he's not telling me.

"What is it?" I ask. "Is something wrong?"

He gets up and closes the door to his office, then returns to his desk. "I need you to keep this quiet. Just between us."

"Okay. Go ahead."

"I've been getting some complaints about Valerie. From both buyers and sellers. And from John, the builder on the condo project."

"I don't understand. Why would anyone complain about Valerie?"

"From what I've heard, she's been losing her temper with clients, even going so far as raising her voice and cursing."

"Are you sure they were talking about Valerie?" I laugh, because what he's saying is completely ridiculous. "Marcus, you know that's not her. Valerie would never do that. She's extremely professional. Whoever's saying this is either exaggerating or making it up."

"It's more than one person. It was several. John said she yelled at him over the phone last week when he couldn't give her a date for when the condos would be completed. She knows a builder can't promise a completion date when we're still this far out. The outside walls aren't even up."

"That doesn't sound like Valerie. I don't know why she would do that."

"Do you know if something's been going on with her? Maybe something in her personal life?"

"Not that I know of, other than my accident. She was really worried about me, but I can't imagine that being the reason she'd yell at John."

"Could it be something else? Maybe a health matter she hasn't addressed?"

"Are you meaning her mental health?"

"Or otherwise, but yes, her mental health, specifically."

"I don't think so. She's never mentioned having any issues, at least not to me."

"Well, something is causing her to act this way. I'm hoping it's stress and she just needs some time away. I'm going to ask her to take some days off, maybe a week, to see if that helps."

"She has a closing next week."

"Not anymore. The buyers backed out, which is a shame because she hasn't had a closing in over a month."

"Let me talk to her before you ask her to take time off."

"Go ahead. It'd be better coming from you anyway. I've been dreading having to discuss this with her. You know how poorly she takes criticism."

"I'm not going to tell her that part. Not yet. I'll start by seeing if I can figure out what's going on with her."

He stands up. "I need to get going, but let me know how it goes with Val."

"Yes, I will." I get up and turn to leave.

"Blaire, wait. Before you go."

I turn back. "Yes?"

Marcus walks over to me and I notice his expression turn grim, almost threatening. "Did you tell someone?"

"What are you talking about?"

Marcus is a large man — over six feet tall with broad shoulders and a heavy build. His size can be intimidating, but I've never been afraid of him. Until now. He's never looked at me this way.

60

He grabs my arm. "Don't play games with me, Blaire. Just tell me the truth. Did you say anything?"

He's referring to his secret, but why does he think I told someone?

"No. Of course not. Why would I?"

"That's exactly what I was thinking. I've given you everything, Blaire. Every new construction project. Every lead. You've made a fortune thanks to me, so I can't for the life of me understand why you'd turn on me."

"I didn't." I lock my gaze on his dark brown eyes. "And I don't like being accused of something I didn't do. I also don't like you taking credit for my success. The money I've made is because of me and my skill as an agent. The projects you've given me wouldn't have been half as successful with anyone else and you know it."

He grits his teeth. "Then how did this get out?"

"How should I know? It wasn't me. Maybe someone saw you and recognized you."

"No, it's not possible. I was in the city. It was dark. And I was dressed as . . . well, we don't need to get into that."

"So what happened? Who knows about this?"

"If I knew that, I wouldn't be asking you."

"Did they say something?"

"It was a message. A text." He grips my arm tighter. "If this is some kind of joke you're playing—"

"I don't play jokes," I say, trying to free my arm from his grasp. "And if you're so concerned about someone finding out, then perhaps you should stop doing this. Live out your fantasies in your head instead of doing it in real life."

He leans closer, his eyes locked on mine. "What I do in my personal life is not your concern. And if you want to keep making millions, I suggest you keep your mouth shut."

There's a knock on the door. It opens and I see Lydia, Marcus' wife, coming in. She's fifty-six, a few years older than Marcus, and very prim and proper. I've only seen her wear designer dresses and suits, nothing casual, and for all the years

I've known her, her jet-black hair has been styled in a chin-length bob, parted on the left side. She's never had a job, but is very involved in the arts and her church, serving on committees and planning charity events.

Lydia stops suddenly when she sees me with Marcus. He's still gripping my arm and standing closer than you should to an employee.

"Sweetheart," Marcus says, letting me go and backing away from me. "What are you doing here?"

"I decided to stop by on my way to do some shopping." She glances at me. "I didn't realize you were . . . in a meeting."

She says it as though she thinks there's something going on with Marcus and me. I almost smile at that, but stop myself before I do.

"It's nice to see you again, Lydia," I say, going over to her. "I love your dress."

She clears her throat. "If you don't mind, I'd like to speak with my husband."

"Of course. I was just leaving." I walk to the door.

"Blaire," Lydia says, in a tone that sounds like a teacher calling your name when you get in trouble in class.

I turn back to her. "Yes?"

Her thin red lips turn up just slightly. "I'm so sorry I wasn't able to attend your party. I had another commitment that night."

"I'm sorry you couldn't make it. Your husband did a wonderful job putting it together."

"That's what I heard." She looks at him. "Perhaps someday you'll plan a party like that for me. Your wife."

"Sweetheart, it was a work event," he says with a nervous laugh. "I mean, yes, we were celebrating Blaire's birthday, but a lot of our clients were there. I needed to be involved with the planning of it."

"Of course you did," Lydia says sarcastically. Her gaze returns to me. "It's so unfortunate what happened. Your little tumble down the stairs? I'm surprised you're able to be up and around so soon."

"I heal quickly." I smile at her. "I'll leave you two be. It was good seeing you, Lydia."

She says nothing back, but watches as I leave, then shuts the door. I pause just outside it and hear her talking to Marcus, but her voice is low enough that I can't make out what she's saying.

"Hear anything good?" Valerie says, catching me eavesdropping outside the door.

"Lydia's here," I whisper to Valerie.

"Did she bring the leash?" she whispers back.

"Stop it." I try not to laugh.

We always joke that Lydia keeps her husband on a short leash, but it's not far from the truth. At work, Marcus is a dominant, take-charge leader, but around his wife, he's like a little boy who does what he's told. I'm sure that's why he feels the need to have his little "side hobby." It's his escape from real life, where he's forced to play the role of the stuffy, conservative real estate broker and put up with his even stuffier wife who spends her days hobnobbing with the wealthiest people in town.

Lydia comes from old money. She's a Rockingham, as in *the* Rockinghams, the family that founded the Rockingham Group. Lydia's great grandfather started the company by buying and selling apartment buildings in Manhattan. The Rockingham Group quickly grew, selling high-end real estate in and around Manhattan and making the Rockingham family one of the wealthiest in the country.

Lydia's father and two brothers run the offices in New York, but Lydia had no interest in running the office here in Connecticut. Her father insisted someone in the family be in charge of it, so Lydia married Marcus, who at the time was a real estate broker who was doing quite well for himself but not nearly as well as he'd do with Lydia in his life. All he had to do was drop her name and people would sign with him. It's human nature. People want to be associated with those who have wealth, power, and status. It's why I chose to work at the Rockingham Group. Before I even moved here, I did my research and decided this was where I would get a job. I didn't even consider other options.

When Marcus married Lydia, he took her last name, knowing the power that comes with being a Rockingham. There are many perks, but there are also downsides, like having to follow his wife's orders. If he steps out of line, he could lose the lavish lifestyle he's accustomed to, along with his job. Marcus is trapped, just like Rob is with Alice.

"How's it feel to be back?" Valerie asks, following me to my office.

"Wonderful," I say with a dreamy sigh. "I couldn't take another day at home." I take a seat at my desk. "I have so much to do. I'd work all weekend if I could, but knowing Adam, he'd come here and drag me home. He's convinced I need to rest more." I look at Valerie as she sits across from me. "Speaking of resting, you must be exhausted after covering for me all week. Why don't you take some time off?"

She laughs. "And do what? I have no life outside of work."

"That's not true," I say, but it actually is true when I think about it. Valerie doesn't really have any friends other than people at work. She doesn't date. She doesn't have any hobbies. "You could sign up for Pilates. You keep saying you want to try it."

"I said that three years ago. I've lost interest." She pauses. "What is this about? Why are you pushing me to take time off?"

"No reason. I just realized you hadn't taken time off since last year."

"Because I don't need to. I like working."

"Do you?" I ask, trying to figure out how to say this. "Or do you ever wish you could do something else?"

"Like what?"

"I don't know. Maybe something in business. You have a degree in it."

"My degree is in finance, and I never intended to use it. My parents forced me to pick something that would get me a respectable job, or what they considered to be respectable. They were extremely disappointed when I went into real estate. They still are, along with being disappointed I'm not

64

married and don't have children." Her shoulders stiffen as she sits up straighter. "They remind me of that constantly, which is why our visits have become less frequent." She eyes me. "Why are you pressuring me to find a new career?"

"I'm not. I just wondered if you ever considered doing something else."

"Why would I do something else? Where is this coming from?"

This isn't going well. She's getting angry. I need to drop it and talk about something else.

"Oh, now that I'm back, I'll pick up Caitlyn at school today."

"Would you mind if I did? I was going to take her to a new store downtown that I think she'd really like. I already told her about it and she's excited to go."

"Um, sure. Go ahead. It'll give me more time to catch up on things here." I wake up my computer and see the long list of emails. "Just have her home in time for dinner."

Valerie gets up and leaves without saying anything. I hope she's not angry at me for suggesting she consider a new career. I wish I hadn't done that, but I didn't know what else to say. To be honest, she's not a very good agent. She should probably do something else.

"These just came for you," Tara, the front desk girl, says, walking into my office with a large floral bouquet arranged in a glass vase.

"They're beautiful," I say as she sets them on my desk. "Who are they from?"

"I don't know. I didn't open the envelope."

"Thanks, Tara," I say as she leaves.

Taking the tiny envelope from the bouquet, I open it and take out the card.

I gasp when I read what's written on it.

I know what you did with him. You deserve whatever happens to you!

Who sent me this? Was it Alice? Did she find out what I did with Rob and now she's threatening me? Or was it someone else? It's possible it's from one of my clients. I deal with a lot of wealthy couples and sometimes the wives can be very jealous, worried I'm trying to steal their rich husbands. I'm not, of course. I'm just trying to make the sale, and often the men are the ones I have to convince. So I smile, compliment them, maybe touch their arm. It's completely harmless. I'd never actually do anything with a married client, but it wouldn't surprise me if a jealous wife assumed I did. But who could it be?

I don't know what this means. Is whoever sent this note planning to harm me? Or is this just an empty threat meant to scare me?

I can't tell Adam about this. The note makes it sound like I cheated, which I did, but I don't want Adam, or anyone else, knowing that. It could destroy my reputation and end my career.

CHAPTER 9

"Are you leaving?" Valerie asks as she sees me coming out of my office with my purse and laptop.

"Yes, I set up a showing for ten. I have an errand to run before I meet them at the house."

"Are you feeling okay? Your face is pale."

"I feel fine. I'll see you later."

I don't have a showing. I'm just too worked up to be in the office right now. I have to find out who sent those flowers and if their threats are real. I need to talk to Rob. Maybe he could search his house for a receipt that would prove the flowers were from Alice. She's the most likely person to do something like this, especially when I think about what Rob said about Alice getting that woman fired. If she has that kind of power, what else is she capable of?

Getting in my SUV, I try to think of where to go. I take off driving and find myself at the house where the party was held. I feel sick seeing it now, knowing I could've died here, but I need to get over it. It's just a house. It wasn't trying to hurt me. It was my carelessness that caused me to fall, along with a lot of champagne.

Now that I'm here, I should check if any progress has been made on the basement. The crew should've been working on it last week.

Going into the house, I stop abruptly as a memory comes flooding back. I see myself walking into the foyer, looking over at the living room, seeing the huge birthday banner above the fireplace.

It's back! My memory is back, or at least part of it. I should've come here days ago. Maybe being in this house is what I needed to get my mind to remember that night.

As I go into the kitchen, an image flashes in my mind of Adam standing by the counter, a bottle of beer in his hand. Valerie is next to him, opening bottles of champagne. They're both laughing about something.

I remember balloons. Pink and gray balloons. They were outside, but I could see them from inside the house as I looked out the sliding glass door. There were flowers too. Lots of flowers in vases. There were some in the kitchen, set up on the center island, right next to where I'm standing.

The images continue to flash in my head, like a film made from static photos strung together instead of flowing from scene to scene. It's overwhelming and making me feel light-headed. I need to sit down, but there aren't any chairs. I close my eyes and take a breath, but my chest feels tight, like there's a band around it restricting my breathing.

Something's not right. I don't feel good. Maybe being here, remembering that night, is too much, too soon. I didn't expect this. I didn't think getting my memory back would make me feel so anxious, almost panicked.

My phone rings, making me nearly jump out of my skin. I see Adam's name on the screen and answer the call.

"Hi, honey," I say in a cheery tone.

"Blaire, hey, I was just calling to check in. I hope I didn't wake you up."

"Oh, um, no. I'm not home. I decided to make a visit to the office."

He sighs. "You said you weren't going back until next week."

"That was only if I wasn't feeling well. But I feel great, and you know me. I can't just sit around at home."

"Are you working a full day?"

"I plan to. Valerie is picking up Caitlyn from school."

"Why aren't you picking her up?"

"Valerie already promised to take her shopping. She didn't want to change their plans."

"Yeah, fine, whatever," he mutters.

"What's wrong? Why are you angry?"

"Because you lied to me. If you were going to the office, why didn't you just tell me instead of trying to hide it?"

"I didn't want to fight with you. If I want to go to the office, I will. I don't have to ask for your permission."

"Yeah, I'm the only one who has to do that."

"What's that supposed to mean?"

"Forget it. Oh, I'm working late tonight. And I'm not *asking* if I can. I'm telling you. You see how that feels? When you don't get a say in the matter?"

"Adam, I—"

"Bye, Blaire." He ends the call.

Why is he acting this way? Why does he care if I went back to work? It's only a day earlier than I'd planned and he knows I go crazy being at home. And I didn't lie to him. I just didn't tell him I was working today. If anyone's lying, it's him. The car dealership closes at five on Fridays. Adam's not working late, so what's he doing? Where's he going after work? To see that woman Rob saw him with?

No. Adam wouldn't do that. He wouldn't cheat. He loves me. He went on and on after my accident, telling me how devastated he would've been if something had happened to me.

Needing some fresh air, I open the sliding glass door and go outside. As I'm standing there, images flash through my mind of people on the patio and scattered throughout the backyard, lingering by the bar tables Marcus must've rented. As I walk around, the memories continue, more like a movie this time rather than a series of images. The couple who bought a house from me last month are telling me how much they're enjoying it and how they love the neighborhood. As we're talking, Marcus comes over and gives me a glass of champagne.

Looking out at the lawn, I see a long buffet table. Rob is there, holding his drink and looking right at me, smiling in a way that says we're more than friends. Where was Alice? Did she see him smiling at me like that?

The woman is crazy. I'm convinced of it. Only a crazy person would send flowers with a threatening note attached. Maybe I could talk to her and convince her nothing happened between Rob and me. As far as I know, nothing did. I honestly don't remember it. I'm taking his word for it, and I have to say, I'm not sure I trust Rob. He's a born salesman. He does and says whatever he has to in order to close the deal. It's possible he told me we slept together so that I wouldn't think twice about doing it again. After all, once you've crossed that line, it gets easier to do again.

A breeze blows and the chill in the air makes me shiver. It's one of those mid-September days that starts out warm and muggy, then a cold front comes through and drops the temperature to more like late fall.

I hurry back inside and shut and lock the sliding glass door. Going over to the fridge, I open it and see bottles of soda and water. They're meant for prospective buyers who come to see the house, but I haven't been able to show it yet. The builder insists on the basement being finished before people see the house, which is foolish, if you ask me. I could easily sell this house without the basement being done.

Taking a water from the fridge, I tell myself to stop wasting time and just go down to the basement. That's why I'm here. To see if any work's been done. But the thought of opening that door to the stairs makes me feel sick to my stomach.

I'm being ridiculous. I'm not going to fall again. I haven't been drinking like I did that night, and this time I'll be extremely cautious, clinging to the railing the whole way down.

I drink some of the water and take a breath.

"Hey."

The loud, deep voice startles me and I drop my water.

I whip around and see Troy standing there, a wrench in his hand.

"Troy!" I say, my heart pounding. "What are you doing here?"

He holds up the wrench. "I left this here that day I fixed the sink. I was just stopping by to get it."

Troy's ripped jeans and weathered gray T-shirt are stained with dirt, and I notice dots of red by his shoulder. Is it blood? Why would he have blood on his shirt? Did he cut himself shaving? It looks like he hasn't shaved in a week. And his hair is a mess, like he just got out of bed.

I'm all about giving second chances, and up until now, I've always thought Troy was harmless, but I'm not so sure anymore. He shouldn't be here. If he really forgot his wrench, why did it take him this long to get it? The party was two weeks ago. He went two weeks without realizing he didn't have his wrench?

That doesn't make sense. He would've needed it before now. So what's the real reason? Why is he here?

CHAPTER 10

"Is something wrong?" Troy asks, tapping the wrench on the palm of his hand.

"No. Nothing." I hear my shaky breath and force out a smile, trying to appear relaxed. "I'm just surprised to see you. I didn't know anyone was here. You startled me. That's all."

His mouth turns up on one side, forming a crooked, somewhat creepy smile. "I seem to do that a lot."

"Do what?"

"Scare people." He laughs a little. "Like your daughter."

My shoulders tense at his mention of Caitlyn. "What about her?"

"That night I came to fix the sink, I think I scared her. She was hiding out in one of the rooms upstairs. She saw me and took off."

"Yes, well, she just didn't know who you were. I'm sure she wasn't scared but just surprised to see someone up there when she thought she was alone." I glance down at the water bottle by my feet, spilling out all over the floor.

"You want me to clean that up?" Troy asks, noticing the bottle.

"No." I look back at him. "I'll do it. You can go."

"You sure?" He gives me that lopsided smile. "I don't mind."

"No. I can do it. I'm sure you have places to be."

He reaches down and picks up the water bottle, then slowly stands up, his eyes following a path up my body. I was already on edge being here alone with him, but having him look at me that way is sending me into a full-on panic.

"Troy, I'd like you to go," I blurt out, squaring my shoulders, my head held high in what I'm hoping is a confident, I'm-not-afraid-of-you stance.

He laughs a little. "What's wrong?"

"I don't know what you mean."

"You're acting like you're afraid of me." He sets the water bottle down on the counter and steps closer to me. "You're not, are you?"

"No, of course not," I say, looking away. "I just have a lot to do and I can't have any distractions."

"Is that what I am to you, Blaire? A distraction?"

"Troy, I don't have time for this," I say, my eyes returning to his. "I'd appreciate it if you'd leave so I can get back to work."

He slowly backs away, a smirk on his face. "Whatever you say, Mrs. Banks." He taps his wrench on his palm in a slow, rhythmic pattern.

I watch him, my pulse going faster, wondering why he isn't leaving. I go around him, but he grabs my arm, stopping me.

"I need this job," he says, gripping my arm tighter as he leans down to my face. "You know how hard it is to find work after getting out of prison? I don't need you telling on me and taking all this away."

"I . . . I don't know what you mean," I say, my voice trembling. "I got you this job. Why would I take it away?"

"Because you know what I did." He looks me in the eye. "But I didn't have a choice. It was either that or not pay my rent. The bitch never even noticed. She has so much fucking

73

jewelry, she'd never know if something went missing." His eyes narrow. "Unless someone told her."

Troy stole jewelry? From one of the homeowners? That has to be what he's talking about, but I knew nothing about it. I guess I shouldn't be surprised. Troy has a history of stealing, and being a handyman who goes into the houses of people with money, he has access to some very valuable items. I wonder how many times this has happened. Has he been stealing since we hired him, or was it a one-time thing? None of my clients have mentioned items going missing so maybe it only happened once.

"Troy, whatever you've done, I honestly didn't know. And if I did, I wouldn't tell anyone. But you need to stop. It's too easy for someone to find out. A lot of the homeowners have security cameras both inside and outside the house. You could easily be caught."

"You think I don't know that?" he says, finally letting me go. "I'm smarter than you think, Blaire. Smart enough to know not to trust someone who tells me they're just trying to give a criminal a second chance."

I take a step back, making my way closer to the sliding glass door. My eyes scan the counters, searching for my phone. Where is it? Where did I put it?

"You think I don't know why you hired me?" Troy walks toward me, eliminating the distance I put between us. "Someone to keep around to do your dirty work?"

"I don't know what you think I'm doing, but I can assure you I'm not doing anything that would require what you're speaking of."

"Maybe not yet," he says, his eyes locked on mine. "But you know it might come to that, and you're not taking chances. You didn't work this hard to get where you're at just to lose it."

That part is true. I *did* work hard, and sometimes I do fear losing everything. I worry I'll wake up and find myself back in Pittsburgh, living in a small, run-down house like my parents have, working some dead-end job and struggling to make ends meet. It's my worst fear, but it'll never come true. I left that life and I'm never going back.

"I looked you up," Troy says. "Before I took the job. I wanted to know why you wanted *me*, a guy who just got out of prison, to work around rich people. Why you'd want me in their homes, knowing what could happen."

"I was giving you a second chance." I stand up straighter. "I believe everyone deserves that. A fresh start. A chance to prove that they've changed."

"Or maybe . . ." He pauses. "You wanted me around to take care of shit if something — or someone — threatens to take all this away." He glances down at my designer suit.

"I don't know where this is coming from, but what you're saying isn't true." I back up and bump into the counter, realizing he's got me trapped there, his tall, muscular body in front of me, surrounding me.

"You can pretend all you want," he says, "but deep down, you know it's true. People like us don't get shit handed to us. We have to work for every little scrap, and once we get it, we'll do anything to keep it."

"I don't know what you—"

"Stop lying," he interrupts. "I told you I did my research. Turns out you're no different than me. You can pretend to be one of these rich bitches living the life of luxury." He leans toward me, so close I can feel his breath on my face. "But under all those fancy clothes, you're the kind of trash those bitches look down on. It's why I like you, Blaire. Or should I call you Barb?"

"Get away from me!" I say, pushing hard against his chest.

He laughs. "Easy. No need to get rough." He takes a step back. "I'm just making sure we're on the same page. You want to keep things good between us? You look the other way. Keep your mouth shut."

"Yes. Fine." I clear my throat and walk away from him, noticing my phone on the counter by the sink. I pick it up and unlock it, preparing to call the police if Troy doesn't leave.

"It's good to see you're back at work. I heard that fall you took could've killed you."

"Yes, well, I'm fine now." My finger hovers over the phone.

"I'll see you around." He gives me that creepy smile before finally leaving.

I wait until I hear him go out the front door, then race over to it and lock it. Locking the door is pointless since Troy has a key, but it still makes me feel better knowing it's locked.

What was going on with him? Troy has never been that way with me. He's always been very polite, almost shy, in all our interactions. I tell him to fix something and he does it. That's been the extent of our relationship. But today, he was someone else. He was threatening and seemed unstable, almost like he was on something. And those things he said, about why I hired him, were nothing short of bizarre.

Why would he say that about me? Why would he assume I'd do something horrible that would need "cleaning up" by someone like him?

Maybe he really was on some kind of drug and didn't know what he was saying. Given that, and how he was acting today, maybe I should consider ending our contract with him. I could have Marcus do it so it wouldn't link back to me.

Going back to the kitchen, I notice a headache forming and go over to my purse to get a pain reliever. As I'm digging around in it, my hand lands on the note that was attached to the flowers. I take it out and read it again.

I know what you did with him. You deserve whatever happens to you!

It had to be Alice who sent this. Who else could it possibly be?

I don't know what that bitch is planning, but if she tries to go after my business, my reputation, the life I've built here, she won't get away with it. I'll go after her with just as much vengeance. I'll destroy her.

Except Alice has the upper hand. She's one of the wealthy elite. Born and raised here, growing up with everything she could ever want without having to lift a finger. I'm an outsider, like Troy said. I hate admitting that, but it's true. As much as I want to be one of these people, as much as I pretend to be, I'm not and never will be. Someone like Alice could use her lineage and clout to destroy me and everything I've worked for.

Maybe Troy was right. Maybe I hired him for a reason I wasn't even aware of until now. Until I realized how useful he could be.

CHAPTER 11

My phone rings and I see Valerie's name on the screen. I take a breath to calm myself, forcing aside my concerns about Alice.

"Hey, Val," I say, answering the call.

"Hey, are you heading back to the office?"

"No, I'm running some errands." I don't want her to know I'm at the house where we had the party. She's told me more than once that I shouldn't go back here until more time has passed. She's worried it'll trigger some kind of post-traumatic stress response, which I suppose it has, but I was able to handle it. What I couldn't handle was having Troy show up here, threatening me and making me feel like I wasn't safe. I still feel shaken by that. I'm not sure what to make of it or how to respond the next time I see him. I'm hoping we'll just go back to how things were, when he was just the quiet and reliable handyman who did his job and didn't cause problems.

"Okay, well, we can chat later," Val says, talking fast, her voice higher than normal.

"Is something wrong?" I ask, wondering if Marcus talked to her about the complaints made against her. I hope he didn't do that. I asked him to wait, but it's possible he did it anyway.

"I'm sure everything's fine," she says, sounding flustered. "I was far away. I really couldn't see that well. Or maybe I misinterpreted it. You know what? That's probably it. Never mind. I shouldn't have called. I'll just—"

"Val, what is going on? What did you see?"

"Nothing. Forget it. It was a mistake to even bring it up. I know he'd never do anything to — well, anyway." Her tone brightens. "Maybe we could meet for lunch."

"Val, seriously? You think I'm just going to forget this? Tell me what's going on."

She sighs. "Okay, but try not to overreact. I could be completely wrong about this."

"About what? What did you see?"

"I needed to get out of the office so I decided to go get a coffee. I was driving down the street by that park, the one close to Adam's dealership? And I, um . . . I saw him sitting in a car. It wasn't his. It was one of the cars from the lot."

"He was probably test driving it. He does that when it's slow at the dealership. Was he alone or with one of the other guys?"

"He was . . ." She clears her throat. "With a woman."

"Oh, then it was a test drive with a customer."

"She looked young. Maybe twenty-five? Aren't his customers usually older? They kind of have to be to afford the cars he sells. The cheapest ones start around fifty grand."

I smile. "Did you forget where we live? We're surrounded by millionaires. And billionaires. Whoever this girl was, I'm sure she could afford the car, or her parents could."

"Yes, I'm sure you're right. It's just . . ."

"Just what?" I ask, a tightness forming in my chest.

"I, um, can't say for sure, but it kind of looked like they were . . ." Valerie pauses. "I don't know how to say this."

"Just say it. Hurry up."

"He was kissing her," she blurts out. "But like I said, maybe I'm wrong. I mean, my eyesight isn't the greatest. I keep saying I should go to the eye doctor and then never get around to it. I should make an appointment."

She keeps rambling on about her eyesight, but I stopped listening the moment she said Adam was kissing this woman. Who is she? And how long has this been going on?

"Blaire?" Valerie says. "Are you still there?"

"Yes. I'm trying to figure this out. How far away were you when you saw them?"

"I was on the street and they were in the lot next to the park. So maybe like thirty feet? I don't know. And I didn't stop and stare. I slowed down just long enough to see it was Adam."

"Are you sure they weren't just talking? If you only got a glimpse of him, maybe what you thought you saw was just the two of them talking."

She takes a moment to answer. "I'm pretty sure it was more than that. She was, um . . . sitting on his lap and, well, there wasn't any distance between their faces."

My throat goes dry, and I feel a knot forming in my stomach. I lean back against the counter, squeezing my eyes shut and taking a breath. "Okay, well, thank you for telling me." I open my eyes. "I should go. I have a lot to do."

"Wait! Blaire. Don't you want to talk about this?"

"Not really. This is between Adam and me. I'll talk to him when he gets home."

Except he's not coming home. He said he's working late tonight, even though his workday ends at five.

"Are you sure?" she asks. "We could meet somewhere. Maybe get a drink. Have lunch. Whatever you want."

"Really, Val, I'm fine. And I have a million things to do. Maybe we could go out next week sometime."

"Yes, definitely. Is it still okay if I pick up Caitlyn at school, or do you want to get her?"

"You can get her but have her home by five. I think I'll take her to dinner somewhere."

Maybe taking Caitlyn out will get my mind off her father cheating on me. I can't believe he's doing this. After all I've done for him. All the work I put in to help us escape the life we came from, the one our parents are still living, the one I promised myself I'd never go back to.

I gave Adam a life of luxury, got him a good-paying job, and this is how he repays me?

CHAPTER 12

The morning's half over and I have so much to do. I can't keep putting this off. I head to the door that leads to the basement but stop before I get there to take a call from Marcus.

"Yes, Marcus," I say, answering his call.

"Hey, did you talk to Val?"

"I tried but didn't get very far. She turned down my suggestion to take some time off. She got rather defensive about it so I let it go."

"Why was she getting defensive?"

"I think she suspected there was something behind it. A reason why I was telling her to take some time away."

"There *is* a reason. She's upsetting her clients. You were supposed to talk to her about that."

"I think it'd be better coming from you. Valerie and I are friends. I don't want to ruin that by telling her how to do her job."

He sighs. "Yes, fine. I'll talk to her. So, where are you right now? I went to your office and Val said you left."

"I had some errands to run. I'll head back to the office soon."

"Hey, I wanted to let you know I'm going over to the house on Lyndale. I'm meeting Nick there to discuss the basement and try to light a fire under him to get it done."

The house he's talking about is the one I'm currently in. Nick is the builder. He's young, probably late twenties, and is still getting used to dealing with contractors. He hasn't yet figured out that you have to constantly check their work and make sure they're showing up. All his projects are delayed by at least six months.

"When are you meeting with him?" I ask.

"In a few minutes. I'm on my way there now."

"Great! We can talk to him together. I'm already here."

"You're at the house?" he asks, sounding surprised.

"I stopped by to check on the progress."

"Blaire, you shouldn't be there. Not after what happened. Let me handle this."

"Marcus, I'm fine," I assure him. "I'll be extra careful this time."

"I'm not worried you'll fall again. I'm concerned about how being there will affect you. It's too soon. You could've died in that house. You can't tell me you don't feel at least some level of trauma being there again."

"First of all, I don't even remember what happened that night. And second, you know I'm stronger than that. I've had plenty of trauma in my life and never let it affect me."

It's not entirely true. Growing up poor, seeing my parents struggle to put food on the table and hearing them fight about money affected me a great deal. But not in a bad way. Growing up that way is the reason I'm so successful. It's what drove me to work hard and have the life I have now.

"So how does it look?" Marcus asks. "Have they done any work? Nick said they had, but I don't believe him."

"I don't know. I haven't been down there yet. I was just about to go down when you called."

"Why don't you wait until I'm there? I'm only a few minutes away."

"Marcus, you're being ridiculous. I'm fine. Being here isn't causing me any stress."

The stress I felt was caused by Troy, not the house, but he's gone now.

"Okay, well, I'll be there shortly," Marcus says. "And Blaire, please be careful."

"I will. I'll see you soon." I end the call and slide my phone into the pocket of my dress slacks.

As I approach the door to the basement, I notice my breaths getting shallow and a tightness forming in my chest. It must be Marcus' comments making me react this way. I was fine before he called.

I reach the door and slowly open it. As I look down at the stairs, images flash through my mind. I see myself falling head first, my body tumbling, over and over, until I reach the bottom.

I gasp and take a step back.

"You're fine," I tell myself, my hand over my chest, feeling my heart beating hard and fast. "It's just a memory. It's good. It means your brain is healing."

My words of encouragement don't help. I'm still panicking, feeling like I'm experiencing that night all over again.

This wasn't supposed to happen. I'm stronger than this. I take a deep breath and step up to the stairs. I grab hold of the railing and am about to lower down to the first step when I feel something. A set of hands, pressing against my back. Shoving me. Forcefully.

I jerk back and slam the door shut.

"Blaire?" Marcus calls out from the other room.

"I'm here," I call out in a fake cheery voice.

I don't want Marcus knowing he was right, that being here would cause me to have some kind of traumatic response. Clearly, that's what happened, but it wasn't real. Nobody pushed me. Why would my mind even imagine such a scenario?

"There you are," Marcus says, finding me in the short hallway between the living room and kitchen, eyeing the door that goes to the basement. He smiles at me. "What are you doing?"

"What do you mean?"

He laughs a little. "Why are you standing in the hall, backed against the wall like that?"

I didn't realize my back was hugging the wall. I step away from it and straighten my shoulders, trying to appear confident and unaffected by what just happened.

"I was on the phone," I tell him. "I called Val to confirm she was getting Caitlyn at school today. They're going shopping."

He gives me a confused look. "Since when does Val spend time with your daughter?"

"She doesn't, usually. She's just been helping me out, getting Caitlyn from school while I recover."

"How kind of her," he says, but I can't tell if he's being sarcastic or genuine. He glances at the basement. "So, how's the progress? Did they do anything?"

"Oh, I never made it down there. I called Val, and then you showed up."

"Let's go check it out." He goes over to the basement door and opens it. "Ladies first," he says, smiling at me.

My heart's pounding as I look at the dark staircase.

What is wrong with me? Why am I acting like this? I'm not going to fall again.

"Blaire?" Marcus says. "Is everything okay?"

"Yes, of course," I say, slowly moving forward until I'm at the top of the stairs. I flip the light switch on, the single lightbulb doing little to illuminate the space.

Grabbing hold of the railing, I lower down to the first step. I'm shaking and my knees feel weak, like they're about to buckle and cause me to fall. I tighten my grip on the railing.

I can do this, I tell myself. *I'm not letting my fears get the best of me.*

I take another step.

"Blaire?" Marcus asks from behind me. I feel his large hand on my back and shriek.

"What's wrong?" Marcus says, racing down to the stair in front of me. "Why are you yelling?"

My knees give out and I sink down on the stair. I'm breathing fast and breaking out in a cold sweat.

"Blaire, I'm right here," Marcus says in a soft, concerned voice. "What happened?"

"I'm fine," I say, hearing my shaky voice. "I just need a minute."

"Marcus!" I hear Nick yell. "Where are you?"

"I'll go distract him," Marcus says.

I nod as Marcus hurries up the stairs.

He doesn't want Nick seeing me like this. As the listing agent assigned to selling this multimillion-dollar house, I need to appear professional and confident, not cowered on the staircase, holding on to the railing for dear life.

"You been down there yet?" I hear Nick say.

"No," Marcus says. "I was about to when you walked in. Oh, and um, Blaire is here too. I hope you don't mind."

"No, it's good. You two are the ones selling it. You should both be here."

I'll be selling it, not Marcus. He stopped selling houses a long time ago. He makes enough money that he doesn't need to. Combine that with Lydia's money and he's wealthy enough to never work another day in his life. I think he only comes into the office to get a break from his wife.

"Let's go check it out," Nick says. "As far as I know, the electrician is the only one who was over here last week, but I called my contractor and said he either gets a crew over here next week or I'm finding someone else."

"Hey, before we go down there," Marcus says. "Could you take a look at the siding out front? I think I saw a crack in one of the boards."

"Which one? Let's go out there and you can show me."

"I need to make a call, but it's on the right side, about halfway up."

"I'll check it on my way out."

"Would you mind doing it now? We might forget if we wait."

Marcus is trying to get rid of Nick to buy me some time. I need to get myself together. I've never had something like this happen before. It felt like a panic attack, although I've never actually had one so I can't say for sure.

"Blaire," Marcus says as I slowly stand up from the stair. "Are you feeling any better?"

"Yes." I turn back and smile at him, keeping hold of the railing. "Where's Nick?"

"Outside, but he won't be gone long. Do you think you can handle this, or do you need to leave?"

"I'll be fine." I turn back toward the basement, my fear creeping back as I look at the stairs.

"Here." Marcus appears beside me. "Take my arm."

Holding onto him with one hand, my other hand gripping the railing, I'm able to make it down the stairs, but the whole time, I keep having that memory of someone's hands on my back, shoving me.

Did that really happen? It couldn't have. It doesn't make sense. Nobody would push me down the stairs. But then why do I have a memory of it? I wouldn't just imagine something like that. Would I?

If it really did happen — if someone shoved me down the stairs — it means they were trying to hurt me, maybe even kill me.

Who would do that? It would've had to have been someone at the party that night. Someone I know, maybe even someone I'm close to, but why? Why would they do it?

I don't have enemies, at least not ones who hate me enough to want to kill me.

CHAPTER 13

"Marcus?" Nick calls out from upstairs.

"Down here," Marcus yells. "Blaire and I are in the basement."

Nick runs down the stairs quickly without holding onto the railing. I tense up watching him, worried he'll trip and fall. I'm always careful going down stairs, and I always hold onto the railing. So how did it happen? How did I fall down the stairs? Was I really pushed? That can't be true. Can it?

"Blaire," Marcus says with an uncomfortable laugh. "You still with us?"

What does he mean? Did he ask me a question? Or did Nick?

"Sorry, my mind wandered. I was thinking of some people who would be a perfect fit for this house." I smile at Nick. "I can't wait to start showing it."

"You still want to wait?" Marcus asks Nick. "Because I know Blaire could sell this place without the basement being finished."

"I want to wait," Nick says, folding his arms over his chest. "If it sells before it's finished, the buyers will want input on finishing the basement and I don't want to deal with that."

Marcus looks around the dimly lit space that's littered with construction equipment. "You've got a lot to get done, and it's looked this way for over a month."

"Yeah, I know." Nick sighs. "The contractor called me back when I was outside. He said he'll have five guys over here tomorrow."

My mind wanders again as Nick and Marcus talk. My gaze lowers to the concrete floor. I remember my head hitting it, hearing the thud it made, feeling the pain slice through my skull, then the blood running down my face.

"So, Blaire," Nick says, drawing my attention back to him. "How's the recovery going?"

"Well," I say, smiling at him. "I was supposed to be off today, but I'm feeling so much better that I returned to work a day early."

"That's great! You know I never heard how it happened. Did you miss a step, or how'd you end up falling?"

"It's probably best if we don't make her relive it," Marcus says to Nick. "It was rather traumatic for her."

"Oh, yeah, sorry," Nick says. "I wasn't thinking."

"No, it's fine," I say, keeping a smile plastered on my face. "Honestly, I really don't know how it happened. It was one of those things where it happened so fast I don't remember what caused it. One minute I was standing at the top of the stairs and the next thing I know, I'm tumbling down them."

"Guess I should be more careful," Nick says. "I'm always running down stairs without even thinking about it, but all it takes is for your foot to land wrong and you could end up in the hospital."

"Blaire was very lucky," Marcus says. "It could've been much worse. I was so relieved when we heard she'd be okay."

Marcus says it with so much care and concern, almost like he was talking about one of his daughters. He's very protective of me, but I don't know if it's because I make him a lot of money or because I know his secret. I'd like to think he cares

89

about me because we're friends, but the cynic in me knows better than to believe that.

"So you're back full-time now?" Nick asks me.

"I will be on Monday. I promised my husband I'd take the weekend off, but he knows that's not realistic in this business. I'm there when my clients need me." I smile at Marcus as I say it.

"Blaire always goes above and beyond," Marcus says, returning my smile before looking back at Nick. "So, going back to our discussion, when will you be able to give us a completion date?"

"Probably after next week. But I honestly can't see it being done sooner than a month from now."

"You've been telling us that since June." I finally focus on the conversation. "We need you to commit to a timeline and stop throwing out arbitrary dates."

Nick shrugs. "Yeah, I know. I'll stay on top of things from here on out."

"Do you have everything picked out for down here?" I ask. "Last time we met, you had some decisions to make on the lighting and bar cabinets."

"Yeah, I've got it all on my laptop. Let's go upstairs and I'll show you what I picked out."

He waits for me to go first, but I can't. My heart's beating out of my chest as I think about making it up the stairs. Going up shouldn't be a problem, but I keep imagining myself losing my balance and falling backward down the stairs.

"You go ahead," Marcus says to Nick. "I need to talk to Blaire."

"Yeah, okay." Nick goes upstairs as Marcus comes up to me.

"What's wrong?" he asks, keeping his voice down.

"Nothing." I shake my head. "I'm fine."

Marcus puts his hand on my shoulder. "I'm worried about you. Maybe you came back to work too soon."

"I didn't. It's just . . ." I pause. "It's this house. Being back here."

"Then maybe you should go. I can finish up with Nick. You don't need to be here."

"No. I want to hear what he's planning before it's too late to make changes."

"If that's what you want." He steps back and waits for me to go first.

I walk over to the stairs and grip the railing. My heart's pounding so hard I feel like I can't breathe. Looking up the stairs, a memory flashes in my head. I see someone standing at the top of the staircase, looking down at me as I lie on the floor, injured and begging for help. It's dark and I can't see who it is, and then the door shuts. Whoever was there shut the door so nobody would find me, or when they did, it'd be too late. I'd be dead.

"Blaire," Marcus says. "What are you doing? Nick's waiting."

I glance behind me and see Marcus there. "Go ahead. I'll be up in a minute."

"Is this about the stairs?"

"No. I just—" I stop, not sure how to explain this in a way that doesn't make me sound crazy or weak, or both.

"Go ahead," Marcus says. "I'll be right behind you if something happens."

Marcus is being very understanding about this. I assumed he'd tell me to get over it and hurry up the stairs, but instead he's being very patient and kind.

"That's good," he says when I'm halfway up the stairs. "I'm right behind you. You can do this. Just a few more steps."

With his encouragement, I make it to the top, my heart calming down the moment my feet hit the wood floor that leads to the kitchen where Nick is waiting.

"I wasn't sure if you were coming," Nick kids as Marcus and I join him at the kitchen island, where he has his laptop set up.

Marcus ignores the comment and looks at the laptop screen. "Let's see what you got."

Nick goes over the materials he's picked out. We've already seen most of them, but that was months ago so it's good to review them again.

"I'll be in touch later this week," Nick says as we walk him to the door.

"You can just call Blaire," Marcus says. "She'll fill me in."

"Sounds good." Nick leaves, going out to his pickup truck parked on the street.

Marcus shuts the door.

"Aren't you leaving?" I ask.

"In a minute." He turns to me. "I think we need to talk first."

"About what?" I ask, my pulse quickening.

"About what's going on with you." His brows furrow as he looks at me with concern. "I think maybe you should see someone."

"Like a psychiatrist?" I laugh, expressing how ridiculous it is for him to even suggest that. "You think I'm crazy just because I didn't go up the stairs fast enough?"

"Blaire, you were terrified. You went up those stairs like you were walking to your death. And you were even more terrified going down them."

"It's perfectly normal for someone to be frightened when having to do something that nearly killed them. I just need practice. After I go up and down the stairs a few more times, I'll be fine."

"And what if you're not? How are you going to show this house to people if you can't go up and down the stairs?"

"When that time comes, which according to Nick won't be for at least another month, I'll have no issue with the stairs." I check my watch. "It's getting late. I need to get back to the office."

I only say that to put an end to this conversation. I hadn't actually planned on going back to the office yet. I still need to clear my head after getting that threatening note, and now I have the added stress of thinking someone pushed me down the stairs.

What if the two are related? What if whoever sent those flowers is the one who pushed me, assuming that really happened and it isn't some false memory conjured up by my injured brain?

Marcus follows me back to the kitchen where I left my purse.

"Are you sure you're okay?" he asks. "Maybe you should take the rest of the day off. You'd already planned to, so I'm guessing your calendar is free."

"It is, which is why I'm using the time to catch up on some things before Monday." I sling my purse over my shoulder, my mind going back to that note in the flowers. "Marcus, did anyone help you make the guest list for my party?"

"Just Valerie. And I guess Adam. Val called him to get input on who to invite. Why do you ask?"

"I was just surprised to see Rob and Alice there."

Marcus gives me a confused look. "Rob and Alice?"

"My neighbors. They live next door. You know Rob. Tall. Dark hair. Really fit. He owns that online diet and fitness program."

Marcus nods. "Yes, that's right. He used to be a trainer at the health club where Lydia goes."

"I didn't know Lydia belonged to that club."

"She belongs but rarely goes." He rubs his jaw. "I guess I do remember seeing Rob at the party, but not his wife."

"Alice was there. Short woman, kind of . . . large."

His eyes widen. "That was Alice? I had no idea. Last time I saw her, she looked nothing like that."

"She's put on some weight the past few years. And she doesn't leave the house much, other than to meet friends for lunch."

"Yes, she was quite the socialite before she got married. But that might've been her parents pressuring her to be that way. Before they died, they were very active in the community, attending various fundraisers and charity events."

Alice's parents died in a plane crash. It was one of those small private planes. It happened twenty years ago, which I found out when I looked her up online. I always do research on people after I meet them, just a quick internet search. I'm not being nosy. I'm just curious about people's backgrounds. And who wouldn't want to know more about the people living right next door to them? It's for safety purposes more than anything else. You need to know if a psychopath is living next door, not that I could find that out online, but you might find something that would indicate the person is unstable or dangerous.

In Alice's case, I couldn't find much. Just the usual things you find online with wealthy people. Articles about donations to this and that charity, photos of Alice and her parents at ritzy, high-society events, and of course, Alice's extravagant wedding to Rob. I didn't find anything that would lead me to believe Alice is capable of attempted murder, but that doesn't mean it's not possible.

People are capable of most anything. All it takes is a strong enough motive and the right circumstances. If Alice suspected I'd been intimate with Rob, she'd have motive to kill me, and the party gave her the time and place to do it. Everyone was outside. The music was loud, so even if I'd been able to scream, no one would've heard me. And when someone finally noticed I was missing, the last place they'd look for me is the basement.

Whoever did this to me thought it out. They planned it. They were watching me that night, waiting for the right time.

If that person was Alice, she would've had to invite herself to the party. She would've had to know the layout of the house. And during the party, she would've had to watch me and wait for me to go into the house at a time when no one else was around.

I can't imagine Alice going to all that work. She's very lazy. That seems like more than she'd be willing to do.

But if she really wanted me dead, it's entirely possible that's exactly what she did.

CHAPTER 14

"So are you saying you didn't invite her?" I ask Marcus.

"Alice? No. Valerie must have. Maybe Adam told her to when she asked him for suggestions for the guest list."

"Adam wouldn't do that," I say, knowing he wouldn't invite someone I don't like.

"Then it had to have been Valerie," Marcus says. "She invited several people on your block. Why are you asking about this? Did you not want your neighbors there?"

"Not those particular neighbors." I glance out the sliding glass door, then back at Marcus. "I don't care for Alice. The way she gossips about people, and she's always so negative. I would've preferred not to have her there."

"Sorry about that. If I'd known, I would've made sure she wasn't invited."

"Do you happen to recall seeing Alice and Rob leave that night?"

"No. As I said, I didn't even remember Alice being there, but honestly, I didn't know that was her. She looks so different from a few years ago. Why do you ask?"

"I'm just curious how long they stayed."

The truth is, I'm trying to figure out if Alice was in the house around the time I fell — or was pushed — down the stairs. But I'm not sure I want to tell Marcus about my memory of someone pushing me. I'm not sure I want to tell anyone, not until I know that memory is real.

I'm starting to think it *is* real, given the response it causes in me every time images flash through my mind. If it didn't happen, I wouldn't react that way. I wouldn't be terrified to go down those stairs. My mind wouldn't be racing to figure out who would do that to me.

It had to be Alice. She was the only person at the party who hates me. And if she thinks there's something going on between Rob and me, it's entirely possible she wanted me dead.

"What's this about, Blaire?" Marcus asks. "I feel like there's something behind these questions. Did something happen that night that you're not telling me? Something between you and Alice?"

"No," I say, laughing it off. "Nothing happened. I just wondered why she was there, but it doesn't matter. It's over now. I'm going to head out. I have an errand to run before I go back to the office."

He holds up his phone. "I need to make a call. You go ahead. I'll lock up."

I leave the house and go out to my SUV, my mind still on Alice, thinking she has to be the one who sent me that threatening note. Determined to find out, I drive to the floral shop that delivered the bouquet.

"Can I help you?" an older woman with white hair and glasses asks as I go into the shop.

"Yes." I walk up to her, a big smile on my face. "I received the most beautiful bouquet from your shop this morning, but it seems the card fell off and now I don't know who they're from. I was wondering if you could tell me so I can thank them."

"Yes, of course," she says, adjusting her glasses before typing into the computer. "It'll just take a minute. Could I have your name, please?"

"Blaire Banks."

The lady stops typing and smiles at me. "The real estate agent. I knew you looked familiar. I see your signs all over town."

"Yes, that's me. So anyway, the flowers were delivered to my office. The Rockingham Group on Harcourt Way."

She types it into her computer, her smile dropping to a frown. "I'm sorry, but it looks like we didn't make any deliveries there this morning. Was it perhaps another day?"

"No, it was definitely this morning. One of the office assistants brought the bouquet to me and said it had just been delivered."

She shakes her head. "Not by us. It must've been a different shop."

"No, I'm certain it was here," I say, remembering seeing the name of the floral shop printed on the envelope.

"It's possible someone picked them up and dropped them off at your office."

I suppose that could be true. Tara didn't actually say the floral shop delivered them. I just assumed they did because that's how flowers are typically delivered to offices. If Alice sent them, she wouldn't be dumb enough to drop them off herself. Maybe she bought them but had someone else drop them off.

"You have a record of who came in this morning, right?" I ask. "Their name would be on the credit card receipt."

"Yes, but I can't give out that information. And believe it or not, a lot of people still pay cash."

I'm guessing those are men buying flowers for their mistresses, who don't want their wives finding out. It's a well-known fact that many of the men in this town cheat, especially the ones who commute to Manhattan. Most of them keep an apartment there, claiming it's necessary for nights when they have to work late and don't want to make the commute back to Connecticut. But everyone — even their wives — knows what really goes on there. It makes me wonder why these men even bother sneaking around, but then I think of Marcus and the thrill he gets from his little secret. The secretive part is what makes it so exciting.

I let out a sigh. "I just feel terrible not being able to properly thank whoever gave me those flowers. Are you sure there's nothing you can do to help me find this person?"

She pauses to think. "What time did you receive them?"

"I think it was around nine?"

She looks up at the ceiling, tapping her lip. "I had several people come in this morning. One was a younger man getting flowers for his girlfriend. Another was an elderly gentleman, getting a small bouquet for his wife's grave." Her eyes dart back to me. "The other two were women around my age. One was getting flowers for her dinner party tonight and the other didn't say the reason. Perhaps she just wanted them for herself."

"What did she look like? Do you remember?"

"Yes, she was very thin, rather tall, and had short blonde hair. And like I said, she was around my age, or maybe a little older."

That doesn't describe Alice. Maybe she hired someone to buy the flowers.

"I really shouldn't have told you that," the woman says. "But I know how embarrassing it is when you receive a gift and the person asks you about it later and you have no idea what they're talking about."

"Yes, isn't that the worst?" I say.

"I'm sorry I couldn't be more helpful."

"I understand. I'll talk to the girl at my office. She might be able to tell me who dropped them off." I smile at the woman. "Thank you so much for taking the time to check for me."

When I arrive back at the office, Tara's at her desk, looking at her phone.

"Tara," I say, walking up to her. "About those flowers I got this morning. Did you see who dropped them off?"

She looks up from her phone. "No, I was in the back, making copies. Why?"

"I'm trying to figure out who sent them so I can thank them."

"Are you sure they're not from Adam?"

"No," I say with a laugh. "We've been married too long for Adam to send me flowers. Even when we were first married, he didn't send flowers. He said they were an unnecessary expense."

Adam still says that, even though we have plenty of money. It's a belief he inherited from his cheapskate of a father, who would never in a million years spend money on flowers or do anything nice for his wife.

"Maybe they were from someone you sold a house to," Tara says. "You know, to thank you for all the work you did. What did the card say? That should help you figure it out."

I can't tell her that, so I say, "It turns out it was blank. Isn't that strange?"

"Huh. Maybe try the flower shop. They might be able to help you."

"I already went there. They said they didn't deliver them. Whoever bought them picked them up and dropped them off here. That's why I was asking if you'd seen who delivered them."

She shrugs. "Sorry I can't help. They were here when I got back to my desk. I didn't even see anyone leaving."

"Well, I guess it will have to remain a mystery."

I go back to my office but can't focus on all the things I need to do. Every time I try, my mind wanders back to the memories I had at the house. Being at the top of the stairs. Feeling someone shove me. Lying on the concrete floor and watching as the person at the top of the stairs closed the door.

I shudder and a chill goes through me as I think about that. Whoever did that to me left me to die. But I didn't.

So what happens now? Are they going to try again?

CHAPTER 15

"Hey, Mom," Caitlyn says, coming into the house holding two large shopping bags. Valerie's behind her, holding Caitlyn's backpack.

It's just after five. I've been home since four, searching the internet for information on Alice. I couldn't find anything new that would support my theory that she's crazy enough to kill someone. I almost called Rob to tell him what really happened the night of my party and how I think his wife's involved but then decided against it. I need more time to think about this before taking action.

"Did you two have fun?" I ask.

"We did," Valerie says, smiling at Caitlyn. "And while we were shopping, we ran into two very cute boys."

Caitlyn smiles and rolls her eyes. "You weren't supposed to tell Mom that."

"Oh. Sorry," Valerie says with a laugh as she sets Caitlyn's backpack down.

"Do I know these boys?" I ask Caitlyn.

"Cameron and Matthew. You've met them. They go to my school."

"I sold Cameron's parents the house on Adams Street," I say to Valerie.

"That's a beautiful house," she says.

"Mom, could we go to dinner tomorrow instead of tonight?" Caitlyn says. "Emma and Kira invited me over and I really want to go. Emma's mom said she'd pick me up."

I'd normally tell Caitlyn no because we already made plans, but it might be good to have her out of the house so I can spend time trying to figure out who's trying to harm me and why.

Maybe I should tell Valerie about this. She knows what it's like to feel like someone's after you. A few years ago, a man was leaving notes on Valerie's car, saying she belonged to him and that she'd be sorry if she ever tried to be with someone else. She didn't know who was doing this until she caught the man on camera. It was someone she'd met online and had only been out with one time. The police arrested him, and luckily, he never bothered her again.

"Yes, you can go," I say to Caitlyn.

"Really?" she asks, like she doesn't believe me.

"Yes. I think I'm just going to stay in tonight. It's been a long day. I'm too tired to go out."

"I'm going to go call Emma and tell her!" Caitlyn runs upstairs with her shopping bags.

"Thanks for taking her," I say to Valerie. "How much do I owe you?" I head to the kitchen where I left my purse.

Valerie follows me in there. "You're not paying me. The clothes weren't much, and I had fun with her." Val laughs. "You should've seen her when those boys showed up. She clearly has a crush on Cameron. She couldn't stop blushing when he talked to her."

"Huh. I didn't know she liked him. But she hates talking about boys with me so I guess I'm not surprised she didn't tell me about Cameron."

"She has good taste. He's a nice-looking kid, and his family's loaded."

"Yes, they paid cash for that house."

It was over three million and they didn't even bother to negotiate the price. Cameron's father is a hedge-fund manager and his mother is an attorney. Cameron's an only child so his parents spoil him, but he seemed like a nice kid when I met him. He was very polite, and his mother said he gets all As in school. I wouldn't mind if Caitlyn dated him, but Adam would hate it. He doesn't want her dating boys who come from wealthy families, which is a problem since that describes every boy at her school.

"So, what are you and Adam doing tonight?" Valerie asks, taking a seat at the kitchen table. It's really more of a breakfast nook with a built-in bench along the window and two seats across from it.

"Adam has plans so it'll just be me here. I'll probably drink some wine and watch a movie."

"Sounds fun! Would you mind if I joined you?"

Having her here would probably be better than being alone all night, especially when I'm worried someone's trying to harm me.

"Sure! It'll be a girls' night." I walk over to the fridge and take out a bottle of white wine. "Should we start with this?"

"Yes, I'd love some. What about dinner?" She gets out her phone. "Do you want to order from the Italian place? You could get that shrimp pasta dish you like so much."

"That sounds wonderful," I say as I pour her wine.

As she orders the food, Caitlyn appears, a duffle bag slung over her shoulder. "I'm leaving. Emma's mom is here."

"What's in the bag?" I say.

"Some clothes. In case I spend the night." She gives me a look, her eyes pleading with me to let her stay overnight. "Can I, Mom? Please?"

"I need to speak with Emma's mom before I agree to this."

Just then, the doorbell rings. I go to answer it, with Caitlyn trailing behind.

"Hi, Jennifer," I say to Emma's mom, smiling at her. "How have you been?"

"Great!" She smiles back. "How about you?" Her smile drops. "I was horrified when I found out what happened. What an unfortunate accident."

It wasn't an accident. Someone shoved me.

"Yes, I'll certainly be more careful from now on," I tell her. "So anyway, I just wanted to confirm that the girls will be at your house all night."

"Yes, they'll be home, and Roger and I will be there to make sure they stay out of trouble." She smiles at Caitlyn as she says it.

"And you're okay with her spending the night?" I ask.

"If she'd like to, then yes. I believe Kira is planning to stay over as well."

I turn to Caitlin. "Call me in the morning and let me know when you're ready to go. Dad or I will come pick you up."

"Yeah, okay, bye." Caitlyn tries to sneak past me, but I catch her before she can and give her a quick hug.

"Have fun! Love you."

"Love you too," she mutters.

As soon as I let her go, she bolts past Jennifer to the driveway.

"Don't you just love this age?" Jennifer kids. "One day they want you around, the next they don't want you anywhere near them."

"Yes, exactly." I'm glad I'm not the only one whose child treats them that way.

She laughs and walks off to her luxury SUV that's still running in the driveway.

"Food will be here in a half hour," Valerie says as I go back to the kitchen.

"Let's be naughty and eat in the living room."

Her brows rise. "Are you feeling okay? You don't even let us drink water in there."

It's because I have a white couch and a white rug. When I moved here, I noticed rich people use a lot of white in their homes, as if to prove they were rich enough not to care if their white furniture and rugs got stained. They'd just buy new. I'm

103

not that rich, or I don't feel like I am, which is why I don't usually allow food or drinks in the living room.

"After almost dying," I say, taking a sip of my wine, "I feel the need to live a little — starting with having dinner on the white couch."

"Don't say you almost died." Val shudders. "It freaks me out."

"It's true. The doctor said I'm lucky to be alive. I could've snapped my neck when I hit the floor, which would've paralyzed me if it didn't kill me."

She shakes her head. "I don't even want to think about that. I still can't believe it happened." She takes a big drink of her wine. "What a freak accident."

It wasn't an accident. I was pushed.

But do I tell her that, or keep quiet?

Picking up the bottle of wine, I say, "Let's take this to the living room." We go sit down and I finish what's left in my glass and refill it, nearly to the top. I gulp some down and sink back on the couch.

"Blaire?" Valerie says, sounding concerned. "Is everything okay?"

Knowing me all these years, she can tell when something's off with me, even better than Adam can. But he's not the most observant person.

"No." I take another drink of my wine. "Things are very much not okay."

She sets her glass on the coffee table and turns to me. "What do you mean? Is this about Adam? Did you catch him with someone?"

"No," I say, thinking I should probably be concerned that Val saw him with another woman, but it hasn't even crossed my mind with everything else that's happened. "I, um, got a strange note with those flowers I received this morning."

"What do you mean? What did it say?"

I look at Val. "The note made it sound like I'd been with another man and said I deserve whatever happens to me."

Valerie gasps. "Oh my God! Why didn't you tell me? I mean, this morning, at the office?"

"I was too shocked and too focused on trying to figure out who might've sent it. Tara didn't see who dropped the flowers off and the floral shop didn't have a record of who bought them."

"I don't understand. Who in the world would do something like that?"

"I think it might be Alice."

"Alice who?"

"My neighbor. That weird woman who lives next door and rarely leaves the house. She's married to Rob, the fitness guy."

"Oh, yes. I met her a few weeks ago." Valerie picks up her wine and takes a sip.

"Where did you meet her?"

"Here. In the driveway. I came over to drop something off. I can't remember what, but anyway, Alice was out getting her mail and yelled over to me that you were out back by the pool."

"Yes," I say with a sigh. "She's always watching me, like she has nothing better to do. I can't stand it. So then what happened? Did she talk to you?"

"She walked over to me, saying she recognized me from my ads. She said she'd met my mother once at some charity event. She seemed normal at the time, but I do remember you saying she was a little off."

"She's more than a little off. She's crazy. Hey, did you invite her to my party?"

"Yes." She cringes. "Sorry. I kind of had to. She saw one of the invites sticking out of my purse and asked me about it. She practically begged me for an invite, so I gave her one. I didn't think you'd be upset since she's your neighbor."

"Yes, well, I wish you hadn't done that." I pour more wine into Valerie's glass. "The woman hates me."

"Why? She has no reason to."

I set the wine bottle down. "She thinks I'm having an affair with Rob."

"What?" Valerie laughs. "That's ridiculous. Why would she even think that?"

I keep quiet and take a drink of my wine.

"Blaire, you didn't . . . I mean, I know you and Adam are having issues, but you're not . . . seeing someone else. Are you?"

The doorbell rings.

"That's our food," I say, getting up from the couch.

As I answer the door, Val goes back to the kitchen. I bring the food in there and find her getting the plates out and some silverware.

"Val, about this thing with Rob. I—"

"You don't have to explain. It's none of my business. And hey, I've never been married. I don't know what it's like." She hands me a plate. "You two got married so young, I get why you might feel the need to be with someone else."

"But that's not why I did it." I take the plate from her and set it on the counter. "Honestly, I don't even remember it."

"What are you saying?" she asks, her brows rising. "That he drugged you?"

"No, nothing like that. I'd been drinking that night. Adam was away at that car show in Boston and Caitlyn was at a friend's house. I went out to a bar and had way too much wine. Rob showed up and offered to drive me home. We went out back to the parking lot and . . . something happened. Something I don't remember, but he remembers it quite clearly."

"Maybe he's lying. Maybe it never happened."

"I'm pretty sure it did. I remember us kissing and things moving beyond that. I just don't remember the actual act. He came over here the next day acting like we'd agreed to have an affair. I had no idea what he was talking about. Apparently, I'd said I wanted to have an affair after we were together that night, but I don't remember saying it."

"And you haven't done anything with him since then?"

"No. I told him I'm committed to Adam and whatever happened that night wasn't happening again."

"But you think his wife found out?"

"She had to have. Why else would she write that in the card?"

"Assuming it was from her."

"Who else would send me that?"

She shrugs. "I don't know. There's a lot of crazy people out there. Maybe one of the wives you sold a house to thinks you have something going on with her husband."

"But why would anyone think that? I'm not out there flirting with men when I'm trying to sell a house."

She walks over to the sacks of food and starts taking containers out.

"Valerie?"

"We should eat this before it gets cold."

I walk over to her. "What do you know? Are people saying things about me?"

She turns to face me. "It was just one woman. She came to the office a few months ago to talk to you, but you weren't there. I asked if I could help her and she said — and these are her words, not mine — 'you can tell her to stay away from my husband.'"

I'm stunned. I can't believe someone actually said that. I'm always extremely professional, so for some woman to accuse me of trying to steal her husband, or whatever this woman thinks I was doing, is both appalling and insulting.

"Who was it?" I ask. "Did she give you her name?"

"No, but she was around thirty-five and very tall with long black hair and some kind of accent. I couldn't tell where it was from."

I nod. "Irina. She accuses every woman of trying to steal her husband. I guess I feel a little better knowing it was her and not someone else."

"Did you sell them a house?"

"No, they ended up moving to Dubai for her husband's job."

We take our food to the living room and Valerie tells me about her day, but my mind keeps wandering to that memory of someone pushing me down the stairs. I desperately want to tell someone about it but don't know if Val is the right person. What if I can't trust her? I could tell Adam, but if he's lying to me and cheating on me, I can't trust him either.

I feel like I can't trust anyone anymore.

CHAPTER 16

It's after eight and Val and I just opened our third bottle of wine. I don't usually drink this much, but with each glass, the day's events seem less overwhelming and I feel myself becoming more relaxed.

"Are you still on painkillers?" Valerie asks. "Because you probably shouldn't be drinking if you are."

"I'm not," I say, sipping my wine. "I stopped taking them this morning."

"It's really amazing how quickly you recovered. I still can't believe you didn't break anything. You're really lucky." She picks up the bottle and refills her glass. "It's scary to think how quickly your life could change after something like tripping on the stairs."

"I didn't trip," I mutter.

"What was that?" she asks, setting the wine bottle down.

"I said I didn't trip." The words flow past my lips before I can stop them. "It wasn't an accident."

"Of course it was." She laughs, swirling her wine around the glass. "What else would it be? You wouldn't intentionally fall down the stairs."

"Someone pushed me." I take a drink of my wine.

Valerie laughs again, but it's an uncomfortable laugh. "I think you're done." She takes my wine glass from me and sets it on the table. "Why don't we quit for tonight? We can drink the rest some other night."

"Val, I'm serious." I turn to her. "I went to the house today, the one where we had the party. While I was there, my memories came back, or at least some of them."

"And? What did you see?"

"I saw you and Adam in the kitchen. I saw the birthday banner hung over the fireplace. I saw people in the backyard. Tables set up. The three-tiered cake. I saw it all."

"And you waited this long to tell me? Blaire, this is great news! You got your memory back!" She sees my expression and her excitement fades. "Why aren't you smiling? Aren't you happy about this?"

"I was until I opened the door to the basement."

"Why? What happened?"

I look at her. "I felt someone shove me. Hard. It wasn't an accident, Val. Someone wanted me to fall down the stairs."

She rears back. "What? No. Blaire, that's crazy. No one would do that."

"But someone did. I saw them at the top of the stairs. I watched as they closed the door, leaving me down there, knowing I was seriously injured, maybe even dead."

"Who was it?" she asks, setting her wine glass down.

"I don't know. It was dark and my vision was blurry from hitting my head. All I really saw was an outline of someone standing at the top of the stairs."

"That doesn't make sense. Nobody would do that. Maybe it wasn't real. Maybe your brain's playing tricks on you, making up fake memories."

"I thought that too at first, but now I think it really happened. Being there today, it was like I was back at the party. Like I was experiencing it all over again. When I realized why I fell — that it wasn't an accident — I was terrified. I couldn't even make it down the stairs. Marcus had to help me."

"Marcus was there?"

"He was meeting with Nick, the builder." I scoot closer to Valerie. "I didn't tell Marcus what happened. And you can't either. I don't want anyone knowing this until I figure out what to do."

"But you told Adam, right?"

"No. You're the only one who knows. You can't tell anyone. Promise me you won't."

"Um, okay, but why wouldn't you tell Adam? He's your husband. He needs to know this."

"What if I can't trust him?" I sit back, feeling sick to my stomach at the very thought of Adam being involved.

"You don't mean . . ." She waits for me to finish the thought.

"It's always the husband. Isn't that what they say? When something happens to a woman? The police always suspect the husband, especially if there are issues in the marriage, and Adam and I definitely have issues."

"Yes, but Adam would never do anything to hurt you."

"I didn't think so, but what if I'm wrong? Think about it, Val. Adam's the one who found me that night. And it took him an hour before he went looking for me. If I'd been seriously injured, I could've been dead by then."

"Adam thought you were at the party. He didn't have a reason to go looking for you."

"He knew I went into the house to talk to Caitlyn. She told me later that she'd gone outside to the party, which means Adam would've seen her. If he knew she was outside, but I was still in the house, why didn't he go looking for me?"

"Maybe he thought you were using the bathroom or getting more champagne."

"For an hour? That doesn't make sense."

"So you think Adam followed you into the house, pushed you down the stairs, left you there, went back to the party, then came back an hour later and pretended to find you?"

"Yes."

111

Although when she lays it all out like that, it sounds less plausible.

"Blaire, that's crazy. Adam loves you."

"And yet he's cheating on me."

"Yes, well, you don't know that for sure. And even if you did, that doesn't mean he'd try to harm you."

"He would if he wanted to get rid of me to be with someone else. And with me gone, he'd get everything. The house. The cars. Our money. He wouldn't have to split it with me like he would if we got divorced."

She pauses to think about that. "I still don't think he'd do it. He just planned that nice trip for you. Adam hates the city, but he took you there because he knows how much you love it. A man who does that isn't going to try to kill you a few days later."

"Then who did it? It had to be someone at the party that night. I was thinking it might be Alice, but she left before I went inside to look for Caitlyn."

"Are you sure? Did you actually see her leave?"

"I didn't see her get into the car and drive off, but I definitely saw her leaving the party with Rob."

"When you went into the house, did you see anyone else in there?"

"No, but Caitlyn said Troy was there to fix the sink. When she saw him, she got scared. That's why she went outside to the party."

"It's him," Valerie says with conviction. "It has to be. The guy's been to prison. He's violent." She shakes her head. "I told you not to hire him. I knew something bad would happen."

"Just because Troy was there that night doesn't mean he did it."

"Blaire, think about it. Everyone at the party was either a friend or family member. None of those people would try to hurt you. The only person who might is your weird neighbor, who you already said was gone when it happened. That leaves Troy."

112

"It's not him. I saw him at the house today. We were alone together. If he wanted to kill me, he could've done it then."

"And have it look like a crime? He's smarter than that. He'd want it to look like an accident so he doesn't end up in prison again. I'm telling you, Blaire, it's him. We need to fire him. We can hire a different handyman, someone who doesn't have a criminal history."

Maybe she's right. Even if Troy didn't do it, I'd feel safer if he wasn't around. He made me very uncomfortable this morning when he cornered me in the kitchen, and I think he did it on purpose. He was trying to scare me. But firing him could turn him against me and he's not someone I want as an enemy.

"Did you go in the house that night?" I ask Valerie. "During the time I was missing?"

"Only to use the bathroom. Wait, are you accusing *me* of doing this?"

"No. I'm just trying to figure who might've been in the house when it happened. Did you see anyone when you went in to use the bathroom?"

"Let me think." She chews on her lip. "Oh, yes, I remember Adam coming in as I was leaving. He said the bartender ran out of his favorite beer so he was getting one from the fridge."

"We didn't have beer in the fridge. Only bottles of water."

"Oh. Then maybe he was in there to use the bathroom."

"But he told you he was getting a beer?"

"I think so. I mean, I'm pretty sure that's what he said. But hey, that doesn't mean anything. Maybe he thought there was beer in the fridge and then found out there wasn't."

"Or he lied. To cover up the real reason he went into the house."

Valerie doesn't say anything. Neither do I.

Adam wouldn't try to hurt me, would he? I'm his wife. We've been together since high school. We have a daughter. He wouldn't want Caitlyn to be left without a mother.

113

But I can't deny the fact that it's possible. These things happen all the time. Men kill their wives. They're always the prime suspect in a woman's murder.

There's a sound at the door. The lock turning. The door swings open and Adam walks in.

My pulse races when I see him, wondering if this man I've spent my entire adult life with, the father of my child, is really capable of murder.

And if he is, how do I keep living with him, knowing he tried to kill me?

CHAPTER 17

Adam looks disheveled, his hair mussed, a thick layer of stubble on his face, his shirt wrinkled. His suit jacket is slung over his arm, and his tie is hanging loose around his neck. Was he with a woman? Is that why he looks that way?

"Blaire," he says, seeming startled by the sight of me on the couch. He shuts the door. "I thought you were taking Caitlyn out tonight."

"She went to a friend's house, so Valerie and I decided to have a girls' night."

"Hey, Val," he says, giving her a nod.

She smiles at him. "Out with the boys tonight?"

"Something like that. I'll leave you two alone. I'm going up to bed."

"Actually, I was just leaving," Valerie says, getting up.

"You are?" I say, panicking at the thought of being alone with Adam.

"I'll help you clean up first." She gathers up her plate and wine glass as Adam goes upstairs.

"What are you doing?" I whisper, following her into the kitchen. "You can't leave me here with him."

115

She puts the dishes in the sink and turns to me. "Blaire, listen to yourself. You're being ridiculous. Adam is not trying to kill you."

"How do you know?"

"I just do, okay?" She dries her hands on a towel. "I'm going to go and let you two talk this out." She picks her purse up from the counter.

"Are you sure you're okay to drive?"

"I'm fine," she says as we walk to the door. "I only had a few glasses. You drank the rest."

I follow her out to her car. "I really wish you wouldn't leave. What if he—"

"He won't," she assures me, glancing up at the house. "I'm telling you, Adam didn't do it." She gives me a quick hug. "Try to get some rest. I'll see you on Monday."

As she drives off, I think about how certain she sounded when telling me Adam wasn't the one who pushed me. Why did she say it that way? With so much conviction? It's almost like she knew who did it. But she couldn't. She would've told me if she knew. Wouldn't she?

Going back into the house, I see Adam coming down the stairs, wearing a T-shirt and pajama pants, his hair wet from the shower.

"Hey," he says. "Did Val leave?"

"Yes." I walk past him to the kitchen to finish cleaning up. Despite what Valerie said, I'm still not certain I can trust Adam. He lied about where he was tonight. How can I trust him if he's lying to me?

"You want some help?" Adam asks as I put the plates in the dishwasher.

He never offers to help. He must be feeling guilty for whatever he did tonight.

"I can handle it," I tell him. "You can go to bed."

"Why don't you come with me? I'm sure you're tired after being at work all day."

"As if you'd let me sleep," I mutter, knowing the real reason he wants me to join him in bed.

"What's that supposed to mean?"

"Nothing. Forget it."

Adam comes up to me, standing closer than I'd like. "I'm trying to make an effort here, but all you do is push me away."

"Really?" I huff. "Is lying to me what you consider making an effort?"

"What are you talking about?"

"You said you were working late. The dealership closes at five on Fridays."

He looks down, rubbing his face. "Okay, fine. I wasn't at work. I went out."

"Where?"

His eyes rise to mine. "To a bar. I had a drink. Got dinner. Then I drove around."

"You really think I believe that?"

"It's the truth," he says, raising his voice. "What do you think I was doing?"

"Well, let's see. You come home with a wrinkled shirt, your hair a mess, and race upstairs to shower. I think it's pretty clear what you were doing tonight."

"Really, Blaire?" He walks away, then turns back to me. "You think I was with a woman?"

"How else do you explain why you looked that way?"

"Because I'm under a lot of damn stress, that's why. I'm not making my sales quota at work. We keep racking up debt buying stuff we can't afford. And my wife almost died. Can you see why I might be a little stressed out right now?"

My muscles relax, my fear of him fading away as I see the worry on his face. The frustration. The exhaustion.

"Why didn't you tell me this?" I ask. "About your job?"

He lets out a harsh laugh. "And have you tell me I'm a loser? Yeah, no thanks. I already feel like shit. I don't need you making me feel even worse."

"Adam, I didn't know." I walk up to him. "I didn't know you were struggling like this. If I had, I would've—"

"Told me to work harder. Told me I'm lazy. Unmotivated. And that I should be spending my time reading books on sales techniques instead of watching TV."

He might be right about that, but it's only because I'm trying to help him. You don't get better at something by sitting around doing nothing. You have to put in the work.

"I'm not you, Blaire," he says, looking at me. "I don't want to work myself to death just to impress people or make a lot of money."

"That's not why I do it. I like my job. I enjoy working."

"Because you like the attention you get for being the top agent. The compliments you get from clients. The sales awards. The big checks you get after you sell a house."

"There's nothing wrong with those things. Who doesn't like compliments and awards? And the money helps us have the life we've always wanted."

"It's the life *you* wanted, Blaire, not me." He motions to the house. "All this is great. I'm not complaining. But look what we gave up to have it. We never see each other. And Caitlyn has to make an appointment to spend time with you."

"That's not true."

"Look at your calendar. I bet you've got Caitlyn's name written in there, like she's one of your damn clients."

He's right. I do, but I'm sure a lot of parents keep a calendar with time blocked out for their children. I can't be the only one.

"I thought after your accident," Adam says, "you'd see there are things more important than money. I thought you'd finally stop working so much, but instead you went back to the office on a day you were supposed to be home recovering. You couldn't even wait one more day."

"Because I love my job. Why can't you get that? I'm not my mother. I can't sit around the house all day, cooking and dusting and ironing my husband's clothes. If that's what you wanted for a wife, that's not me."

"That's not what I want. I just want a wife that isn't gone all the time. I want a wife I can sit down and have dinner with at night. A wife that wants to do stuff with me on the weekends."

"Nights and weekends are my busiest times. You know that, Adam. It's just part of the job."

He nods, looking defeated. "You coming to bed?"

"Not yet. I think I'll stay down here and watch some TV."

He doesn't offer to watch with me, but I didn't think he would. He's frustrated with me for not agreeing to what he wanted, but it's just not possible. He knows I have to show houses when people are able to see them, not when it's convenient for me.

As I watch him leave, I'm tempted to go with him. I keep saying I'll work on our marriage, but then I never do. This is my chance, but part of me still doesn't trust him. Was he really just driving around all night, and if so, why did he come home looking like he'd just had sex?

Maybe it's time for me to accept that my marriage can't be saved. I love Adam, and always will, but I don't love him the way a wife should love her husband. The passion between us is gone. We're living like roommates, passing each other on our way to and from work, only talking when we need to. But I've been with Adam for so long that imagining a life without him doesn't seem possible. I don't want a divorce, but it's not fair to either of us to keep living this way. We each want more than the other person can give.

If I loved Adam the way I should, I'd be upstairs right now, telling him what happened today. I would've told him about that threatening note and called him the moment I got my memory back. But I didn't. And I'm still not sure if I will.

That says a lot about our marriage. And doesn't give me much hope for our future.

CHAPTER 18

Saturday morning, I wake up on the couch. I fell asleep watching TV and never made it upstairs. I'm sure Adam's angry about that, but I wasn't ready to sleep next to him, not after that tense conversation we had.

I go to the kitchen and get the coffee started, then check my phone to see if Caitlyn texted. She didn't, but I didn't think she would this early. It's not even eight.

"Hey," Adam says, coming into the kitchen, shirtless and wearing jeans.

I watch him as he goes to the fridge, noticing his body and realizing he's not in bad shape for someone his age. He isn't as fit as Rob, but almost no man is that fit so it really isn't fair to compare the two.

"Do you want breakfast?" Adam asks. "I could make us some eggs."

"I'd like that," I say, gazing at him.

He gets the eggs out and notices me staring at him. "What are you looking at?" He glances at his chest. "You want me to put a shirt on?"

"No." I smile a little. "I prefer you like that."

I don't know what happened between last night and now, but I'm suddenly very attracted to Adam.

"You want scrambled?" he asks, not picking up on my flirting. "Or I could do omelets."

"Whatever you want," I say, walking up to him.

"I'll just make scrambled. It's faster. I want to try to get some yard work done this morning before it rains." He cracks the eggs into a bowl. "You got any appointments this morning?"

"No, but I need to pick up Caitlyn at Emma's house. She'll text me when she's ready to leave." I stand beside him. "Adam?"

"Yeah?" He continues cracking eggs.

"Could you stop for a moment?"

He glances at me. "Why? Am I doing it wrong?"

"No, I'd just like you to stop." I grab a dish towel. "Here."

He takes the towel and dries his hands, finally noticing the look I'm giving him. He slowly smiles. "What's going on?"

"We're home. Alone together. I thought maybe we could . . ." I run my hand over his chest.

"Are you serious?" he asks, smiling more.

I hop up on the counter and pull him toward me. "If you'd rather finish with the eggs, I totally understand."

"The eggs can wait."

We kiss, and he lifts me off the counter and carries me to the living room. We make love on the couch, the same couch where just hours ago I was convinced he was trying to kill me. I spent last night thinking about that, wondering if it was even possible, and decided it wasn't. Adam isn't a killer. He's not violent. He's only been in one fight, and that was in high school when a guy tried to grope me in the hall. Adam beat him up and landed himself in detention for a week. He protected me, and I know he still would today.

"What are you going to do in the yard?" I ask Adam as we're having breakfast.

"Just clean up the leaves. The pool guy's coming on Wednesday to close the pool up for winter."

"Oh. Good. Thanks for taking care of that." I pause. "About what you said last night. About your job. Do you want to talk about it?"

"Not really. I'll figure out what to do. I was just upset about it last night."

"Do you think they might let you go?"

He shrugs. "Maybe."

He says it like he doesn't care if he loses his job, which irritates me, but I try not to react, not wanting to ruin the moment. It's been a good morning. We haven't gotten along this well in years.

My phone dings with a text from Caitlyn saying she'll be ready to go in an hour.

"I'm going to head outside," Adam says, getting up from the table. He takes his plate to the sink.

"You go ahead. I'll clean up."

He walks over to me and gives me a kiss. "Thanks."

"It's only fair I clean up since you cooked."

"That's not what I meant." He looks me in the eye. "I was thanking you for this morning. This is all I wanted, Blaire. To spend time with you, even if it's just us having breakfast." He smiles. "What we did on the couch was good too."

I smile back. "Go. The leaves are waiting."

After I clean up the kitchen, I change into yoga pants and a sweatshirt. It's a cool fall day but not yet chilly enough for a jacket. I admit, it *is* nice to have a Saturday morning free to do what I want instead of rushing off to an open house or to the office to do paperwork.

Instead of my usual power walk, I go at a more leisurely pace, noticing the leaves on the trees, which are just starting to change color. I breathe in the crisp fall air and try to forget about the events of the past few weeks and just relax.

"Well, look who's up and about," I hear Alice say.

Just when I was finally feeling relaxed, Alice appears. She was getting her newspaper from her driveway when she spotted me. She's one of the few people in the neighborhood who still gets a newspaper delivered.

"Hi!" I say, giving her a quick wave and picking up speed as I approach her house.

"I heard about your accident," she says, walking down to meet me on the sidewalk.

I stop and force out a smile. "Yes, well, I'm fine now and I really need to get going so—"

"What happened? Did you just miss a step?" she asks, pulling her housecoat closed. It's a pale pink housecoat that looks like something my mother wore when I was growing up, and on her feet she's wearing pink rubber sandals. She looks much older than her age, especially when she dresses like that.

"I really don't know," I say. "It all happened so fast."

"I had an aunt who died that way." Alice clutches the newspaper to her chest. "Poor thing snapped her neck and died instantly. You're lucky that didn't happen to you." I swear I see a smile briefly appear on her round, chubby face.

"I was very lucky." I glance at my house. "Well, I need to go—"

"Some people think Aunt Edna didn't fall," Alice says. "They think her son pushed her. He was an only child. Greedy little brat. Always trying to get Aunt Edna's money. And he did, so who knows? Maybe he really did kill her."

"I'm sorry to hear that," I say, wondering why she's telling me this. Is it just a coincidence she told me a story about someone being pushed down the stairs, or is she giving me some kind of message? Hinting that she was the one who pushed me? But she couldn't have. She'd already left the party.

"Well, I'll let you get back to your exercise," she says, giving me a wave and a smile.

"Yes, have a nice day." I start to head to my house but then stop and turn back. "Alice?"

"Yes?" she says, now standing on her porch.

I shouldn't say this. I should keep quiet. But I want her to know I'm on to her and not afraid of her.

"I just wanted to thank you for the flowers."

She gives me a confused look. "What flowers?"

"The ones you sent to my office. It was a beautiful bouquet."

"I'm not sure what you mean. I didn't send any flowers."

Why is she lying? I know they're from her. Who else would send me a note like that?

"I'm quite certain they were from you," I say, walking up her driveway. "And that note you included. It was so very kind." I give her my sweetest smile.

"I really don't know what you're talking about. I never sent any flowers." She opens the door to her house. "Now, if you'll excuse me, my program is on."

She goes inside and shuts the door.

That's odd. She seemed to have no idea what I was talking about. She's either a really good liar or she was telling the truth and the flowers weren't from her.

But then who sent them? Who else could it be?

CHAPTER 19

Monday morning, I arrive at the office at nine. I'm usually here before eight, but I had an early meeting with a woman who's getting divorced and needs to sell her house. She was very distraught and wanted to talk about her husband's affair. If I'd let her, I would've been there all day, so I told her I had a meeting to get to but would get the paperwork going to list her house.

The day has just begun and I already have a new listing. Marcus will be pleased. I've already brought in twice as many listings this quarter as anyone else in the agency. More than once, I've considered leaving this place, getting my broker's license and going out on my own, but that would mean I'd have to move. The Rockingham Group owns this region. It'd be nearly impossible to start from scratch and try to compete with them. I'm confident I could do it, but it'd be a lot of effort for less money.

"No, he gave it to Blaire."

I stop when I hear my name. I'm standing in the hall outside Donna's office. She's one of the other agents. She's several years older than me. She started working here soon after I did.

"Are you kidding me?" Donna says with disgust. "He gives that woman everything! And now she gets the new condo development too?"

Who else is in Donna's office? Who is she talking to?

Just as I'm thinking that, I hear Valerie's voice.

"I was furious when I found out," Val says. "I mean, why is it always her? I know she's a good agent, but she already has more listings than anyone else. She doesn't need an entire condo project too!"

I can't believe Valerie is talking behind my back! And if Val was this angry about me getting the condo project, why didn't she tell me that instead of congratulating me?

"This has been going on for years," Donna says. "Marcus gives her every new construction project. He doesn't even consider the rest of us." She lowers her voice. "I told you something was going on with them. This just proves it."

"I hate to say it, but I think you're right. And like you said, I think it's been going on for years."

I can't believe what I'm hearing. Val knows I'm not sleeping with Marcus, but instead of telling Donna that, she's agreeing with her! How dare she!

Soon this rumor will spread to the entire office. Maybe it already has. It sounds like this isn't the first time Donna thought I was messing around with Marcus. Has she already told everyone? I'm sure she has. She's the office gossip.

"Do you think her husband knows?" Donna asks.

"No. Adam is clueless. But I know they have a horrible marriage. I wouldn't be surprised if they got divorced."

"Interesting," Donna says, sounding intrigued. "What else do you know?"

"Not much. Blaire doesn't like talking about her personal life. I have to keep refilling her wine glass to get her to talk. Oh, I was over there Friday night, and remember those flowers she got?"

"Yeah, what about them?"

"There was a note attached."

Val better not tell her. I told her that in confidence.

"What did the note say?" Donna asks.

"Something about her cheating on Adam and that she deserves whatever she gets."

Donna gasps. "Do you think it was from Lydia?"

"It had to be. Just imagine how embarrassed Lydia would be if anyone found out Marcus was having an affair with Blaire. It's bad enough he's cheating, but it's even worse if people found out it's with Blaire. She's not even from around here. She's a cheap cut of hamburger pretending to be prime rib."

Donna laughs. "That's hilarious and so true. But I'm surprised Lydia would be so subtle. Sending flowers with a note? What's that going to do?"

"Scare her away from Marcus? I don't know, but Blaire was all worked up about it last Friday. She was convinced her neighbor did it."

"Who's her neighbor?"

"The woman who's married to that fitness guy. Rob something. He has that diet program that's always being advertised. Didn't you try that last year?"

"She lives next to *him*? That man is gorgeous. I wouldn't mind having him next door," she says with a laugh.

"Blaire feels the same way. Don't tell anyone this, but . . . she's sleeping with him. She thinks his wife found out and sent her those flowers."

I'm fuming. I can't believe Valerie is saying these things! Things that were only supposed to be between us! I have to end this right now.

Going up to Donna's door, I knock a few times, a big smile on my face. "Hey, girls. I'm hearing lots of chatter in here." I go into the office. "What are you two talking about?"

"Val says you got assigned to the new condo project," Donna says, glancing at Valerie. "Congratulations."

"Thank you. You probably don't know this, but the builder specifically requested that I be the one assigned to it, given my history of selling properties quickly at or above asking price."

127

"Is that so?" Donna says, like she doubts what I'm saying is true.

"Why else would I get such a lucrative project? Did you think I was sleeping with the boss?"

Donna glances at Val and clears her throat. "No, of course not. Everyone knows you're our top seller. It makes sense you would get the project."

"You know, maybe if you two spent less time gossiping and more time getting out there and selling houses, you'd be rewarded for your hard work, just like I was with the condo project." I smile at them. "Have a great day!"

I leave Donna's office and go down to my own, my head held high, refusing to let their comments get to me. When you're at the top, people will try to bring you down. It's human nature, a way for people to feel better about themselves. I'm used to people at the office talking about me, but I didn't think Val was doing it. I really thought we were friends. Not close friends, but still friends.

I've had Valerie over for dinner many times. I've invited her to spend holidays with us. I asked Adam to change her tire when she had a flat on her way home from work. I've helped her get through numerous breakups, taking time away from my family to be with her. I've been a good friend, and this is how she treats me?

Going into my office, I shut my door, not wanting to look at the traitor in the office across from me. Why did she do it? Why did she tell Donna those things about me? Is it jealousy? Is she that jealous of my success that she's willing to turn people against me? Make them all hate me?

There's a knock on the door.

"I'm busy!" I yell, assuming it's Valerie trying to find out how much I overheard. She'll deny ever saying it and try to pretend we're still friends, but we're not. As of now, our friendship is over.

The door opens.

"I said I'm — what are *you* doing here?"

It's Rob, and he's wearing a suit. I'm not used to seeing him in anything but gym clothes. My pulse quickens and I feel myself getting warm. He looks extremely good in a suit.

"We need to talk," he says, coming into my office. He shuts the door behind him.

"Talk about what?"

He walks up to my desk. "What the hell did you say to my wife?"

"Nothing. I mean, I might've mentioned the flowers." I point to them on my desk. "I thought they were from Alice, but she said they weren't."

"Yeah, and now she thinks I'm the one who sent them. She's been yelling at me all weekend, accusing me of having an affair." He throws his hands up. "What the hell were you thinking, Blaire?"

"I honestly thought they were from her. They were dropped off last Friday and there was a card attached." I reach in my purse and pull it out, handing it to Rob.

He reads it and hands it back. "This isn't from her."

"How do you know?"

"Because I know my wife and that's not her style. A note isn't going to do anything. If she wanted to get back at you, she'd go after your career. Your reputation. Something that could destroy everything you've worked for."

"She'd really do that?" I stand up. "And you're just telling me this now?"

"I told you how she got that woman fired. The one I'd been with who Alice knew from college?"

"Yes, but I thought that was a one-time thing."

"As far as I know, it was. I don't think she's done anything else."

"But, clearly, she's capable of doing something, and if she knows what we did—"

"She doesn't. She can accuse me all she wants, but she doesn't have proof."

"That doesn't mean she wouldn't try to do something to me."

"Maybe, but she'd be more careful with you than someone else."

"Why?"

"She's checked your background. She knows where you came from, how you grew up. Rich people use their money to protect them, but that only works with other rich people. People like you use other methods." He smiles a little. "I think Alice is afraid of you."

"That woman is not afraid of me," I scoff. "She could use her money to hire someone to go after me if she really wanted to."

"She could, but I don't know if she'd actually do it. Alice doesn't mess with people unless she knows she can, and she's not sure about you. She doesn't know what you're capable of."

"I think you're wrong about her. When I talked to her on Saturday, she told me a story about her aunt falling down the stairs, then said her aunt might've been pushed."

"Yeah? So?"

"Why would she tell me that, knowing what happened to me the night of the party?"

"I don't get the connection. What happened to you was an accident."

I could tell him it wasn't, but I don't think that I should. I'm not entirely sure I can trust Rob. I think we're friends, but I thought Val was a friend too, and then she turned on me.

"I'm just saying it was odd she'd tell me that story about her aunt when I was almost killed the same way."

"You're reading too much into it," Rob says. "It was just a story. She tells it to everyone."

He doesn't get what I'm trying to say, but that's understandable since he doesn't know what really happened.

"The night of the party," I say, "did you and Alice leave right after we talked?"

"Yeah. Why?"

"I just wondered."

He pauses. "Actually, I guess it was a few minutes later. I waited in the car while Alice went back inside to use the bathroom. She didn't think she'd make it all the way home."

"So Alice was in the house? For how long?"

"I don't know. I wasn't paying attention. I was going through emails on my phone."

It could've been her. Alice was in the house around the time I went in there to look for Caitlyn. And Alice is a very large woman. She could've easily used her strength and body weight to shove me with enough force to send me tumbling down the stairs.

"I have a meeting to get to," Rob says, glancing at his watch. "I just wanted to ask about those flowers. And to tell you to stay away from Alice."

"Believe me, I try to. She's the one always wanting to talk."

"Well, try to avoid it if you can." His phone rings. He takes it from his suit jacket and silences it. "I need to go. See you, Blaire." He leaves my office.

Alice *was* there that night, in the house. Did she see me go inside and then tell Rob she needed to use the bathroom? It's possible she saw that as her chance to get rid of me.

Rob doesn't think Alice knows about us, but I know she does. I can tell. The question is, does she hate me enough to kill me?

CHAPTER 20

"Blaire?" Valerie opens my door and steps into my office, holding a coffee cup from the place down the street. "I got you your favorite drink."

"I don't want it," I say, keeping my eyes on my computer monitor. "And I'm in the middle of something, so please leave and close the door on your way out."

She sets the cup on my desk and sits down. "Blaire, what's wrong?"

"Val, I can't do this right now. I have a showing this morning and I have a lot to do before I go over there."

"Are you free for lunch? It's my treat. Wherever you want to go."

She's really trying. She knows I heard more than she wanted me to. She can apologize all she wants, but it won't make a difference. After what she said about me to Donna, I'll never trust her again.

"I can't do lunch, and I really need you to leave so I can finish this."

She gets up, her shoulders hunched, looking like a puppy who just got scolded. She walks to the door. "Oh, hey, why was Rob here? Your neighbor. Is he selling his house?"

132

I ignore her and type something into the computer.

"Okay, well, we can talk later."

I'm not talking to her, not unless I have to, for something work-related. I'm furious with her for what she did. It's not only unprofessional but also childish. Donna and Val sounded like two high school girls gossiping in the locker room.

My office phone rings.

"Hello," I answer in the upbeat tone I use with clients. "This is Blaire Banks. How can I help you?"

"Blaire!" Marcus barks. "Come to my office. Now!"

"Um, yes, I'm on my way." I get up and walk down there, wondering what this is about. Maybe it's something personal. He often confides in me when he's having issues with Lydia, which is basically all the time. He hates that she's always telling him what to do, how to dress, how to run the business. But he won't divorce her, saying he doesn't want to break up his family. The truth is, he's not willing to give up being a Rockingham.

"Good morning, Marcus," I say as I go into his office, shutting the door behind me.

Marcus is standing in front of his desk, wearing a dark gray suit, his hair looking like it's just been cut. Lydia is very particular about Marcus' appearance. She insists he keep his hair at a certain length and his face free of any stubble.

"This needs to stop," he says, storming up to me. "Do you hear me? I'm done with your threats!"

"What threats? I have no idea what you're talking about."

"You think this is funny?" He waves his hand around. "Is this some kind of game to you?"

"I don't know what you're referring to, but I will not be talked to this way." I stand up straighter and look him in the eye. "If this is about your little secret, you can stop right now. I've told you before, I don't care what you do in your spare time. I have much more important things to worry about. And if you're that fearful of someone finding out, then stop. Just stop doing it."

"You know I can't do that," he says, sneering at me. "It's my only outlet. The only time I can let myself go. Do you have any idea what it's like to be a grown man who can't make a single decision for himself?"

"Yes, I know, and I'm sorry for that, but it's the choice you made. You either have to live with it or get a divorce."

He lets out a harsh laugh. "Lydia Rockingham doesn't get divorced. She's a pillar of the community. An example of what everyone aspires to have. The perfect marriage. Two beautiful children. A thriving business."

"And yet you're miserable," I say, putting my hand on his arm. "I truly am sorry, Marcus. I know how difficult this must be."

I pretend to be concerned, but honestly, I don't feel sorry for Marcus. He got himself into this situation. He knew marrying a powerful, wealthy woman like Lydia meant giving up his freedom. He wants the perks that come with being part of Lydia's family without the sacrifices. I've made nothing but sacrifices to get where I'm at, and you don't see me complaining.

"What is this about?" I ask. "Did Lydia say something?"

"No, it's nothing like that." His eyes pause on me a moment, then he turns and walks back to his desk. "Never mind. I was overreacting. Forgive me for wasting your time. You can go back to work now."

That was strange. He went from being angry and accusatory to acting like nothing happened.

Marcus has always been honest with me, but now I feel like he's hiding something. Does he no longer trust me? Does he really think I told someone?

"Marcus, I promise you, I've said nothing. I wasn't even sure you were still doing it. And really, it's none of my business."

But I know he'd still tell me about it. He can't seem to help himself. Every time he goes there, he comes back and tells me, either to relieve his guilt or so that he doesn't have to carry the burden of his secret alone. Either way, it works out well for me. Being the person he confides in has benefited me a great deal over the years, in ways Marcus doesn't even know about.

He nods, a polite smile on his face. "Thank you, Blaire. I've always appreciated your discretion regarding this matter. And you're correct. I haven't been engaging in those activities." He laughs a little. "I don't know what I was thinking. I was just being paranoid, I suppose. With Addison's wedding coming up, I've been overly concerned that everything goes perfectly for her. I wouldn't want any skeletons coming out that would ruin this important time in her life."

"I completely understand." I smile. "Does that mean Addison picked a date?"

"Yes. The wedding will be next May, but the planning has already begun. As you can imagine, Lydia insists on it being as extravagant as possible. She's hired a very expensive wedding planner. The best in the business." He gazes at the family photo on his desk. Despite his flaws, Marcus is a wonderful father. He loves his girls more than anything.

"Well, I suppose I should get back to work," I say.

Marcus gets up and walks over to me, standing very close, his eyes on mine. "Thank you, Blaire, for all you've done."

"Of course," I say, not sure what exactly he's thanking me for, and feeling uncomfortable that he's standing so close.

"I'm sorry for my earlier behavior. I haven't been feeling quite like myself lately."

"It's fine, Marcus. I understand."

The door opens and Lydia appears.

"Oh!" she says, looking surprised to see me. "Hello, Blaire. I thought Marcus was in here alone. His secretary said he was free."

"He is." I step away from him. "I was just leaving."

Her thin lips rise to a tight smile. "I seem to keep walking in on you two during what appears to be some rather intimate conversations."

Marcus nervously laughs. "I would hardly describe our conversation as intimate. We were discussing the commission percentage for the new condo project. The builder wants to negotiate."

"I assume you told him no," Lydia says, in a tone that sounds like she's speaking to her child and not her husband.

"Of course, dear," Marcus says. "We agreed on the standard terms."

"Good," she says. "Very good."

I walk past her to the door. "Nice seeing you, Lydia."

She watches me leave but doesn't say anything.

On my way back to my desk, I check the time. I need to get going. The house I'm showing this morning belongs to a bachelor businessman who has a tendency to not pick up after himself. That's a nice way of saying he's a slob. Before each showing, I have to arrive early and clean the place up. Picking up dirty socks and putting dishes away is not my job, but I do it and without complaints. It's one of the many reasons I'm a top agent. Even if I despise a client, I put on a smile, keep a pleasant attitude, and don't complain. After all, I only deal with these people for a short time. Once the house is sold, I'm done with them, and because I'm so easy to work with, they refer all their friends to me. So, although I hate doing it, I'll clean up after a grown man if it means more business will come my way.

Driving to his house, which is in a very exclusive neighborhood, I notice a car behind me. A shiny black sedan with tinted windows. The man driving it is wearing a black suit, chauffeur's hat, and dark sunglasses. He must work for one of the wealthy people in the neighborhood I'm going to because he's been behind me for several miles now, on streets that aren't main thoroughfares.

I turn left, and the sedan does as well, getting very close to my bumper.

"Hey, back off," I say, glancing at the driver in my rearview mirror.

As if he heard me, he darts out from behind me and moves into the other lane, the one meant for opposing traffic.

"What is he doing?" I say to myself, watching as he speeds past me, then veers back into my lane. He slams on the brakes, forcing me to do the same.

He stops the car in the middle of a residential street.

What in the world?

I honk my horn, a few light taps.

The car doesn't move, but I think it's still running.

I honk again, then wonder if he's having car trouble. I'll just go around him.

But just as I'm about to, the driver's door opens. The man gets out of the car and walks toward my SUV.

With his sunglasses and hat, it's hard to get a good look at him. I can only see part of his face. He's not smiling. He looks very serious, and he walks with intention as he approaches my door.

What the hell is going on here? Looking behind me and to the side, I don't see anyone around. No cars. No one walking on the sidewalk.

It's daylight and we're in a nice neighborhood so I shouldn't be worried, but I'm starting to feel like I might be in danger.

The man is at my window now, with no expression on his face, causing a chill to go through me. I try to figure out a way to get out of there, but with the sedan in front of me and the man beside me, I'm trapped.

He raises his hand and I notice he's wearing black gloves. He knocks on my window several times, hard.

"What do you want?" I yell through the glass.

He knocks again, not saying anything.

"I can't help you," I tell him. "I need to go. I'm late for an appointment."

He stares at me from behind his dark glasses and reaches into his pocket.

Oh, God, does he have a gun? Is he planning to shoot me?

But instead of a gun, he pulls out an envelope. He holds it up to the window.

"What is it?" I yell, my heart pounding.

The man doesn't say anything. He just remains there, holding up the envelope.

"What do you want?" I yell. "Tell me who you are!"

He doesn't answer but taps the envelope on the window.

"I'm not taking it! I don't want it! Go away!"

He glances at my windshield, then back at me.

"Just leave me alone!" I say, my voice shaky. "Get away from me or I'm calling the police!" I get my phone out, unlocking it and making it look like I'm about to call.

The man steps over to my windshield, places the envelope under the wiper, and walks back to his car. I lift my phone to take a photo of his license plate but see there's something covering it. Some kind of black cover that blends in with the car.

The driver gets in the car and speeds off.

I wait until he's out of sight, then unlock my door and get out of my SUV. I grab the envelope from under the wiper and toss it on the ground. There's probably nothing in it. This had to have been some kind of prank. Probably some rich, spoiled teenager trying to scare people because he has nothing better to do. A boy at Caitlyn's prep school got in trouble last year for scaring an old lady by showing up at her house every night and tapping on her window. He said he did it because he was bored and likes scaring people. I really despise spoiled rich kids, which is why I'm strict with Caitlyn and don't give her whatever she asks for.

I'm buckled in my seat and about to drive off when my curiosity has me wondering what's in the envelope. I look out my side window and see it sitting there in the street. Should I pick it up?

No. I'm not falling prey to some silly prank. The person behind it is probably watching me right now, seeing if I'll open it.

I drive off, then slam on my brakes.

What if it's not a prank? Whoever did this obviously targeted me. That driver followed me for several miles.

Whatever's in that envelope is meant for me. I need to know what's in it.

Backing up my SUV, I stop next to where I left the envelope in the street. I open my door, snatch the envelope from the ground, and toss it on the passenger seat.

A car comes up behind me and taps on its horn. I quickly put on my seatbelt and drive off, heading to the house where I'm doing the showing. It's only a few blocks away, and when I get there, I park in the driveway and turn the engine off.

I grab the envelope and rip it open, certain it's going to say something stupid like *gotcha* or *you fell for it*, indicating it was all a joke.

But when I pull out the small white card, it reads:

Dear Blaire,
  You're a lucky girl. But your luck's about to run out.
This is your last warning.

CHAPTER 21

I drop the card, my hands shaking, heart pounding. I look back at the street, making sure that car didn't follow me. My eyes search the perimeter of the house, around the manicured hedges, the flowering shrubs, for anyone who might be lurking, waiting to attack me.

Who would do this? Who would give me that note? It had to be the same person who sent me the flowers. The same person who pushed me down the stairs.

Should I call the police? But what would they do? Sending a threatening note isn't a crime, is it? I could tell them someone pushed me down the stairs, but how would they find who did it? The party was weeks ago, and given my head injury, the police may not trust that my memories from that night are accurate. And what if the press found out? I don't want this making it into the news with some headline that reads "Blaire Banks, top agent at the Rockingham Group, believes someone tried to murder her at her birthday party." What if people thought I made it up? That I was mentally unstable? It could ruin the reputation I've spent my entire adult life building.

My potential buyers will be here in an hour. I need to go inside and get the house ready, but I'm afraid to go in there.

What if someone broke in and is hiding in the house, waiting to kill me?

Staring at my phone, I think of who I could call for help. It's just before ten. Adam's on his way to work, but the dealership isn't usually busy before noon.

"Hey, babe," he says, answering my call. "Everything okay?"

He asks because I rarely call him during the day. If I do, it's usually because of an issue with Caitlyn, like she's sick and one of us needs to pick her up at school.

"I'm not sure," I tell him.

How do I explain this to him? I can't tell him about the note. Until I know who sent it and what it's about, I don't want to involve Adam. I haven't ruled Alice out as the one who's behind this, and if I tell Adam that, he'll suspect there's something going on with Rob and me. It's the only reason Alice would do this.

"What do you mean?" Adam asks. "Where are you right now?"

"I'm at the house on Tremont. I have a showing in an hour and I need to tidy up the house before they get here. But I saw this man and he, um, seemed kind of suspicious. I was wondering if you could come over here."

"And do what?"

"Maybe just check around the house before I go in."

"The guy's still there?"

"Well, no, I don't think so. I'm just being cautious."

"Yeah, it's just that I'm meeting with someone in like five minutes. I'd have to cancel."

"Who are you meeting with?"

He pauses. "Just some guy buying a car. He's picking it up this morning and we need to do the paperwork."

The way Adam hesitated before answering makes me wonder if he's lying. I hate that our relationship has come to this, with both of us hiding things from each other.

"So you can't come over?" I ask.

"I will if you really need me to, but if the guy took off, I don't know what I could do to help."

Just being here would help. When your wife is scared, you show up to make her feel better. To protect her. That's what I want to say, but I don't. I should've known better than to call Adam. I can't count on him.

"Don't worry about it," I say. "I'm sure it was nothing. Sorry to bother you."

"You're not bothering me. I just—"

"Adam, it's fine. I need to go. I'll see you tonight." I end the call, frustrated but not surprised he wouldn't help me. I'm partially to blame for that. I always try to be independent and do things on my own. Adam's not used to me asking for help.

Grabbing my purse, my phone gripped tightly in my hand, I get out of my SUV and hurry to the entrance of the large, two-story brick house. I unlock the door, go inside, and lock the door behind me.

Standing in the foyer, I listen for any sounds of someone sneaking around. I don't hear anything, so I slowly walk over to the living room. The place is a mess, as usual, with socks, dress shirts, and ties tossed on the floor and draped over the furniture. Throw pillows from the couch are piled up on the coffee table next to an open bottle of bourbon.

How does a man who makes millions a year live like this? If he can run a company, why can't he pick up his socks? I feel sorry for his future wife, although I don't know what woman would want to marry a slob like him. Then again, enough money can make some women overlook the messiness.

Cleaning the house temporarily distracts me from my fear of whoever sent me that note, and by the time the potential homebuyers arrive, I'm able to put on a cheery smile and act as though everything's fine.

"I really like it," the wife says after I've shown her and her husband the house. We're in the kitchen now, which looks out at the wooded backyard. "But I don't care for this kitchen. It seems dated. How old did you say this house was?"

"It was built in 2000," I say, "but as you can see, it's been very well maintained. And as for the kitchen, it'd be easy to remodel. There's so much space, you could do most anything. I could put you in touch with a contractor who specializes in kitchen remodels. He does an excellent job."

The woman looks at her husband. "What do you think?"

He shakes his head. "I don't want the mess of a remodel. We'll have to find something else."

"Of course," I say. "I'd be happy to show you some newer houses that wouldn't need any updating."

I smile at the couple but am secretly annoyed. I've shown them at least thirty houses and we've looked at more than a hundred online, and they've found problems with all of them. I suggested they custom-build to get exactly what they want, but the husband said he doesn't want the headache of a custom-build.

"Could you show us some more options later this week?" the wife asks.

"I'll go through the listings and let you know," I tell her. "I'm sure the perfect house is out there. We just have to find it." I walk them to the door. "Enjoy the rest of your day!"

They leave, and I shut and lock the door.

What a waste of time. I spent an hour cleaning this place, and the couple was only here for ten minutes. I knew the wife would complain about the kitchen, but when she saw the house online, she insisted they look at it.

Going upstairs, I turn off the lights in the bedrooms and office. As I'm coming back down, I freeze when I hear someone walking around. Is it the couple? Are they back? No, it can't be them. They left, and I locked the door.

I hear it again, the sound of footsteps. It sounds like they're coming from the kitchen. I have to get out of here, but if I make a run for it, whoever's in the house will hear me and catch me before I make it to the door.

I can't get out of here without being caught. Even if I could, I can't drive away. My keys are in the kitchen, along with my phone.

I'm trapped. And I can't call for help.

CHAPTER 22

The heavy footsteps get louder and faster as they go through the house. I need to hide. Maybe I could make it to the coat closet. The door to it is still open from when I showed it to the couple.

Taking off my heels so they don't click on the wood floor, I slowly descend the last two stairs to the main level.

"Blaire?"

Whipping around, I see Clark, the homeowner, behind me.

"Clark!" I force out a smile, my heart pounding from thinking he was an intruder. "I thought you were in California."

"I was, but I had an issue come up at the office here and had to fly home."

"I'm sorry to hear that. I hope it isn't anything serious."

"No, just some issues with the project I'm working on, but it wasn't something that could wait. I just came by the house to drop off my bags and get something to eat."

Why didn't he tell me he was coming home? I specifically asked him to let me know when he'd be at the house so I don't bring people over when he's here.

"Are you having a showing today?" he asks.

"I just did. Unfortunately, they decided it wasn't the right house for them."

"It's been on the market three weeks now. Shouldn't you have sold it by now? That's why I hired you, Blaire. You're supposed to sell houses faster than anyone else."

He seems to have forgotten that I almost died a few weeks ago, not long after I listed his house. Valerie showed it to a few people while I was recovering, and a few other agents showed it, but I'm sure none of them cleaned the place up. No buyer will want this house if it looked like it did when I got here today. That might be acceptable at a lower price range, but this house is priced at over two million.

"I had some health issues that delayed things," I say. "But I'm back at work now and will put all my efforts into getting it sold."

"I'm counting on it. Don't make me regret hiring you." He winks at me like he's joking, but he's not. If this house doesn't sell soon, he'll tell everyone he knows that Blaire Banks isn't as good as she claims. As soon as I met Clark, I knew I'd regret working with him, but he got my name from a referral and I never turn down referrals.

"I'll get my things and let you have some privacy," I say. "I'm sure you're tired from the trip."

"Not really," he says, taking his tie off and tossing it on the floor. "I slept on the plane." He looks around. "I see you picked the place up." He smiles at me. "I love how you gals like to clean, because I sure as hell don't."

Most of us "gals" don't enjoy cleaning, especially for a rude, condescending jerk like you. Those are the words going through my head, but the ones coming from my mouth are much more pleasant.

"I just wanted it to look nice for the showing. I need to get going, but it was good seeing you, Clark. I'll get some more people over here this week. Hopefully, one of them will make an offer."

"Yeah, they better," he says. "I'll see you, Blaire."

He goes upstairs while I go to the kitchen to get my things. In the short time he was here, he managed to spill his protein drink on the counter and dirty the floor with crushed cracker crumbs. The box of crackers is sitting by the sink, left open, of course. I find myself rolling my eyes, Caitlyn-style, as I leave the kitchen, passing by the tie Clark left on the floor.

Heading back to the office, I keep checking my rearview mirror for that black sedan. I take a different route this time, avoiding the more remote residential areas and taking the busy main streets. The car dealership Adam works at is just up ahead. I pull off the road and drive into the lot. I'm not sure why. I didn't think this through. It was more of a gut instinct, a feeling that told me I should stop and see if Adam's there.

"Blaire," Dale, the manager, says as I walk into the dealership. "This is a surprise."

Dale is the owner's cousin and has worked here since high school. He's almost seventy years old now. He's spent his whole life at this job. I met his wife, Doreen, at a charity event soon after I moved to town. When she told me what her husband did, I immediately thought of Adam and how much more he could make selling luxury vehicles than changing oil at a local garage, which was his job at the time. After the event, I went up to Doreen and asked if she'd like to have lunch sometime, telling her I'd love to know more about growing roses, which I'd learned by talking to her earlier was one of her passions. She even volunteered at the botanical center in town, giving tours of the rose garden.

Doreen and I had lunch that week, and a few days later, Dale called Adam and offered him a job at the dealership. Adam doesn't like sales so he was reluctant to take the job, but he took it because he knew I wanted him to and we desperately needed the money.

"Hi, Dale," I say. "How have you been?"

"Good. Very good. Doreen and I just got back from vacation." He leans back and folds his arms over his chest. "Went to Hawaii for a few weeks."

"How nice. Was this for a special occasion?"

"It was our fiftieth wedding anniversary," he says proudly.

"That's wonderful. Congratulations!"

"Thank you. You and Adam are at what . . . almost twenty years?"

"We're past that. It's been twenty-two years. We were married right out of high school."

"That's right," Dale says, nodding his head. "You two were just kids when you moved here. I still remember seeing Adam come in here his first day and thinking he didn't look old enough to drive, let alone sell cars."

I smile. "Yes, he did look young for his age. Speaking of Adam, is he here?"

Dale looks back at the offices. "I'm not sure. I saw him earlier with that lady but haven't seen him since."

"What lady? A customer?"

"I don't think so. She didn't look at any cars. She was in his office. Let's go back and check if he's here."

"Oh, I can do it. I don't want to take up your time."

"You're not. The only thing I had on my schedule is getting a donut from the break room." He laughs and pats his stomach. "Not that I need it." He motions for me to follow him. "Come on back."

We walk past the showroom to the hallway where the offices are located. Adam's is the last one, near the door that leads to the employee parking lot. He could easily sneak out and nobody would notice.

"Looks like he's not here," Dale says, poking his head in Adam's office.

"What about the woman he was with? Did you see her leave?"

"No, but she might've left when I was out doing a test drive. She was here the other day too. I thought maybe she was your insurance lady. With Caitlyn turning sixteen soon, you'll have to get her added to your policy. You pick out a car for her yet?"

"I'm not sure she's ready to drive. She's afraid to after she tried backing out of the driveway and hit the mailbox."

Dale laughs. "That's right. I forgot about that. At least it was only a mailbox."

"Unfortunately, it frightened her enough that now she won't even let Adam take her out again."

"That's a shame. But hey, saves you from buying another car. Even with Adam's discount, they aren't cheap, and the insurance on a teenager is outrageous."

"That's for sure." I look out the back window for Adam's car but it's not there, which means he's not out on a test drive. So where did he go?

"Well, I should get back to work," I say to Dale. "Oh, and don't mention to Adam that I stopped by. It's so rare that I surprise him like this and I don't want him feeling bad that he wasn't here."

"Sure, I understand. Hey, you want a donut before you go? They're fresh. Brought them in myself this morning."

"Thank you, but I think I'll pass."

"Let me walk you out." Dale takes me back through the showroom to the parking lot out front. "So, how are you feeling?" He shakes his head. "Sorry, I should've asked you that as soon as I saw you."

"It's fine. You weren't here when it happened. I didn't expect you to ask. But the answer is I'm feeling much better. I took last week off to rest, and today is my first official day back at the office."

"Doreen and I felt terrible when we got back into town and heard the news. Doreen was going to send you a card, but I suppose it's a little late for that."

"That's sweet of her, but not necessary."

"Well, let us know if there's anything we can do."

"Just be extra careful when going down the stairs," I say with a smile as I open my door.

"Will do." He steps back and gives me a wave. "Good seeing you, Blaire. You take care."

Dale and Doreen are a very nice couple. When Adam and I were younger and struggling to make ends meet, Doreen would invite us over for dinner and send us home with leftovers. They were like our substitute parents back then. As our lives got busier, we didn't go over there as much and now it's probably been a couple years since we've been to their house.

I can't imagine Dale telling Adam he might have to let him go. Even if Adam's sales were down, Dale wouldn't fire him. That decision would have to come from someone else, like maybe Dale's cousin, the owner. He owns several dealerships but isn't very involved with them. He's retired and lives in Florida. He comes up here every few months and will stop by the dealership, but it's more to say hi to the staff, not interfere with the business.

Was Adam lying about possibly losing his job, or were there changes at the dealership he didn't tell me about? Maybe they hired a consultant to cut costs and Adam was targeted for having low sales. But I would think Dale would tell me that, unless Adam told him not to.

Still in the parking lot, I get out my phone and call Adam.

"Hey, babe," he answers. "Did that guy show up again?"

"No, I think he took off. Hey, I was thinking we could meet for an early lunch. I could stop by the dealership and pick you up."

"I would, but I'm swamped. I've got all this paperwork to do and I've got a guy in the showroom waiting for me to take him on a test drive."

"Yeah, okay. I'll see you tonight." I end the call, feeling like I want to punch something, or *someone*, specifically Adam if he were here.

Why is he lying to me? Where is he? And who is that woman he was meeting with?

CHAPTER 23

"Marcus wants to see you," Tara says as I'm walking into the office. She's typing on her computer, but glances at me briefly, her fingers still moving.

"Right now?" I ask.

"That's what he said."

What does Marcus want? He better not be calling me in there to accuse me again. I honestly have no idea what he was talking about when he summoned me to his office earlier. He made it sound as if someone was threatening to tell his secret. But it wasn't me. Maybe he's just being paranoid.

"You rang?" I say with a hint of sarcasm as I go into Marcus' office. He's looking at his computer monitor, typing on his keyboard.

"Shut the door, please," he says.

I close the door and walk over to his desk, sitting down across from him. "Twice in one morning. What am I in trouble for now?"

He stops typing and turns to look at me. "We have a problem."

"We?" I huff. "Marcus, no offense, but your problems are your own, and I'm tired of being brought into them."

"Would you stop talking and listen?" he barks.

I put my hands up in surrender. "Go ahead. I'm all ears."

"It seems there's a rumor going around the office that you and I are having an affair."

"Yes. I heard."

His brows rise. "You knew about this?"

"I overheard Valerie talking to Donna when I came in this morning."

"Valerie was the one who started this? I thought you two were friends."

"Apparently not." I try to hide my hurt feelings over Valerie's betrayal.

"Why didn't you stop her? Tell her she was wrong?"

"Why would I? Once something like that gets out, it's too late. You know how people are around here. They hear a rumor, they assume it's the truth."

"Yes, well, this can't be allowed to continue. It's affecting morale. A few people are even talking about leaving."

"So go out there and tell people it's not true. Maybe if you say it, they'll believe you."

"I can't just say it. I need to show it through my actions."

I don't like the sound of that.

"Meaning what, exactly?"

He sits back. "I'm taking you off the condo project."

"You're *what*?" I bolt up from the chair. "You can't be serious!"

"Blaire, people think this affair we're supposedly having is causing me to give you special treatment. And I have to admit, it doesn't look good when I give you every new construction project that comes in."

"I'm your top agent! Why *wouldn't* I get the new projects? My sales record is better than anyone here. I've received awards. Clients flood your inbox with compliments, saying how much they love working with me."

"While all that is true, I'm still taking you off the project. It's the only way to convince people there's nothing going on between us."

"That's not going to convince them!" I say, throwing my hands up. "They'll think whatever they want. Spreading lies about me is their way to get back at me for being more successful than them. And you're letting them get away with it!"

"I'm making a statement. Taking an action that will put an end to this. Think about it, Blaire. If we were truly having an affair, there is no way you'd let me get away with taking the project from you. Everyone knows that. By giving it to someone else, it's proof we aren't together."

"So you're saying I'd force you to give me the project if we were sleeping together?" I stand up straighter. "If that's what you, and everyone else, think of me — that I use coercion to get projects instead of skills and hard work — then I guess I should prove you right." I smile at him. "Perhaps I should tell people this little secret I have about you."

"You wouldn't," he says through gritted teeth.

"I might, if you don't give me the project back. According to you, and the rest of the office, that's how I work."

"This is about more than people in the office. Think about my wife. If this rumor continues and Lydia finds out, it could end our marriage. Is that what you want? To have my marriage end because of a rumor?"

"Don't blame me for that. If your marriage isn't strong enough to survive a rumor that isn't even close to being true, then perhaps you shouldn't be married." I fold my arms over my chest. "You're not taking this project from me. The builder requested me. You can't tell him you're giving it to someone else."

"I already did."

"Without talking to me? You've gotta be kidding."

"I spoke with him an hour ago. Told him you were too busy to manage a project that big."

I'm speechless. I can't believe Marcus did this. He is not getting away with it. I will make sure of it.

"I've assigned the project to Karen."

Karen's new here and a very good agent. Not as good as me, but she brings in a lot of business.

"Valerie will be assisting," Marcus says, "but Karen will be the one in charge."

"You put Val on the project?" I say, raising my voice. "Last Friday you were considering firing her!"

"This will be her chance to prove she's worthy of staying here. If she doesn't improve, she'll be let go. I've told Karen that, and she'll be providing me with a weekly update on Valerie's performance."

"How did you explain this to everyone? What reason did you give for why the project was taken from me?"

"I told them you were overworked and needed something to be taken off your plate."

"Nobody would believe that. Everyone knows I would gladly take more work over less."

"Which is why I told them I felt as though I had to do it, to keep you from working yourself to death. You need time to recover from your accident. You had a serious injury. You could've died. I know you don't want to, but for the sake of your health, you need to rest. Work a more reasonable number of hours."

"Don't try to pretend you care about me. This isn't about my health. This is about letting some petty gossip win over the truth. If you truly cared about me and valued me and all that I've done for you, you'd fire those women for spreading lies about us and let me keep the project."

"I'm sorry you're upset about this, Blaire, but my decision is made." He turns toward his computer and wakes it up, then starts typing.

"I'm not letting you get away with this." I storm out of his office.

How dare he take that project from me! A project worth millions!

Marcus has always looked out for me and treated me with respect, rewarding my hard work and encouraging me to grow and be an even better agent. But something's changed.

Taking this project away is a punishment, but for what? I've done nothing to deserve this.

I go straight to Valerie's office and knock on the door. "Valerie, I need to speak with you."

She doesn't answer so I try the door. It's locked.

"She's not here," Tara calls out from down the hall on her way into the copy room.

"Of course she's not," I mutter to myself.

I go across the hall to my office and shut the door. I set my purse down and sit behind my desk.

Could this day get any worse? I find out my so-called friend is spreading lies about me behind my back, then get yelled at by Marcus for something I still don't understand. Then a car follows me. I get a threatening note. I spend an hour cleaning a house that nobody wants, and I find out my husband's lying and likely cheating on me. And if that wasn't enough, Marcus takes my project from me.

There's a knock on the door. "Blaire? It's Karen. Do you have a minute?"

Now that Karen has my project, I really don't want to talk to her, but I can't just ignore her. She'll need the file I started for the project and it would be unprofessional for me to keep it from her.

"Come in," I tell her.

She slowly opens the door. "Am I interrupting something? We could set up a time to meet later."

"No, it's fine. I just got back to the office. I'm just getting my computer going." I hit the button to turn it on.

She sits down across from my desk. "I wanted to let you know I had nothing to do with this. The condo project? I assume Marcus talked to you about it."

"Yes." I smile at her. "Congratulations! It's going to be a very lucrative project."

"Blaire, I know you're upset that Marcus assigned it to me, but I'm just as shocked as you are. I wasn't expecting this. I wasn't even aware the builder signed with us until this

154

morning, when I overheard people talking about it." She leans toward me and lowers her voice. "And I don't believe any of that nonsense about you and Marcus. I can't stand office gossip. It's why I left the last place I worked at."

"I appreciate you saying that," I tell her, although I'm not sure if she's sincere or just saying that to get on my good side so I'll help her with whatever she needs to know about the project. "Unfortunately, it doesn't change the outcome." I straighten my stance, shoulders back. "I think you'll do a wonderful job, Karen. You're certainly the best person here to take over a project of this scale. At least when it comes to that, Marcus made a wise choice. But you might have some issues with Valerie."

"Yes, I've heard she can lose her temper with clients." She sighs. "I'm not sure how to deal with that. I'm not great at having difficult conversations with colleagues, which you can probably tell, given how nervous I am right now."

"You're doing fine," I assure her. "Let me get you the files I started."

Getting up, I go over to the cabinet and pull out the stack of files.

"That's a lot," she says as I hand her the files. "You've done your research."

Because I'm a good agent. Better than anyone else here, which is why this project should be mine.

"Go through them and let me know if you have any questions," I say, sitting back at my desk.

"I will. Thank you." Karen gets up and walks to the door. "Any advice on dealing with Val?"

"Just watch your back."

"That's concerning," she says with an uncomfortable laugh. She looks down, then back up at me. "I'm sorry she said those things about you. I'm sure it came as quite a shock. I heard you and Valerie used to be quite close."

"I wouldn't describe us as close. More like casual acquaintances."

That's not really true. Val and I were friends for many years, and we actually *had* become close after my accident. Almost dying made me realize I need more people in my life, people I can count on. Real friends. I thought Valerie might be one of those friends, but she deceived me.

I never should've trusted her, but I did. I confided in her. She's the only person I told about someone pushing me down the stairs. I'm not certain what she'll do with that information, but if she could use it against me, I'm sure she would.

CHAPTER 24

I remain at the office for the rest of the day. I assumed Valerie would return at some point, but she didn't. Clearly, she knows what she did is wrong and is afraid to face me. At least that's what I thought, until I got home and saw Valerie's car in the driveway.

What is she doing here? Does she think she can just show up at my house, apologize, and everything will go back to normal? I should've called Adam and told him what happened and not to let her in the house, but I didn't anticipate her showing up here.

"Blaire," Valerie says, greeting me at the door to my house like she lives there. She smiles and steps aside. "Come in. We've been waiting for you."

"Get out," I say, glaring at her as I go into the house.

"We ordered dinner," Valerie says in a cheery tone, ignoring my order for her to leave. "It just arrived. We were just about to sit down to eat."

"Mom," Caitlyn says, racing up to me. "Val got us sushi from that place downtown. That one we never go to because Dad says it's too expensive?"

I look at Val. "You can certainly afford it now that you've been given the condo project."

"Mom, can we eat?" Caitlyn asks. "I'm starving."

"Go ahead. I need to speak with Valerie."

Caitlyn's eyes bounce between Valerie and me, sensing the tension between us. "Um, yeah, okay. What about Dad? Should I tell him we're eating?"

"Caitlyn, please," I say, growing impatient with her. "Just go."

She heads to the dining room.

"Get out of my house," I say to Val. "And don't come back here again."

"Blaire, what is going on with you?" she says with a laugh. "Is this about the condos? That's business. It's nothing personal."

"Business?" I huff. "Telling the office I'm sleeping with the boss is business?"

"What did you say?" Adam asks as he comes down the stairs.

I hope he didn't hear what I said about sleeping with the boss, but from his angry expression, I'm thinking he did.

"Valerie's been spreading lies about me," I say, my eyes on Val. "We can talk later, Adam. I need to talk to Val."

"Blaire, what the hell is going on?" Adam asks.

My eyes dart to his. "I said I'll talk to you later. Caitlyn's waiting for you in the dining room."

He sighs, shaking his head.

Valerie watches him go. "You should really be nicer to him. If you're not, he's going to leave you." She looks back at me. "Or maybe he's already planning to."

She says it like she knows he is, like she's certain of it. But how would she know? Is she following him? I wouldn't be surprised if she was. Nothing she could do would surprise me now that I know what she's capable of.

"What's going on here, Val?" I ask. "Were the last twenty years a lie? Were you putting on an act that whole time? Pretending we were friends when you were plotting against me?"

"Oh, please, we were never friends," Val says, giving me a Caitlyn-like eye roll. "At least not close ones. You wouldn't let us be. You don't trust anyone enough to let them in, even your own husband."

"Stop talking about Adam. You don't know anything about my relationship with him. And as for me trusting people, look what happened when I did." I step closer to her. "I confided in you. I told you things I haven't told anyone. And then you turned on me! Spread lies about me in the office! Why would you do that?"

She glances around to make sure we're alone before looking back at me. "Do you really think people weren't already talking about this? For years, people have assumed you and Marcus were sleeping together. It's because he gives you absolutely everything. Every new construction project. Listings that come in. It's all the other stuff too. Do you think people don't notice all the private meetings you two have? The looks you give each other? The whispers in the hallway?"

"We're talking about business. Nothing else. And we are not giving each other looks. If people think that, they're seeing what they want to see, not what's actually true."

"What about your party? Marcus spent a fortune on that, and he spent months planning it. Has he ever done that for anyone else?"

"Turning forty is a major birthday. Marcus just wanted to do something special for it."

"Carol turned fifty last spring. Did he throw her a big party? No. He got her a dozen donuts and a coffee mug."

"Carol hasn't worked for him as long as I have. I've been there for twenty years."

"So have I, and what did I get when I turned forty? He took me to dinner. And invited you!" She shakes her head. "I can't believe you're angry at me for this. I was doing you a favor."

"Are you serious? How was stealing my project from me a favor?"

"I didn't steal it. I'm not even the lead agent. Marcus gave it to Karen and made me her little sidekick. I'll basically be doing all the grunt work while she gets all the glory."

"Stop complaining. It's not going to make me feel sorry for you. This project is worth millions and you'll be getting a cut of that."

"And why does that bother you so much, Blaire?" She motions around her. "You have everything you could ever want. A family. A beautiful home. I live alone in a condo overlooking a parking lot. I could use this money to finally get a house."

"It's not my fault you haven't been as successful as me. All you had to do was put in the work and you would've made as much as I have the last twenty years."

"You really think that? You really think I'd be as successful as you by just working more? Without Marcus giving me handouts?"

"My success is *not* because of Marcus," I say, narrowing my eyes at her. "I did it all on my own."

"You can't be serious," she says with a laugh. "Blaire, you've made a fortune off new construction and it's all because of Marcus. Because he keeps assigning you those projects. Introducing you to developers and builders. Do you see him doing that with anyone else?"

"I'm his top agent. He knows he can trust me to manage projects and get properties sold faster than anyone else."

"You're not getting it, Blaire. You can't see how this isn't fair because you're the one benefiting. If someone else were getting all the perks, you'd be suspicious too. You'd think there's something going on."

"But there's not. You know that, Val. You know I have absolutely no interest in Marcus. He's like a brother to me."

"And he just proved that by not giving you this project. That's what I'm trying to tell you. By getting this rumor about you two out in the open once and for all, and having Marcus finally address it by giving the condo project to someone else, the rumors will end and people will stop hating you."

"People at the office don't hate me."

"They do. You just don't know it. You don't know what they say about you when you're not around."

I shrug. "I don't care what they say. And I don't care if they hate me. They're only being this way because they're jealous. I would've rather had the rumors continue and people hate me than lose the condo project. I can't believe you did this to me. I really thought we were friends."

"We were. We still could be." She puts her hand on my arm. "I was honestly trying to help you. I was trying to protect you."

"Protect me?" I yank my arm from her. "From what? Making money?"

"From whoever did that to you," she says, lowering her voice. "From whoever pushed you down the stairs."

"How does what you did protect me?"

"People from the office were at your party. What if one of them is the person who pushed you? Because they were jealous of you and wanted to get rid of you so they could finally have a chance at getting a project that comes in? One that would've gone to you?"

"Are you speaking about yourself? Because now that I know you betrayed me, I'm thinking it's quite possible that you're the one who pushed me."

She gasps. "How could you say that? You know I'd never do that. I'd never do anything to hurt you."

"You just did. By turning against me and taking my project."

"I didn't do that to hurt you. I did it to end the rumors and protect you, but if you're choosing to make me the villain, then fine. I'll leave. There's clearly nothing I can say that will change your mind."

"No, there isn't. So go. Get out of my house."

She walks back to the kitchen to get her purse, then I hear her in the dining room. "I'm sorry I can't join you for dinner," I hear her say, "but I hope you enjoy the sushi."

"It's so good," Caitlyn says. "Why can't you stay?"

"I have some things to do at home."

"What about this weekend?" Caitlyn says. "Are we still getting manicures?"

161

Manicures? Why was Valerie making plans with my daughter without talking to me first?

"I'd love to," Valerie says. "But you'll have to talk to your mom. Make sure it's okay with her. I'll see you later."

Valerie walks through the house, passing me on her way out, neither of us saying goodbye.

Going into the dining room, I take a seat at the table and drink the wine that Adam poured.

"What's going on with you and Val?" Caitlyn asks.

"Nothing. Everything's fine." I smile at her. "So how was school today?"

"Mom, tell me the truth. Why are you and Val fighting?"

"We just had a disagreement about something at work. It's nothing serious."

"So I can still go for manicures with her this weekend?"

I glance at Adam, who won't look at me, his eyes on his dinner plate. "I don't know yet. I'll think about it."

"Mom, why can't I go? Just because you're fighting with her doesn't mean I can't hang out with her. Valerie's fun. I like her. And you'll be working Saturday, so you won't even have to see her."

"Let it go," Adam says in a curt tone, glancing at Caitlyn. "If your mother doesn't want you seeing her, you're not going. End of story."

I'm surprised Adam's taking my side on this. He usually stays out of my arguments with Caitlyn, especially now that she's in her teen years and argues about pretty much everything.

Caitlyn keeps quiet for the rest of dinner, then gets up from the table.

"Take your dishes to the kitchen," Adam tells her.

"Fine," she mutters, picking up her plate and glass and leaving the dining room. I hear dishes clanking in the sink, then the sound of her going upstairs.

"So, what's the story?" Adam asks. "With you and Val?"

I pick up the wine bottle from the table and refill my glass. "She told everyone at work a lie about me, and because of it, I lost the condo project."

"What was the lie?"

I don't want to tell him. Even if I tell him it's just a rumor, there's a chance he'll think it's true, which will damage our already-crumbling marriage.

But I need to tell him. I have to explain before he hears this from someone else.

I look at him across the table. "People at work think I'm having an affair."

His shoulders stiffen and his brows draw together. "With who?"

"Marcus."

Marcus...

CHAPTER 25

"People really believe that?" Adam's shoulders relax and he laughs. "The guy's not even your type."

That's not the response I was expecting. I thought Adam would be angry or at least ask questions about how the rumor started, in an attempt to find out if it's true.

"I'm also married," I point out. "Which is the primary reason why that rumor is both insulting and ridiculous."

"Well, yeah, but if you were going to cheat, it wouldn't be with some overweight old guy who's boring as shit."

"You think Marcus is boring?"

"Yeah. All he talks about is real estate."

"I talk about real estate."

"Yeah, but not all the time. And Marcus is fat and even more out of shape than I am."

"I wouldn't say he's fat, but he has put on weight the past few years. And he's never been someone who works out." I cock my head. "Why do you think I'm only attracted to men who are in shape? I've never made comments about that."

"You don't have to." He pats his stomach, which is larger than it used to be. "Ever since I got a gut, you lost interest in me."

"That's not true," I insist.

"We went from doing it five times a week to once a month, if that. I'm not stupid, Blaire. I know you're not attracted to me anymore."

"Adam, of course I'm attracted to you. Our lives have just become much busier than they used to be. We're both working a lot, taking Caitlyn to all her activities, trying to keep up with the house and the yard work."

"People make time for the stuff they want to do." He picks up his empty plate and gets up.

"You're leaving? You don't even want to know what happened?"

He sighs and sits down, setting his plate back on the table. "Marcus gave the project to Val and now you two are fighting. Am I right?"

"Well, yes, kind of. He actually gave the project to Karen. She's only worked with us for a year, but she's been an agent for a long time. She was at my party, but I don't know if you met her. Anyway, Valerie will be working on the project with her, but Karen will be in charge."

"Why'd he give the project to someone else? Is Marcus trying to prove the rumor isn't true?"

"Yes, but all this is doing is rewarding gossip that never should've been allowed in the first place. He should be punishing the people who were spreading the lies, not me."

Adam shrugs. "So you'll find other properties to sell. You always do. Just let it go and move on."

He doesn't get it. This isn't just about the project or the money. It's about Marcus turning against me and letting the people who were spreading lies about us win. Taking this project away from me could harm my reputation. What if people find out I was taken off the project and start to question my abilities? What if they find out Karen replaced me, and she becomes the new star at the Rockingham Group? My whole business could be destroyed by this one decision that Adam seems to think is no big deal.

"I'm going to take a bath," I say, getting up. "Try to relax."

"Go ahead. I'll clean up."

I pause, wondering if I should ask him where he was today. I almost do but then decide against it, knowing he'd probably just tell me another lie.

I'm starting to think it's not possible to save my marriage. I keep telling myself it is and that Adam and I can get back to how we were, but it's been so long since things were good between us that I don't even remember that time.

After my accident, when I was in the hospital, Adam was so worried about me. He kept saying how he didn't know how he'd go on with his life if he lost me. But sadly, I think those were just words he felt he had to say, and he didn't really mean them. I think, in his head, he's already moved on. Or maybe it's not just in his head and he's moved on with someone else, some other woman.

Going upstairs, I pass by Caitlyn's room. We were getting along great the week I was home recovering, but now we're back to her being mad at me all the time.

Walking over to her door, I knock a few times. "Caitlyn, can I come in?"

"I guess," I hear her say.

Opening the door, I see her lying on her bed, hugging the giant stuffed bear she's had since she was a little girl. She said she uses it as a pillow now, but I think the real reason she still has it is because she's not ready to give it up.

"About your plans with Valerie," I say, sitting next to Caitlyn. "I'm sorry, but I don't want you going out with her. If you really want to go for manicures, we can go together."

"Just forget it. I don't need to go." She turns away from me, facing the wall. "Are you and Dad getting divorced?"

Her question takes me by surprise. She knows Adam and I are having issues, but we've never once brought up divorce.

"No. Why do you think we're getting divorced?"

"You barely talk to each other anymore." She flips around so she's facing me. "Except when you're arguing."

"That's not true. Your dad and I were talking just now, when we were having dinner."

"That was for like five minutes and now you're up here and he's down there. You couldn't even stand to be around each other for more than a few minutes."

"Honey, every marriage goes through tough times. Your dad and I will talk this out and eventually things will go back to normal."

"But what's normal? You guys have been this way for as long as I can remember and it's only getting worse. Do you even love him anymore?"

"Of course I do. Your dad was my first boyfriend. My first love."

"That doesn't mean you love him now. People change a lot from high school."

"Yes, but—"

"Are you cheating on him?" She sits up. "Are you cheating on Dad?"

"No. Why would you even ask that?"

"I've seen how you look at that guy next door. The one with all the muscles? Rob, or whatever his name is. He's always staring at you when you're outside, and I've caught him checking you out when you're out back by the pool."

"Rob is our neighbor. That's it."

"You don't have to lie to me. I'm practically an adult. And most of my friends' parents are having affairs, so it's not like I'd be surprised if you and Dad were."

"You think your father's having an affair?"

She shrugs. "Maybe."

"Why? What makes you think he might be seeing someone?"

"When he picked me up at soccer last week, I smelled perfume. And it wasn't yours."

"Maybe he just gave someone a ride. One of the women he works with. Maybe she had car trouble."

Caitlyn rolls her eyes. "He works at a car dealership. The woman could get a loaner if her car didn't work."

"I suppose that's true, but that doesn't mean your father is having an affair."

"Do you think he is?"

I hesitate, not sure how to answer that. "I think you should stop worrying about this."

"If you were having an affair, would you tell me?"

"Caitlyn, enough of this." I stand up. "These are not the types of conversations we should be having."

"You wouldn't tell me," she says, looking down. "Which means you and that guy next door are—"

"No. We're not. And stop saying that we are. There is nothing going on with Rob and me."

"Then tell his wife to leave me alone."

"What do you mean? What did Alice do?"

"She keeps asking me about you. Like asking where you are or why you got home so late. Or she'll ask if I saw Rob over here or if I've heard you two talking on the phone."

"Why didn't you tell me this?"

"She told me not to." Caitlyn looks down. "She gave me money so I wouldn't tell you."

"She paid you to keep this from me?" I ask, furious that Alice did that. "How much?"

"A hundred dollars," Caitlyn mutters, not looking at me.

"Total?"

"Um, no. Each time she asked."

"Which was how many times?" My voice gets louder as I struggle to contain my anger.

"I don't know. Five or six?"

"That woman has given you six hundred dollars to get information from you and you didn't think you should tell me?"

"Mom, I didn't tell her about you and him! I swear."

"There's nothing to tell! Nothing is going on between the neighbor and me."

"It's getting loud in here," Adam says, standing at Caitlyn's door. "What are you two talking about?"

"Nothing," I say, not wanting Adam to know about this. He's already suspicious of Rob after seeing him flirt with me. Telling him about Caitlyn and Alice would make him even more suspicious. "We were just talking."

"I just wanted to tell you I'm going to the store," Adam says. "We're out of milk."

"Okay, thanks, honey."

When he leaves, Caitlyn scowls at me. "Why'd you lie to him? Because it's true? You're having an affair with that guy?"

I take a calming breath. "For the last time, Rob is a friend. That's it. I'm not even sure if I'd call him that."

"Then why didn't you tell Dad what we were talking about?"

"Because when you tell someone something, even if it's not true, it gets in their head and they start wondering if maybe it's possible. I'm not going to do that to your father. Just imagine if you were dating a boy at school and heard a rumor that he was seeing another girl. How would you feel?"

"I don't know because you won't let me date," she says, rolling her eyes.

"But if you were, how would you feel? Even if people told you the rumor wasn't true?"

"Bad, I guess. Hurt."

"Exactly. Which is why your father doesn't need to know about Alice and her suspicions. I don't want you talking to her again. Or accepting her money. Do you understand?"

"Yes," Caitlyn mutters, following it with another eye roll.

"If she approaches you again, I want to know about it."

"Yeah, got it."

I leave her room, furious at Alice for involving my daughter this way. I should go over there right now and tell her to stay away from Caitlyn, but I doubt she would listen. Alice does what she wants. I just hope Caitlyn listens and doesn't let Alice bribe her again.

After a long, hot bath, I get into bed and watch TV. Adam gets home just before ten and comes into our room.

"You were gone a long time," I say.

"I drove around. It's a nice night." He takes off his shirt on his way to the bathroom.

"Did you get anything besides the milk?"

He comes out of the bathroom. "The what?"

"At the store, did you get anything besides milk?"

"I never made it to the store. I guess I forgot."

He forgot? That's the whole reason he left, or so he said.

If he didn't go to the store, where was he tonight? He was gone for hours. He wouldn't be driving around for that long.

I'm tired of wondering what he's up to. I need to find out what he's hiding.

CHAPTER 26

The next morning, I work from home and wait for Adam to leave. Soon after he does, I get in my SUV and follow him, but to my surprise, he drives straight to the dealership. I'm not sure what I was expecting. If he saw a woman last night, he probably wouldn't go see her this morning as well.

Continuing down the street, I notice a coffee shop up ahead and decide to stop. With so much going on, I haven't been sleeping and desperately need some caffeine.

After I get my coffee, I'm heading to the door to leave when I hear someone calling my name.

"Blaire! Over here!"

The voice is coming from the back of the coffee shop. I look over and see Rob sitting at a table with his laptop. He's wearing a light gray suit and glasses with a thick black frame. I've never seen him wear glasses before. They look really good on him.

"Hey, Rob," I say, walking over to him. "I was just leaving."

"Stay a minute." He smiles and motions to the seat across from him.

I almost tell him no, but then I remember I need to talk to him about what his wife has been up to and how it needs to stop.

I sit down and set my coffee on the table. "We need to talk about Alice."

"What about her?" He takes off his glasses and sets them on the table.

"It seems she's been paying my daughter for information about us."

"She *what*?" he asks, sounding as shocked as I was when I found out.

"Caitlyn said Alice asked her if she's seen you at my house or heard us talking on the phone. She's been giving Caitlyn money for answers."

"I can't believe she'd do that." He shuts his laptop. "No, actually I can. The woman is crazy, especially when she thinks I'm fooling around on her."

"You need to talk to her, Rob. She can't be going to my daughter and paying her to spy on us."

"Yeah, well, unfortunately, she doesn't listen to me. And she really doesn't like you. I probably shouldn't tell you that, but I'm sure you already know. Even before she suspected there was something going on with us, she had something against you."

"Yes, I know. It started soon after I moved in. She's always commenting on my body, saying I need to cover up."

"She hates any woman who's thin and in shape. It reminds her of how she used to look, back when she and I met."

"A lot of women in the neighborhood are fit."

"But you're the one I can't stop looking at." He smiles a little. "I try not to, I swear, but I can't seem to stop."

"You need to. I'm serious, Rob. I don't trust Alice. She seems very unstable." I pause. "Do you think she'd ever hurt me? Physically?"

"No," he says, like the very idea is ridiculous. "I told you, if she wanted to hurt you, she'd go after your job or your reputation."

"That can't happen. You need to get her under control. Maybe start acting like a husband again. Buy her flowers. Take her to dinner."

"Are you kidding? I don't even want to be near her. All she does is complain."

"Well, suck it up, because you need to convince her you want *her* and not me."

"I can't convince her of that. It's too late. She knows I don't see her in any kind of romantic way. And it's not just about how she looks, but what she's doing to me. Trapping me in this marriage. It disgusts me. When we're out in public and she makes me pretend we're a couple, I have to imagine she's someone else just to get through it."

"Have you talked to a lawyer yet?"

"Yes, and she referred me to someone else. Some guy who handles situations like mine, where there's a company involved. I haven't talked to him yet." He takes a sip of his coffee. "Did Adam get his issue figured out?"

"What issue?"

"His legal issue. He was leaving the lawyer's office when I was going in for my appointment."

"Adam was seeing a lawyer?"

"Yeah. You didn't know?"

"Um, no. He didn't mention it."

Why was Adam meeting with a lawyer? Is he planning to divorce me? Without telling me?

"Do you have the lawyer's name?" I ask.

"Leslie. I have her card if you want it."

"Yes, if you don't mind."

He reaches into his laptop bag, pulls out a business card, and hands it to me. "You can keep it. I don't need it anymore."

"Thanks." I get up. "I need to get going, but keep me updated on Alice."

"Yeah, I will." He opens his laptop. "Good seeing you, Blaire."

When I get into my SUV, I put the lawyer's address into the navigation system, then head to her office. She'll probably be meeting with someone when I get there, but I'm willing to wait.

"Yes, I'm here to see Leslie Shaumburg," I say to the receptionist.

"Do you have an appointment?" she asks.

"No, I just need to speak with her. It won't take long."

"I'm sorry, but you'll have to make an appointment." The woman looks at her computer. "She has an opening in a couple weeks."

"I don't think you understand. I'm not looking to hire her. This is a personal matter. I just need a few minutes of her time. Is she meeting with someone now? Because I don't mind waiting. Maybe I could catch her between appointments."

"She's meeting with a client off-site, but if you give me your name and number, maybe she could call you."

"Yes, fine." I take out my business card and hand it to her.

"Blaire Banks?" The woman smiles at me. "I knew you looked familiar. You're on that billboard. The one just outside of town."

"That's me," I say, smiling back. "If you could tell Leslie to call me today, I'd really appreciate it."

"I can't promise anything, but I'll tell her."

As I'm leaving the building, I notice a woman getting out of a silver luxury sedan. She's wearing a dark suit and a very serious expression. I'm guessing that's Leslie, but I could be wrong.

"Leslie?" I say, walking up to her.

"Yes." She stops abruptly. "Do I know you?"

"No, but you know my husband. Adam Banks?"

"Oh. Yes." Her lips purse. "I'm sorry, but I need to be going." She takes off.

I follow beside her. "I need to know why Adam was talking to you. If he's in some kind of trouble . . ."

She stops and turns to me. "Mrs. Banks, this is extremely inappropriate. If you want answers, you should talk to your husband, not harass his attorney."

"Are you saying he's still working with you? What is this about? Why does he need a lawyer?"

"I can't answer that. You'll need to talk to him."

"He won't tell me. He's obviously trying to hide whatever's going on here."

"I'm sorry, Mrs. Banks, but I can't share private information about a client."

"But I'm his wife." Still following beside her, I take out her card. "This says you do family law, so does that mean . . . divorce?"

We reach the door to the building and she stops and turns to me. "As I said before, if you want answers, you'll have to talk to your husband. That's all I can say."

She goes into the building. I don't bother following her. She's not going to tell me anything. Adam won't either.

But I don't think I need him to. I think I already know the answer.

Adam is divorcing me.

Why didn't he talk to me before starting the process? How could he make a decision like that without even letting us have a discussion about it? Is he trying to take Caitlyn from me? Is that why he's being so secretive about this?

What else is he going to try to take from me? The house? Our savings?

Knowing this is what Adam's been up to, I suddenly feel like he's a stranger. The Adam I thought I knew would never do this, which makes me wonder what else he's capable of.

What if he really was the person who pushed me down the stairs? What if he did it to get rid of me, to avoid having to divorce me so that he ends up with everything?

I didn't want to believe my own husband would try to kill me, but I'm starting to wonder if he did.

"Are you feeling okay?" Tara asks when I arrive at the office.

"I'm fine," I say, smiling at her. "Just a little tired. I'm still catching up from being gone last week."

Donna appears, coming out of the copy room, a smug grin on her face. "Blaire. I'm surprised to see you here. I assumed you were home resting. Marcus told us you were feeling overworked."

"When have I ever complained about working too much?" I say in a cheery tone. "That was just a little fib I told Marcus so he'd take me off the condo project." I walk over to Donna. "A much more lucrative project came up and I wouldn't have had time to do both. What about you? Do you have any new listings?"

"No," she mutters.

I frown. "I'm sorry to hear that. It's been what . . . two months since you got a listing?"

"I might be getting one this week," she says, sounding hopeful.

"Wonderful!" I say, walking away. "Good luck with that."

Hopefully, that little lie I told Donna will spread around the office and everyone will be wondering what this new project is that I'm supposedly getting.

It was risky to put that out there, but I'm confident it'll happen. I'll talk about it in our meeting today. It's scheduled at four at our usual spot.

Marcus doesn't know. Nobody does.

It's my little secret. One I've kept for twenty years.

CHAPTER 27

"Mrs. Banks," the butler says, greeting me at the door, a slight smile on his wrinkled face. The man must be close to eighty now. He seemed elderly when I met him twenty years ago, but I was much younger then and anyone with wrinkles seemed old.

"Hello, Albert," I say, smiling back at him. "How have you been?"

"Very well," he says, but even if he wasn't well, he wouldn't tell me. The help are trained to keep their problems to themselves and do their jobs without complaining.

I often wonder how I'd treat my staff if I had the kind of money to hire butlers and maids. I'd like to think I'd be friendly and kind and want to know about their personal lives, but maybe I wouldn't. Money changes people, and it's not always for the better.

"How about you, Mrs. Banks? I assume things are well?"

"Yes," I say, knowing you don't share your problems with the help. Everyone has a place. A place in the hierarchy. I learned that on my first visit. I made so many mistakes back then. It's because this world is so different than the one I came from.

Albert steps aside and I walk into the large open foyer of the mansion. Even though I've been here many times, I'm still in awe every time I see it. The shiny marble floors. The crystal chandeliers. The long velvet drapes outlining the windows. It's not at all my style, but it fits the Rockingham family perfectly.

The mansion was originally built to be the Rockingham's summer home. Now it's only used for parties or the occasional family gathering. None of them live here, but I can imagine them back in the day, lounging on the leather sofas and chairs, sipping bourbon while discussing how their investments were performing. Maybe that's not what really happened, but it's always how I picture their lives when I come here.

"Is she ready for me?" I ask Albert.

"I believe so," he says, walking me to her private study. There are at least twenty rooms in this house and I've only been in half of them, all on the first floor. I'm not allowed upstairs. "She had a phone call to make before you arrived."

"That's fine. I don't mind waiting."

Albert stops at the door to the study and knocks three times. "Ms. Rockingham, your guest has arrived."

"Yes, Albert," she says from behind the door. "Let her in."

He opens the door and I see Lydia behind her desk. It looks like she's writing a note. My mind immediately flashes back to that chauffeur shoving a note at my car window. It couldn't have been from Lydia. She wouldn't send me a note like that. Would she?

"Please sit down," she says as she continues to write.

Taking a seat across from her, my eyes go to her gray tweed suit jacket and the crisp white shirt underneath. On the jacket's lapel is a pin of the Rockingham family crest. Lydia always has it on, letting everyone know she's a Rockingham. I've never understood that. Everyone knows she's a Rockingham. She doesn't need a pin to prove it.

I patiently wait as she finishes writing her note, watching her form elegant cursive letters with her black fountain pen.

She ends the note with her signature, then sets down the pen, slides the note into the envelope, and places it to the side.

Finally, her gaze goes to me. "Blaire. You look tired."

Lydia is very honest with her opinions about me, especially when it's just the two of us. She can be quite critical, but I'm used to it and have come to appreciate it. I strive to be the best, and I know Lydia's honesty will help me get there.

"I've been under a lot of stress," I say, sitting up straighter. Lydia hates poor posture. It's one of her most common criticisms of me and the reason why I'm constantly reminding myself to push my shoulders back. "It's affecting my sleep."

"Perhaps you should see a physician who could prescribe something so that you could get some rest."

"I already have something. The pills I took when I was working on the Hanover development."

It was a new construction project, only six homes, but all over five million. Lawrence Hanover, the developer, was a horrible man who would call me in the middle of the night to ask questions, just because he knew he could. I had to get sleeping pills so I could sleep in short spurts during the day to make up for all the sleep I missed at night.

"Lawrence was very demanding, wasn't he?" Lydia says. "I do remember him causing you problems. But I think you'd agree it was worth it in the end."

She's referring to all the money I made when the houses sold. Looking back, it was definitely worth it, but at the time I couldn't wait for it to be over.

"Have you recovered from your little accident?" she asks.

"For the most part, yes. The doctors say it can take months for the brain to fully heal."

"Marcus tells me you're not yet back to working full-time."

"I am. I just haven't been at the office much."

She cocks her head slightly. "Is there something you're not telling me, Blaire?"

"In regard to what?"

"Anything." She stares at me, waiting for an answer.

"I'm not sure what you mean," I say, my heart thumping faster.

Knowing Lydia this long, I should no longer fear her. She's proven time and time again that she's on my side, and yet I have this underlying feeling that I can't trust her. But can you really trust anyone? Apparently, I can't even trust my own husband.

"This relationship doesn't work, Blaire, unless you're completely honest with me."

I pause to think of what to say. Lydia's very good at reading me. She can tell when something's going on, even when I try to hide it. But how much do I tell her?

"It's Adam," I say. "I think he might be having an affair."

She laughs. "Is that all?" She leans toward me. "Blaire, dear, I would hope by now you would know that men cheat. All of them. Even if it's just in their thoughts, it's happening nonetheless." She sits back. "Does he know about you and the neighbor?"

I look at her in utter shock. How does she know about that? How could she possibly know what I did with Rob?

"If he knows," she continues, "then it's perfectly natural for him to want to do the same. Men are childish that way. The whole you-did-it-first argument to justify their cheating, when the reality is, if they'd been a proper husband in the first place, we wouldn't need to look elsewhere." She smooths her hair, even though there isn't a single strand out of place. "We're getting off topic. The point is you can't allow your husband's infidelity to interfere with your goals. I don't know why you even stay with that man. He's an embarrassment, Blaire. You'd be much better off with someone better suited to you. Someone smart. Successful. Ambitious."

"It's not that simple. I've been with Adam since high school. We have a daughter."

"You're letting sentimentality override logic. Think as though you were advising someone else in this situation. Would you tell someone like yourself to stay with a man like Adam?"

"Well, no, I suppose I wouldn't. But I still love Adam. It's hard to let him go."

"You love the idea of him. You love the idea of being with this man you claim to have fallen in love with as a teenager and spending the rest of your life with him. You love the fantasy, Blaire, not the actual man."

She's wrong. I do love Adam, just not the way I used to, the way I should.

"I know what you're thinking," Lydia says in a nonchalant way. "Go ahead and ask."

I stare at her, confused. "I'm sorry, but I don't know what you're referring to."

"Marcus. You're wondering why I stay with him. Knowing what I know."

"I assume it's because a divorce would look bad or doesn't match with your beliefs. You're very involved with your church and—"

"Is that really what you believe?" She laughs a little. "That I stay with Marcus for religious reasons or because I care what others think?"

"I thought it might be one of those, but if it's not, what's the reason?"

"Marcus is predictable. I know what to expect with him. I'm never left guessing, which means I can focus on my own pursuits rather than wasting time doing silly things like following my husband to work."

Was that just an example, or did she know I followed Adam to work this morning? Is Lydia spying on me? And if so, when did it start? How long has she been watching me?

"I know everything Marcus does." Her lips slide up to a slight smile. "All his secrets."

"Yes, well, I'm glad I'm able to help. It's never good for a husband to keep secrets from his wife."

That's what I tell myself to justify why I do this. It helps relieve the guilt I feel for betraying Marcus.

Lydia folds her hands and places them on her desk. "Blaire, dear, I feel it's time you know the truth about this little arrangement of ours."

"The truth?" I ask, having no idea what she's talking about.

"This arrangement isn't real. It never was."

"What . . . what do you mean?"

"I never needed you to spy on Marcus for me. I've always known where he goes, what he does. Even before I met you." She pauses, that slight smile appearing again. "Did you really think I'd trust you with such an important task as keeping tabs on my husband? You were practically a child when we met. Barely out of your teen years. I didn't even know you, so why on earth would I give you a task as important as that?"

This doesn't make sense. She's saying that everything I've ever told her about Marcus she already knew? Then why have I been doing this all these years?

My arrangement with Lydia started soon after I began working for Marcus — after I learned his secret, which I discovered by accident when I went to Manhattan to shop for a new suit. I'd figured out that if I wanted to sell more expensive houses, I needed to look successful, and wearing the right clothes would help me do that. It was a Saturday, and after a long day of shopping, I was tired and wanted to get home. I somehow got on the wrong train and ended up in a part of the city I hadn't been to before. I looked around, seeing if I recognized anything. I didn't, so I decided to go back to the subway. As I was walking down the street, a woman came out of an alley and bumped into me.

"Sorry," she said, but her voice was deep like a man's.

I glanced up at her face and saw that it wasn't a woman. It was Marcus. Dressed like a woman.

He hadn't noticed it was me and began walking away, so I ran up to him and said, "Marcus?"

When he realized who I was, he was shocked, then horrified that I'd caught him dressed like that. He grabbed my arm and dragged me back to the alley and made me promise to never tell anyone. I said I wouldn't, but my mind was already spinning with ways I could use this to my advantage. From the way Marcus was panicking, I assumed I was the only person in his "other" life who knew about this. I knew that had value. I just wasn't sure how much, or how to best use it.

After I agreed to keep his secret, Marcus let me go and disappeared through a side door in the building attached to the alley. I later learned that the door led to a private sex club in the basement. A place for wealthy men to live out their fantasies without anyone finding out.

Although it was shocking to learn that Marcus was doing these things, I didn't judge him for it, and I completely understood why he couldn't let anyone find out. He's a Rockingham, after all. His very conservative wife and her family would never approve of Marcus dressing like a woman and doing who-knows-what in the basement of a building in New York City, the place where the Rockingham real estate empire began and is still thriving. The place where Lydia's parents live, and her two brothers. I could only imagine what the press would say if they found out what Lydia's husband was doing. It'd be all over the society pages and a huge embarrassment to the family.

So I did as I was told and kept Marcus' secret. I kept it from everyone. Except the one person I knew who would reward me for this information.

CHAPTER 28

When I met Lydia, I knew she was the key to my success, or the kind of success I wanted for myself. I could easily be successful on my own, but I knew my success would be limited because of who I was and where I came from. I wasn't one of the local elite. I didn't come from a prestigious family. I didn't go to a fancy prep school or Ivy League college. To overcome that, I'd need someone on my side. Someone rich, powerful, and well-connected. I wasn't dumb enough to think someone like that would assist me out of the goodness of their heart. I needed to give them something. Something they would value enough to want to help me.

The first time I came to the Rockingham mansion, to the room where I'm in now, was the day I told Lydia her husband's secret. She seemed surprised but also pleased. With me — and my willingness to tell her something that could easily get me fired if Marcus found out.

He never did. And to this day, Marcus doesn't know about my arrangement with Lydia. He doesn't know she's aware of his secret. When he sneaks away to Manhattan, he tells her he's going to see an old college friend, or meeting with investors looking to buy property in Connecticut. It's always some excuse he thinks she'll accept, and she does, but only because she already knows the truth. As long as she knows where Marcus is and what he's up to, she allows him to continue going to that club and doing whatever he does there. The other reason she allows it is that this gives her yet another way to control him. If he ever steps out of line or challenges her, she can tell him she knows what he's been doing and threaten to expose him. She'd divorce him first, of course, then tell everyone why she had to do it, thus destroying Marcus' life while also preserving her family's reputation.

Until this moment, I assumed I was the reason Lydia knew what Marcus was up to. I'm always giving her updates, repeating whatever Marcus tells me about his secret life. But now Lydia's telling me she didn't need me. That she already knew.

This is very concerning. If Lydia knew what Marcus was doing all this time, then why has she been helping me? I thought telling her about Marcus was the price I had to pay to get on her good side. To make her assist me in my career. For years, she's been working behind the scenes, dropping my name to her high-profile friends, getting me invites to exclusive events, introducing me to wealthy developers and builders looking for an agent to handle the sale of their latest project.

Marcus thinks he's the reason I get so much business, but it's really his wife's doing, along with my persistence and hard work. Like, for example, the condo project. I met Nadine, the builder's wife, at a women's luncheon last spring. Lydia introduced us and sat me next to her. By the end of the lunch, I'd convinced Nadine I was the right person to sell the condos. A few months later, Marcus assigned me to the project, acting as though it was his idea, but it really had nothing to do with him. I was the one who persuaded Nadine to tell her husband to give me the job. I earned that project, with Lydia's help.

"If you knew what Marcus was doing," I say to Lydia, "then why did you pay me after I told you?"

Lydia gave me a check for five thousand dollars after our first meeting. After that, she paid me with sales leads rather than actual money, which was fine with me. Having access to all the rich and powerful people she knows has made me a fortune over the years.

"The money was a reward for being loyal to me," Lydia says. "What you did that day showed you were smart. You had just met Marcus and me and yet you already knew I was the one in charge. The person who could make things happen for you. You took a risk and betrayed Marcus to get to me." She smiles a little. "It was very cunning. Very smart. It's the reason I took you under my wing and helped you get ahead. In a lot of ways, you remind me of myself. We may have vastly different backgrounds, but we're both ruthless when it comes to achieving success. The only difference is that I prefer to remain in the background while you prefer the spotlight. I would rather keep my hands clean while you're not afraid to get dirty."

"What about more recently?" I ask. "Did you know what Marcus was doing before I told you?"

"Of course, dear. I have professionals tracking him, telling me where he goes and what he does. I have since the day we got married."

"Then why have you been having me keep watch over him?"

"To make sure your loyalty remains with me and not Marcus. I know you have a soft spot for my husband. Perhaps you even feel sorry for him, having to live this double life. But I can assure you, Marcus is not suffering. He has everything he could ever want."

"I don't understand." I move to the end of my chair, my eyes on Lydia. "When you say you're testing my loyalty, what exactly does that mean? What is it you want from me?"

"You're my protégé, Blaire. Did you really not know that? After all these years?"

"Well, yes, I know you've taken on the role of guiding me in my career, but I thought it was because I was giving you information about Marcus. But if our arrangement wasn't real, then I don't know why you've been helping me all these years."

I pause a moment to think. "Unless you thought I might expose Marcus' secret and—"

"Blackmail me? Threaten to tell people about Marcus if I didn't continue to help you?"

"Yes, but you know I'd never do that. I've proven that to you the last twenty years."

"I'm not that naïve, dear. I know you would do whatever is necessary to preserve the life you've worked so hard for. There's no need to pretend otherwise. It's another way we're similar." Her lips curl up into a smile. "I have no doubt you'd resort to blackmail if necessary, but you see, dear, it wouldn't affect me. If you exposed Marcus' little secret, I'd simply divorce him and deny I had any knowledge of his involvement in those activities. He's not a true Rockingham. People wouldn't count his behavior against us. We'd still have our dignity. It's Marcus who would be destroyed, and I wouldn't feel the least bit bad about it. After all, what kind of man sneaks off like that to engage in such activities? Cheating is one thing, but what he's doing in that dungeon, or whatever you call it, is simply disgraceful."

I'm growing more concerned as she talks. I thought we had a deal. I keep tabs on Marcus and report back to her, and in return, she keeps business coming my way. But if that was never the deal, what's really going on? Why do we keep meeting? What does she want from me?

"Forgive me for asking this, but I need to know . . . do you have someone keeping watch over me? Like you're doing with Marcus?"

"No." She eyes me. "Why? Do I need to?"

"No, of course not. I just wondered why you made that comment earlier about Rob. My neighbor."

"Oh. Yes. His wife, Alice, spoke to me at the hospital charity event last week. She didn't come out and say you were sleeping with her husband, but she hinted at it clearly enough that I got the message."

"Who else did she say this to?"

"As far as I know, just me. I don't know why she'd tell anyone else. I'm the one who has the power to ruin your career. I assume that was her intent. Given my active involvement with the church, she knows I'd frown on such behavior and might consider it reason enough to let you go."

Alice was trying to get me fired? Without even having proof that anything happened? I knew that woman was out to get me. Rob needs to get her under control, and fast.

"There's nothing going on between Rob and me," I say. "Alice is just paranoid. She's been accusing me of being with her husband for months now."

"I don't care either way. I'm hardly one to judge, given what Marcus is doing."

"Going back to what you said. About knowing what Marcus was up to. I still don't understand why you've kept this arrangement of ours if you didn't actually need me."

"It's good to have people around who will do anything to get ahead. People who have a lot to lose. Wouldn't you agree?"

"I don't know what you're getting at. Is there something you want me to do?"

"Just keep doing what you're doing. You don't need to tell me about Marcus' trips to the city. As I said, I have professionals hired for that. What I need is for you to get closer to him. Get him to confide in you. Get him drunk if you have to. Whatever is necessary to get him to talk. He trusts you, Blaire, more than his own family. It's because of this secret he thinks you're keeping. He assumes if you've kept that quiet all this time, you'll keep his other secrets too."

"What other secrets? What do you think he's hiding?"

She picks up her fountain pen and runs her fingers along it, back and forth, as she looks at me. "My husband complains to you about me. Says I'm controlling. And that he feels stuck. Trapped in his marriage. Is that true?"

I hesitate, not sure I should tell her.

"Your honesty will be rewarded, Blaire."

I nod. "Yes. He does say those things. But to be fair, I'm sure Adam complains about me. All men complain about their wives, just like we complain about them."

"But not all men do something about it."

"Meaning what? Are you saying you're concerned Marcus is going to ask for a divorce?"

"No. He'd never do that. He has far too much to lose. Marcus came from wealth, but not the kind he has now. And he doesn't have to work for it, which is good for him because he's incredibly lazy." She pauses. "Did I ever tell you that my father wouldn't allow me to take over that office?"

"No. I just thought you didn't want to."

"I didn't. I find real estate painfully boring. The idea of showing people house after house while listening to them complain about every little thing sounds like a horrible way to spend my time. But regardless, my father could've at least offered me the opportunity when he opened an office here. He didn't because he felt the office wouldn't survive if I were running it. He believed wealthy men looking to buy property want a male broker in charge. So I married Marcus, a man my father couldn't stand, to get back at him. When Marcus took over the office, it immediately failed and my father blamed *me* for it, saying I should've married someone smarter and more business-savvy. I had to get the business making money again just to prove my father wrong." She smiles. "Fortunately for me, Marcus gave a young ambitious woman a challenge and she not only met it but exceeded it."

"Wait, are you saying I saved the office from going under?"

"The money you brought in, with my guidance and connections, got my father off my back. He, of course, gave Marcus the credit and continues to do so." She huffs. "My father hates Marcus but would rather credit him with the office's performance than me. And Marcus happily took the credit. He'd never admit that you are the one making him look good." She pauses. "You do know that challenge he gave you when you started was meant as a joke."

I keep quiet and wait for her to explain.

"He was making fun of you," she says. "Two listings in a month from a brand-new agent? Someone who's not from around here and was barely twenty years old at the time? He was joking with you. He didn't think you'd actually take him seriously. He said it to scare you off. He was trying to get rid of you."

I think back to that day. During my interview, Marcus seemed very distracted. He kept looking at his computer screen. I assumed he was just a very busy man, but thinking back now, his behavior was showing that he was bored and wanted me to leave. I gave him the speech I'd prepared about the research I'd done on the local market and my plan for how to grow my sales, but he didn't seem to be listening. When I was done, he challenged me to get two listings in a month, and I was determined to do it. I never considered that was his way of getting rid of me.

"I knew he was joking," I say, not wanting Lydia to think I was too naïve or stupid to know what Marcus was doing. "But I was determined to get those listings."

"Which completely shocked him." She laughs. "I remember him coming home that night, telling me about you, saying he didn't know how you did it. Even his best agent couldn't bring in listings that fast. That's when I knew I had to meet you. And when I did, I was quite impressed."

"Thank you, Lydia. That means a lot. I respect your opinion a great deal."

"I know you do," she says, her lips turning up.

"So what exactly are you wanting me to find out about Marcus?"

"Before we go there, you mentioned wanting to discuss something at our meeting today. What is it?"

"Oh. Yes. The condo project. Marcus took me off it."

Her brows draw together. "I don't understand. The builder specifically asked for you to take the project."

"Yes, but people around the office believe Marcus gave it to me for another reason."

"Which is what?"

"There was a rumor going around that I'm . . ." I pause, not sure how she's going to react to this. "That I'm sleeping with Marcus."

190

She laughs, harder and longer than I've ever heard her laugh. "And people actually believed this?"

"They think that's why Marcus keeps giving me all the new projects that come in."

Her expression turns serious. "That's very odd. And rather concerning."

"Do you mean the rumor?"

"Marcus doesn't listen to rumors. He abhors gossip. He used to punish our girls when they were younger if he heard them gossiping. So it makes absolutely no sense for him to take action based on a rumor he knows isn't true. Did you talk to him about this?"

"Yes. He said he didn't want the rumor getting back to you, and that taking me off the project was the only way to put an end to it."

"That's clearly a lie. He knows I wouldn't believe a rumor like that."

"Are you sure? Because he seemed very concerned you'd find out, almost as concerned as you finding out what he does at that private club." I pause. "I know you don't believe this, but I think he's a little afraid of you."

"Good. He should be, especially if I find out I'm right."

"Right about what?"

"It involves the reason you're here today. What I need you to do."

"Which is what?" I ask, wishing she'd just hurry up and tell me.

"I need you to get Marcus to confide in you about what he's planning and if he's really going to do it."

"I'm not sure what you mean."

"I've been monitoring his computer for weeks now and have noticed some rather questionable searches. About pills. Toxic fumes. Poisons."

"I don't understand. What are you trying to tell me?"

She looks me in the eye. "I believe my husband is planning to kill me."

CHAPTER 29

As I leave the Rockingham mansion, Lydia's words replay in my head. *I believe my husband is planning to kill me.*

She can't honestly think that. Marcus wouldn't kill her. Even if he wanted to, he wouldn't actually do it because he knows he'd never get away with it. The husband is always the prime suspect, and a lawyer could easily convince a jury that Marcus killed his wife to get her money. Marcus would spend the rest of his life in prison. Besides that, Marcus isn't a killer.

Lydia is just being paranoid. A few suspicious internet searches don't make someone a murderer. Last year, I heard a story on the news about a woman who poisoned her boyfriend, which prompted me to look up poisons on the internet, but I didn't plan to use that information to harm someone.

How am I supposed to get Marcus to talk about killing his wife if he has no plans to do so? That was not how I thought my meeting with Lydia would go. I was hoping to ask her if she knew of any new developments in the area that could be my replacement for the condo project, but after she told me she thought Marcus might be planning to kill her, I didn't feel it was appropriate to bring up.

I'll have to do my own digging to see what properties are scheduled for development. I've gotten to know several of the developers in the area. Maybe it's time to contact them again and schedule a lunch. I'll have to do it soon. I'm sure by now Donna has spread the word to everyone in the office about the new project I told her about, the one that's bigger and better than the condo project. I wish I hadn't told her that.

As I'm driving back to the office, I try to figure out what to say to Marcus to get him to confide in me about whatever it is he's up to. I don't think he's up to anything, other than keeping Lydia from finding out about the rumor that Marcus and I are having an affair. It's almost comical that he's afraid she'll find out. It just proves he has no idea that his wife and I are scheming behind his back. If he isn't smart enough to figure that out, he's definitely not smart enough to plan his wife's murder.

If anyone was capable of carrying out a murder, it's Lydia. Marcus is the one who should be worried, although I can't imagine Lydia killing Marcus. She's got him trained to do whatever she says. It'd be too much work for her to train someone new. Plus, she wouldn't want her daughters to be left without a father.

The more I think about Lydia's assignment, the more annoyed I become. I really don't need this headache right now. I have so many other things to worry about, like my failing marriage and the crazy neighbor lady who's out to destroy me. Then there's the looming issue of who pushed me down the stairs the night of my party.

What if it didn't really happen? What if my injured brain created a memory that isn't real? Have I been worrying all this time about nothing?

"Hi, Blaire," Tara says as I go into the office. "I have a message for you."

I walk up to her desk. "What is it?"

"A man called a few minutes ago wanting to talk to you. I told him you weren't here but gave him your number. Or you could just call him back." She hands me a piece of paper with a phone number written on it, along with a name.

"Stuart Margolis?" I say, staring at the name. "That can't be right. Are you sure this was the name?"

"That's what he said. He even spelled it out for me." She cocks her head. "Why does that name sound so familiar?"

"Stuart is a real estate developer in New York. You might've seen his name in one of the real estate publications we get. He's very wealthy. Worth well over a billion."

"I think I know who he is. Older man? Bald? Wears those thick red glasses?"

"Yes, that's him." I smile at her. "I'll go give him a call."

Going down to my office, I notice Valerie's office door is partially open. I see her at her desk, looking down at a file. I was hoping she wouldn't be here. I'm not ready to deal with her.

I go into my office and shut the door. Getting out my phone, I put in Stuart's number. I saw him at a charity auction a few years ago but didn't get a chance to talk to him. I'm curious why he would call me. As far as I know, he doesn't own any property in Connecticut.

"Blaire Banks," he says, answering my call. "Just the woman I was hoping to speak with."

How does he know me? And how did he know it was me who was calling?

"Mr. Margolis, I must say, this is a bit of a surprise. I don't believe we've ever officially met."

"You're correct. We haven't, but a friend of mine knows you quite well and encouraged me to call you about a property I'm interested in."

"What friend are you referring to, if you don't mind my asking?"

"She'd prefer to remain anonymous. Is that a problem?"

"No. Of course not. I just like to call and thank anyone who refers me. So, about this property you're interested in. I assume it's here in Connecticut?"

"Yes, it's the old Truttell mansion. I'd like to buy it and renovate it. Once it's done, one of my business associates is going to rent it out for events and give me a cut of the profits. We've done the research and found there's a need for those types of historic mansions for weddings and other special events."

"The Truttell mansion would be perfect for that, but unfortunately, it's not for sale."

"It is for the right price. That's where you come in. Tell me what you think it's worth and I'll make an offer."

"We can make an offer, but Mr. Truttell has no plans to sell it. He doesn't need the money, and he's told me, and every other agent, that he's going to stay in that house until he dies."

"I'm disappointed in you, Blaire. I was told you were a go-getter. That you didn't take no for an answer."

He's challenging me, and I never turn down a challenge. Whoever referred him to me knows this and probably told him to say that.

"You're right, Mr. Margolis. I will get you that house. As for the price, the last assessment had it valued at twenty-five million."

"That's it?" He laughs. "It'd be twice that in New York. Let me know when the paperwork is ready to sign. It was a pleasure speaking with you, Ms. Banks. Have a good day."

"You as well," I say, but then notice he already ended the call.

That was strange. A billionaire calls me out of the blue to buy a mansion that's not even for sale? And why did he call the main office number instead of my cell phone? He could've easily found my number online. It's all over my website.

This had to be Lydia's doing. She's giving me an early reward for the information she's hoping to get about her husband. Or maybe it's an incentive to do the assignment quickly, before it's too late. This is so ridiculous. Marcus is not planning to kill her.

"Knock, knock," Valerie says, tapping on my door as she opens it. "Hey, Blaire. Can we talk?"

"About what?" I give her a fake smile. "How you made up a rumor about me so that Marcus would give you the condo project?"

"Blaire, don't be like that." She comes into my office. "I know you don't believe me, but I truly was trying to help you. Everyone already assumed you and Marcus were having an affair. All I did was bring attention to it so Marcus would address it and put an end to the rumor."

"Val, just stop with the lies. We both know this was about you and what you wanted. And it worked. You got the project. Congratulations." I wake up my laptop and type in the password. "I need to get to work. And so do you, with all those condos to sell."

"I don't know why you're so angry about this." She puts her hands on her hips. "You'll still come out ahead. You always do." She pauses. "Why was Stuart Margolis calling you? Is he the one funding this new project of yours?"

Donna clearly spread the word about my fake new project.

"How do you know about Stuart?" I ask, my gaze going from my laptop back to Val.

She shrugs. "I noticed the note on Tara's desk. She said it was for you."

That's why he called the front desk. Lydia must've told him to, so that everyone would know I had something in the works. Something big, with someone important.

I didn't ask Lydia for this, but she did it anyway. I'm pleased, but also concerned. Lydia's help comes at a price. I thought that price was following her husband around, but it turns out I was wrong about that. Instead, Lydia has been using me for some other reason, and I don't think it's just for my outstanding sales record that boosts the overall performance of the office. I don't know what she wants with me, and I'm a little afraid to find out.

"My business with Stuart is confidential," I say. "I need to make a call, so please leave my office."

She walks up to my desk. "Is this how it's going to be now? You're ending our friendship over this?"

"I think we agreed that we were never really friends, which was confirmed when you stabbed me in the back. And yes, this is how it's going to be. We don't need to speak unless it's business-related."

"Fine." She shrugs. "But you're going to end up alone. I hope you're okay with that, because you're about to lose everyone. Adam is going to leave you. Caitlyn will leave and go to college. I was your only friend. Now all you'll be left with is work. Is that really what you want?"

"What you're describing sounds like you. Single and alone with no friends?"

She scowls at me. "I don't know why I even bothered to be your friend. All you care about is yourself and what you can get from people. You deserve whatever happens to you." She storms out of my office and slams the door.

I remain seated, her words echoing in my head.

You deserve whatever happens to you.

It's what was written on that note. The note that was in the flowers.

It wasn't Alice who sent them. It was Valerie.

CHAPTER 30

"Why did you do it?" I ask, going into Valerie's office.

She was just about to sit down but rises back to standing. "Do what?"

"Send me those flowers with that threatening note."

She laughs. "You think I'm the one who did that? Seriously?"

"What you said just now. About me deserving whatever happens to me. That was written in the note. It had to be you."

"It was a coincidence. I did not send you those flowers. I'm offended you would even think that."

I walk up to her. "Stop lying and just admit it. Admit you did it and tell me why."

"I'm not admitting anything. I'm telling you I didn't do it."

"It had to be you. Why else would you say that? The exact words from the note?"

"It's a common saying. And maybe it was in my head from when you told me what was in the note. I don't know, Blaire, but I promise you, I did not send those flowers."

"You said you know what I did with him," I say, still not believing the note wasn't from her. "Were you referring to Marcus? Were you hoping people in the office would see the note and it would support your story that I'm having an affair with Marcus?"

"No!" She goes around me to the door, holding it open. "You need to leave. I'm not going to keep listening to you accuse me of something I didn't do."

I meet her at the door and look her in the eye. "This isn't over. I'm going to prove that you did this."

"Go ahead and try. But just remember, you have a lot of enemies, Blaire. More than you know." She leans toward my ear and whispers, "I'm not surprised someone pushed you down the stairs."

I rear back, wondering if she's the one who did it. Did Valerie push me that night? Was she just pretending to be my friend while plotting to kill me? Is she really that evil? I didn't think so, but anything's possible.

"Stay away from me," I say, pointing my finger at her face. "And stay away from my family."

Leaving her office, I go back to mine and take a moment to calm down. Valerie can deny it all she wants, but she had to have been the one who sent the flowers. I don't know why she did it, but I'm not going to waste time trying to figure it out.

With so much going on, I'm struggling to keep my mind on work, but I can't put off dealing with Mr. Margolis' request to buy that mansion. If I get this deal to go through, he'll consider doing business with me in the future and might refer me to his wealthy friends.

"Yes, this is Blaire Banks," I say when the maid answers my call. "Can I speak with Mr. Truttell?"

"I'm sorry, but Mr. Truttell isn't available," she says.

"Do you know when he'll be back? I'd like to schedule a meeting with him."

"He doesn't take meetings unless he's the one initiating them."

"Well, perhaps you could give him my name and number so he could call me back."

"Yes, I'll do that," she says in a patronizing tone. She's never giving him the message. I'll have to find another way to reach him. "Goodbye, Ms. Banks." She ends the call.

Mr. Truttell isn't going to meet with me. He's known around town as a reclusive millionaire who rarely leaves his house. His maid lives with him and gets him whatever he needs.

Why would Lydia set this up? She had to have known Mr. Truttell would never agree to meet with me and definitely wouldn't allow me to sell his house. As I told Mr. Margolis, Mr. Truttell plans to die in that house.

My office door swings open and Marcus storms in. "We need to talk."

"I'm in the middle of something," I tell him.

He comes over to me, staring down at me in my chair. "I'm done playing games. I need this to stop."

"Need *what* to stop?"

"This!" He shoves his phone in my face, showing me a series of photos attached as text messages.

"What are the photos of? I can't tell."

He huffs. "You know what they're of! You're the one who sent them!"

"I really have no idea what you're talking about."

He races over to shut the door, then comes back and hands me his phone. "Why would you send me those?"

The first photo shows Marcus going into the building in New York, the one that has the private club. The next few photos show him leaving, coming out the side door and into the alley. There are other men in the background. Some are dressed in suits, some in drag, and one is wearing a trench coat and has makeup on his face.

"I didn't take these," I say.

"Really, Blaire?" he says, sarcastically. "Then who do you suppose took them?"

The people Lydia hired, but I can't tell him that.

"I don't know." I hand him his phone back. "Maybe it was someone who knows about one of the other men. Maybe this isn't even about you."

"Then why send them to me?" he scoffs. "I'm obviously being targeted." He leans down to me. "And the only person who'd want to blackmail me with these is sitting in front of me."

"I did not do this." I stand up. "And if you're that worried about me exposing your secret, you wouldn't risk provoking me by taking me off the condo project."

"That was to protect Lydia."

He keeps talking, but my mind goes back to those photos.

"Can I see those again?" I reach for Marcus' phone.

"Why? You already have copies."

"No, I don't. Just let me look at them again."

He hesitates but then gives me the phone. I find the photo showing an older man coming out the side door, the club's entrance, wearing a trench coat and makeup. It's him. I knew I recognized him. It's Mr. Truttell.

Getting out my phone, I take a picture of the photo.

"Hey!" Marcus snatches his phone from me. "What are you doing?"

"I have to go. I need to meet with someone."

He grabs my arm. "We had a deal, Blaire. You tell anyone about this, you're—"

"Yes, I'm aware of our deal. Now let go of me."

He takes his hand off my arm and backs away. "I mean it, Blaire. Stop with the messages. I don't know why you're doing this, but it has to end."

"For the last time, I did not send those messages."

Going past him, I leave my office, prepared to make the biggest single deal of my career. Commission-wise, the condos would've made me more money, but that project is a lot more work. This is one deal worth over a million in commission, and it's something no one else has been able to do. Truttell has received hundreds of offers over the years, but he refused to sell.

Or he did. Until today.

CHAPTER 31

I'm home just after five, ready to celebrate the Truttell sale with a very expensive bottle of champagne. I did it! I made the sale!

When I arrived at the mansion, Truttell wouldn't even let me past the gate. There was a security camera there, so I held up my phone so Truttell could see the photo I got from Marcus. The gate immediately opened and Truttell was waiting for me at the door.

He would've agreed to a price of twenty-five million, but I bumped it up to thirty. Mr. Margolis can more than afford it, and I decided I deserved a higher commission after losing the condo deal.

"Blaire?" Adam says from the other room. "Is that you?"

"Yes, I'm in the kitchen."

He walks in as I'm pouring myself some champagne. "You're not working tonight?"

"No. I'm celebrating." I go up to him, taking a sip of the champagne. "I just sold the Truttell mansion."

"Seriously? What happened? Did Truttell die?"

Even Adam knows Truttell never planned to sell that house. Everyone knows. Just wait until people find out I convinced him to sell it. I'll be a local celebrity.

"He didn't die. I had a very wealthy client willing to pay whatever it takes to get the house and Truttell agreed to it."

"Why? The guy's loaded. He doesn't need more money."

"I convinced him it was time to move out of that drafty old mansion and get something more modern. Given the sale price, he'll have enough money to get whatever he'd like. And I will be making a very large commission." I set my glass down and put my arms around Adam. "Celebrate with me." I give him a kiss. "We'll have some champagne. Order in dinner. Then go upstairs."

He looks at me. "Are you drunk?"

"No. I just thought we could spend some time together."

I should be angry at Adam for seeing that lawyer, and part of me is, but the other part wants to save my marriage.

"Are you only doing this because you made that sale? Because you're in a good mood?"

"Adam, don't read something into this. I just want to be with you." I kiss him. "I miss you." I hand him my glass. "Take this and let's go sit down. I'll get another glass."

I meet him on the couch with my glass of champagne. "Where's Caitlyn?"

"At a friend's house. That tall girl with the pink hair."

"Elise," I say. "Did Caitlyn say when we need to pick her up?"

"She's spending the night there."

"On a school night?"

"I told her she could. It was my idea." He sets his glass on the coffee table. "I wanted time alone with you. So we could talk."

The way he says it, so seriously and without looking at me, I'm starting to get worried. Is this it? Is he going to tell me he's filed for divorce?

He leans forward, resting his elbows on his knees. "Blaire, I—"

"Wait! Don't say it."

He looks at me. "You don't even know what I'm going to say."

"Just please, let me talk first."

He sits back and turns to me. "Go ahead."

"I know things haven't been good between us for a long time. And I know a lot of that is my fault. I get caught up in work and forget that I need to be here, at home, spending time with you and Caitlyn."

He looks confused and a little shocked, like that was the last thing he thought I'd say. "Do you really mean that?"

"I do. I just don't know how to make it happen. I want to move up in my career, but that means spending less time at home."

He lets out a frustrated sigh. "Blaire, why isn't this enough? We have a huge house. Nice cars. Our kid's in private school. We have way more than we ever thought we'd have. You don't have to keep working so hard."

"But I want to. I enjoy it. I like making money and buying the types of things I never thought I could afford. You know how much we struggled growing up. We never had anything. Now we can buy whatever we want."

"And look what it's done to our marriage. We don't even talk anymore."

"We're talking right now." I pause, looking at Adam. "I need to tell you something. Something I should've told you as soon as it happened."

He shakes his head. "I don't want to hear about that."

"About what?"

"About you and—" He stops suddenly. "Never mind. Just tell me what you were going to say."

"The night of my birthday. When I fell down the stairs. It wasn't an accident."

"What are you talking about?"

"Someone pushed me." I grab Adam's hand. "I know this sounds crazy, but I swear, someone was behind me. I heard their footsteps, then felt their hands on my back right before I tumbled down the stairs."

"Blaire, nobody would do that, at least not the people who were there that night. They were either our friends or people you work with."

"Yes, and one of them pushed me."

"Are you sure this isn't a side effect of you hurting your head? The doctor said the memories you get back may not be real. Maybe that's what happened. You had a fake memory."

"I've considered that, but I really think it's real. It happened the day I returned to the office after my week off. I went to the house where we had the party and had a memory of that night. It was like I was reliving it. I could feel myself being pushed. And when I was lying on the floor in the basement, I looked up and saw a shadow at the top of the stairs. The person who pushed me was there, Adam. They knew I was injured. For all they knew, I was dying. And they left me there. They shut the door and walked off."

"No." Adam gets up and paces the floor. "That can't be right. It doesn't make sense. Nobody we know would do that."

"What about Troy? He was there that night to fix the sink."

"The handyman?"

"Yes. He thinks I'm going to tell on him for taking jewelry from one of the homes."

"He's stealing from people?"

"As far as I know, it was only one time, but he's worried I'm going to tell on him. Is that reason enough to kill me?"

"And risk going back to prison? I'd say no, but I don't know how the guy thinks." Adam comes back to the couch and sits down next to me. "Why did you wait so long to tell me this? And why the hell didn't you tell the police? If you're right and someone tried to hurt you, there's a good chance they're going to try again."

"I didn't want to involve the police. There's nothing they can do. It happened weeks ago, and there's a chance they wouldn't believe me. They could say I imagined it because of the damage to my brain. Like you just did."

"Blaire, I'm sorry." He holds my hand. "I shouldn't have said that. I believe you. I really do. I just didn't want this to be true. Why the hell did you keep this from me? Why didn't you tell me sooner?"

"I, um . . . well, it's just that you're the one who found me."

"Yeah? So?"

"I thought maybe . . ." I close my eyes, not wanting to see his face when I say this. "That maybe you were the one who—"

"Are you serious?" he yells, yanking his hand from mine. "You thought I tried to kill you?"

Opening my eyes, I see his jaw tightening, his face getting red.

"Adam, I'm sorry. It's just that we weren't getting along and—"

"And I decided to kill you so we wouldn't fight anymore?" He huffs and looks away from me. "I can't believe this. We've been together since high school. We have a daughter. How could you even . . ." He shakes his head and blows out a breath.

"I didn't want to think it was you, but you've seen those crime shows on TV. How many times is it the husband? And nobody suspects him. They always say how shocked they are that he would do something like that."

Adam looks at me, his expression turning from anger to hurt. "I would never do that to you. I'd never do anything to hurt you. Even if I was angry with you or hated you, I would never hurt you."

I keep quiet, not sure what to say. I didn't want to tell Adam my suspicions about him, but if I want a chance at saving our marriage, I need to be honest and put it all out there.

"Blaire, I know we're broken. And I don't know how to fix us. But I know that what we've been doing is only making things worse. We're both hiding stuff from each other. Doing things we shouldn't be doing." He rubs his jaw. "I wish we could go back to the point where everything went wrong and start all over again."

"I don't know when that would be. It seems like we've been this way for so long. But I'm tired of it. And I'm tired of hiding things from you. I need someone to talk to and you were always that person, until we grew apart."

"Let's start right now. Tell me what's going on with you, Blaire. You're not sleeping. You're always on edge. Is that because you're worried about someone coming after you again or is there more you haven't told me?"

"There was a note. It was delivered with some flowers." I tell him what the note said and how I think Valerie sent the flowers, but that she's denying it.

"It wasn't Valerie," Adam says, leaning back on the couch.

"Then it had to be Alice. She always thinks women are trying to steal her husband. It's completely ridiculous, but you've seen how crazy she can be. Or maybe she—"

"It wasn't Alice."

"No, I really think it was. She—"

"Blaire, it wasn't her." Adam looks at me. "It was me. I'm the one who sent the flowers."

CHAPTER 32

"You sent the flowers?" I stare at Adam, not understanding how that's even possible. It doesn't make sense.

He sighs. "It was stupid, but I didn't know what else to do."

"Adam, why would you do something like that? Do you know how much that scared me? Especially after I realized someone tried to kill me the night of my party."

"I didn't know about that. I wasn't trying to scare you. I was trying to stop you."

"From what?"

He looks down. "From leaving me for Rob."

"Rob?" I say, pretending to be confused. "Rob is just a friend. A neighbor."

"Blaire, don't lie to me. We just said we'd stop hiding things from each other."

"Adam, there's nothing going on between Rob and me."

"Maybe not now, but there was." He gets out his phone, taps on the screen a few times, and shows me a photo.

No. It can't be. How is that possible? It was dark. We were alone.

"How did you get that?" I ask.

208

"Someone sent it to me." He takes his phone back. "It was a text from some strange number. When I called it, the line was dead. I'm guessing it was a burner phone." He shows me his phone again. "There's more. You can flip through them."

I take his phone. There are eight photos of me with Rob the night we were together. We're in the parking lot behind one of Rob's gyms. I'm standing with my back against his SUV. Rob is in front of me. He's kissing me in the first photo. The ones that follow become more intimate, the last one showing my dress pushed up around my waist and Rob with his pants down. It's clear what we were doing.

"It was only one time," I say, as if that'll make Adam feel better. "And I honestly don't remember doing it. I was at a bar, having a glass of wine, waiting for a potential client to show up, but she never did. I was going to leave, but then Rob came in and joined me at the bar. I drank too much and couldn't drive home so Rob gave me a ride. He had to stop at the gym to pick something up and somehow we ended up . . . well, you've seen the photos." I give him his phone.

"I didn't want to believe it." He sets his phone on the table. "I didn't want to believe you'd do that to me. When I saw those photos, I was ready to divorce you. But instead, I did something else. Something I'm not proud of."

"You were with another woman," I say, my throat burning from holding back tears. It hurts knowing he did that, but I hurt him too by being with Rob.

Adam looks at me. "You knew?"

"Valerie saw you with her. At the park."

"Shit." He rubs his face. "Blaire, I swear to you, nothing happened. It could've, and it almost did, but I couldn't go through with it. I kept thinking of you, and how I didn't want to lose you."

"So you and this woman didn't . . ." I don't even want to say it.

"No. I took her home. Haven't talked to her since."

"And there was no one else?"

209

"No." He pauses. "But I did go see a lawyer."

I grip his arm. "Please tell me you didn't start the paperwork. We can work on this. We don't have to get divorced."

"I didn't do anything. I just talked to her. Found out my options. I didn't want you taking Caitlyn from me."

"Adam, I would never do that. You know I wouldn't."

"Do I?" He looks me in the eye. "I feel like I don't know you anymore, Blaire. You've become someone else since we moved here. Sometimes I don't even recognize you as the woman I married. You don't even have the same name." He gazes down at the floor. "The woman you are now would do anything to win. If winning in a divorce meant taking Caitlyn from me, I knew you'd do it. I couldn't let that happen."

Is that really what he thinks of me? That I'd use my own daughter as a pawn in our divorce? I immediately think of Lydia. That's something she would do. She uses people to get what she wants, including me. I thought I was giving her dirt on Marcus in return for her sending clients my way. But this whole time she's been using me, controlling me, getting me to do exactly what she wants. She does the same with Marcus. So do I. He does what I want because I know his secret.

Does that mean I'm no better than Lydia? Am I becoming someone just like her? I used to admire her, but now I'm seeing her differently. Questioning my involvement with her.

"I never should've sent you that note," Adam says, drawing my attention back to him. "It was after I got those photos. I was so damn angry. I always thought there was something going on with you and Rob. The way you looked at him. The way he was always flirting with you. And then I had proof. I assumed you'd leave me for him so I sent you that note, thinking it'd make you end it with him."

"I deserve whatever happens to me? Adam, when I read that, I thought someone was going to hurt me. Or kill me."

"That's not what it meant. It was supposed to mean you'd end up alone and unhappy and . . ." Adam sighs. "I wish I'd never sent it."

"What about the other note? Was that from you too?"

"What other note?"

I tell him about the car that followed me and the man in the chauffeur uniform who left the note on my windshield.

"Blaire, what the hell?" Adam gets up and walks around the room, unable to sit still. "How could you not tell me about this? And why didn't you call the police?"

"I didn't think they'd do anything. The car took off and the license plate was covered up."

"You still could've given them a description of it and had them test the note for prints."

"The man was wearing gloves, so there wouldn't have been prints. It happened the day I called you to come over to that house where I was having a showing. Remember how I told you about that man lurking around? The man wasn't actually there. He'd driven away. I just wanted you to show up. I was scared."

He stops and looks at me. "Why didn't you just tell me that? I would've been there."

"Adam, you knew I was scared. I never call and ask you for help. Just the fact that I did shows how much I needed you that day."

He shuts his eyes and pinches the bridge of his nose. "How did we get here, Blaire? How did we get to this place where we don't even care about each other? Where we're so damn wrapped up in ourselves that we don't even notice when the other person needs us?"

"I don't know." I get up and walk over to him. "But I don't want to be this way anymore. I want us to get back to how we were, before our marriage fell apart."

Adam opens his eyes and looks at me. "Are you just saying that, or do you mean it?"

"I'm saying I want to give us another chance. Maybe it won't work out and we'll find out we're better apart, but I'm not ready to go there yet."

"I'm not either. I love you so much." He wraps his arms around me. "No more secrets, okay? From here on out, we tell each other everything."

211

I nod but know I can't agree to that. I'll tell him what I can, but some things need to remain a secret. Adam doesn't need to know about Marcus and his secret life or about my relationship with Lydia. Those secrets don't involve him. I wish they didn't involve me either.

Knowing what I know now, I want to end my involvement with Lydia, but I'm worried she won't let me. She called me her protégé. She made that comment about wanting to stay in the background and keep her hands clean. To me, that means she wants me to do her dirty work. I don't know what that would be, but I don't want to find out.

Lydia has the money and power to control me, much like she controls her husband. I finally know what Marcus feels like, fearing Lydia and wondering what she'll do next. I'm guessing she's the one who sent Adam those photos. It had to be her. She said she wasn't having me followed, but I don't believe her. She's probably been spying on me for years, having whoever she hired take photos of me doing things she could later use to blackmail me.

She's never liked me being with Adam. She says he's unmotivated and unsophisticated. She's always telling me I could do better than him. She thinks he's holding me back from my true potential. So it makes sense that she would send Adam those photos in the hope that it leads to us divorcing. If I hadn't found out my deal with Lydia wasn't real all these years, I would've thought Alice sent those photos, but now I'm almost certain it was Lydia. It had to be.

"Should we order dinner?" Adam asks. "Or do you want to talk some more?"

I smile at him. "I'd kind of like to go upstairs."

"I'm confused." He looks around. "What happened to my wife?"

I swat his chest. "Stop it," I say with a laugh. "Or I'll change my mind."

We go up to our room, and I'm with my husband because I want to be, not because I feel like I have to. Maybe it was the thought of him leaving that made me feel that spark again. Or maybe after everything that's happened the past few weeks, I realize how much I need him. Whatever the reason, it caused a change in me and how I feel about Adam. I'm now committed more than ever to getting my marriage back. Adam is too.

The only way it won't work out is if Lydia interferes again. I'm going to have to tell her that despite her feelings about Adam, it's my life and I've chosen to stay with him.

I'm just afraid she won't listen. When Lydia wants something, she gets it. And she doesn't want me with Adam.

CHAPTER 33

"Thank you for meeting with me," I say to Lydia, trying to appear relaxed when the reality is I'm a nervous wreck.

I've spent all morning working up the courage to tell her this, but I still don't feel ready. The woman frightens me, and I hate myself for that. When I left my old life behind for this one, I promised myself I wouldn't let these people intimidate me. To succeed, I had to be on their level and not believe they're better than me. For the most part, I've kept that promise, except when it comes to Lydia.

"You sounded quite distressed on the phone," she says, crossing her legs. "Please be aware that this won't be allowed again. I arrange the meetings, Blaire, not you. Is that understood?"

She's never spoken to me this way, as though she's in charge and I have to go along with whatever she says. Something's changed, and it started when she revealed that she knew all along what Marcus was doing. My fake assignment to spy on him was just to test me, to see how much I'd tell her. To make me betray Marcus and place my loyalty with her. To make me dependent on her connections and referrals for advancing my career.

She deceived me, and I fell for it. All these years, I let her condition me and control me without even knowing it was happening. Which brings us to now. I want out. I don't want to do this anymore. As much as I love the money and success, I'll give it all up if it means getting Lydia out of my life.

"Actually, I don't believe we'll be needing any more meetings," I say.

"And why is that?" she asks, sipping her tea.

I take a breath, hoping it'll calm me down enough that my voice doesn't sound shaky. "I've decided to leave the Rockingham Group. I'm not a good fit there anymore."

"I see." She sets her teacup down. "And what would you do if you left?"

"I've decided to get my broker's license and go out on my own."

She laughs. "You would never survive. The Rockingham Group owns this region and continues to expand."

"Yes, I realize I'll have to move, but I spoke with my husband and we feel this is the right decision."

"So this was Adam's idea."

"No, we both agreed to this. We don't belong here. We never have."

"You mean Adam doesn't belong here."

"No, I—"

"Blaire, I told you that man was holding you back. And now he's trying to take your career. Don't you see what's happening? He's jealous of your success so he's trying to convince you to leave all this behind."

"That's not what this is about. Adam and I just need a change. We need to work on our marriage and we can't do that if I'm never around."

I hope she buys that reasoning, but she looks doubtful. What I told her about my marriage was true, but it's not the main reason I'm quitting.

"And you think by going out on your own, you won't have to work as hard?" she asks in a condescending tone.

"I know I'll have to work hard, but I won't have to report to a broker. I can work as much or as little as I'd like."

"You'll be working even more than you do now. You can't help yourself, Blaire. You're very competitive. You're driven to be better than anyone else. It's why I chose you."

Why I chose you. Her words send a chill through me.

"Lydia, I appreciate all that you've done for me over the years, but it's time for me to make a change. I've given it a lot of thought and I know my decision to leave is the right one."

"I'm sorry, but I cannot allow it. I didn't put in all this time and effort with you just to have you walk away."

"But it's not your decision. It's mine. Being here isn't right for me anymore. It's not right for my family."

"Perhaps you should've considered that when you agreed to our original deal." She picks up her teacup. "You knew what you were doing. You knew taking favors from someone like me comes with a catch."

"The catch was that I spy on Marcus for you. And I did. I told you when he'd go to that club and when he'd ask me to cover for him. I told you what he did there, or as much as I knew, based on whatever details he gave me."

"I didn't need you to tell me those things. I already knew."

"But I didn't know that until the other day. I thought our deal was mutual. That we were both getting something out of it."

"Did you really think I'd rely on you, and you alone, to tell me about my husband?"

"Yes. I really did. I had no idea you'd hired people to watch him."

"Then you're not as smart as I thought you were." She sips her tea, then sets her cup down. "I suppose you haven't figured out my connection to the club either."

"I'm not sure what you mean."

"The club Marcus goes to? I own it."

"What was that?" I ask, certain I must've heard her wrong.

"I own the men's club in New York. The one Marcus goes to. I know how often he goes. What he does there. I know everything."

Lydia owns the club? I can't believe this. I've been telling her about this club for years, sharing whatever information Marcus will give me. And this whole time, she already knew. She knew more than I did. Because she owns it!

"I opened it years ago," she continues, "knowing it would be useful. You see, wealthy men are really no different than other men when it comes to their desires. They might even be *worse* than other men." She sighs. "The things I've seen. I won't go into it, but let me just say, they do dark and filthy things at that club. And then I use those things to make them do what I want. Only if I have to, of course."

"Is this how you've gotten me so many property deals? By blackmailing these men?"

"Goodness, no," she says with a laugh. "Those deals are far too small. The information I gather from the club is used for larger, more important deals. Deals you'll soon be helping me with."

She smiles, and another chill runs through me.

"Lydia, no. You don't seem to understand. I'm leaving. I'm not going to be working with you anymore."

"You don't work *with* me, Blaire. You work *for* me, and you will continue to do so. You don't have a choice."

"Yes, I do." I sit up straighter. "It's my life, and I need to do what I feel is right."

"And you believe you can just run off like that?" She waves her hand in the air. "Without any consequences?"

I keep quiet and wait for her to explain.

"People like you don't get attention from people like me unless we see value in you and what you can do for us. You've made the Rockingham Group extremely successful the past twenty years, more than it ever would've been if you'd never walked into that office. I certainly played a part in your success, but it was you, Blaire, who took those opportunities and expanded on them."

"I appreciate the compliment, but I still can't stay."

"You will. You will get your broker's license and eventually take over the office."

She wants to put me in charge? Was that her big plan? The reason she was helping me?

This would be a huge step up in my career. I'd make more money than I ever dreamed of. But I told Adam I was quitting. We talked it over and decided to leave here and start somewhere new. We agreed it's what we need to do for our marriage. The other reason, which I didn't tell Adam, is that I need to get far away from this place and the mess I've gotten myself into here.

"What about Marcus?" I ask.

"He'll be the face of the company, as dictated by my father's insistence that a male Rockingham be in charge, but you'll be the one leading the office and doing the work. Marcus will pop in now and then but won't be there every day. He'll essentially be retired, but we won't be calling it that."

"Does Marcus know this?"

"Of course, but he didn't feel now was the time to tell you. He wanted to wait, but with this news of you wanting to leave, I felt you should know."

This is what I've always wanted. Doing this would mean I'd made my way to the top. I'd be in charge of one of the most well-known, successful real estate offices in the country. I'd make a fortune and people around here would finally treat me like I'm one of them.

But at what cost? Letting Lydia control me? I don't want to live that way.

"I'm flattered by the offer," I tell her. "But I can't accept it."

"I'm not asking you to. I'm telling you. This isn't a negotiation."

My heart's beating out of my chest, but I'm trying to remain calm. Trying to hide my fear.

"Why me?" I ask. "Why can't you find someone else?"

"Because someone else doesn't know the things you do, Blaire. You realize you know far more than you should. About me. Marcus. The club I own. The steps I've taken to get you this far in your career. You can't just walk away from that."

"I'll never tell anyone. I promise. I won't even tell Adam."

"Your word isn't enough. I need you here, where I can keep an eye on you." Her lips curl up into a smile. "You wouldn't want me telling the police how you blackmailed poor Mr. Truttell into selling his mansion, would you?"

She knows about that. So I was right. She set the whole thing up. She sent Marcus those photos, knowing he'd show me. Knowing I'd see Mr. Truttell in the background and use the photo to blackmail him.

Why did I do it? I knew it was wrong but did it anyway. I figured Truttell deserved it for going to that club. But why does it matter that he goes there? He's not married. He can do whatever he pleases. It wasn't right of me to use that against him, but I wasn't thinking that way when I did it. I made him a villain so I could make the deal, get a huge commission, and look good at the office.

"You set that up," I say to Lydia, wanting to see if she'll admit it. "You sent Marcus those photos, knowing he'd think they were from me. You knew he'd show them to me and knew I'd see Truttell in the background."

"I was quite pleased you followed through so quickly," she says, not seeming the least bit guilty that she forced a man out of his house. "I've been waiting years to get him out of that place. It's such an eyesore. The man has more than enough money to fix it up, but he refuses to. When I finally found a buyer, I was thrilled. And it was perfect timing, with you needing something to replace the condo project."

"I shouldn't have done it. It was blackmail. I forced him to sell."

"You didn't force him. When he decided to join that club, he was putting himself at risk. He knew that. Anyone there could tell on him. Another member. One of my staff."

"It still doesn't make it right."

"What's happening to you, Blaire?" she scoffs. "You've always been focused on the deal, willing to do whatever it takes to get it."

"This is different. I broke the law. I could go to prison."

"Then I guess you'll need to do as I say." She pauses. "Unless you want me turning you in."

She set me up, and now I'm trapped here. My only other option is to turn myself in, but that would mean going to prison. Saying goodbye to my career. Losing everything I worked for.

There has to be a way out of this, something I'm not thinking about.

"You need to get used to it," Lydia says. "This is a dirty business. There's a lot of money involved and you don't get rich by playing by the rules. Just think of yourself, Blaire, and how you made it this far. You're an excellent agent, but you wouldn't be nearly as successful as you are now if I hadn't been sending clients your way and introducing you to the right people. The other agents at the office didn't have that advantage and yet I never heard you complain that it wasn't fair. You were betraying your boss. Using his secret to make him give you all the new business that came in." She laughs a little. "You've been playing dirty this whole time. Did you not realize that?"

I didn't think of it that way. I told myself I was helping Lydia by telling her about Marcus, and in return, she was helping me with my career. But the truth is Lydia is right. I got ahead by playing dirty, using people to my advantage. I've become like her, which is exactly what she wanted.

"You should run along," she says, getting up from her chair. "I want that paperwork for the Truttell sale finalized today. Oh, and call up the builder on that new construction house. That property has been sitting there far too long. It needs to be put on the market. Marcus has done nothing to speed things along so I'm putting you in charge of it."

She's talking to me like she's my boss. Is this how it's going to be now? She expects me to take orders from her?

"You'll need to tell Marcus that," I say. "I can't take over his project without him knowing."

"I'll deal with Marcus. You get that house on the market and sold." She walks to the door of the study. "You can show yourself out."

As I'm leaving the mansion, I think about when I arrived here an hour ago. I thought this was it, my last meeting with Lydia. The last time I'd come to this mansion.

But it didn't turn out that way. Lydia isn't going to let me leave.

I had a plan. I was going to get out of here, get a fresh start. But now that plan is never going to happen.

What am I going to tell Adam?

CHAPTER 34

Lydia

I'm losing my patience with Blaire. How dare she try to leave here after all I've done for her?

Where is this coming from? It has to be that idiot husband of hers. He probably threatened to divorce her if she didn't agree to move away with him. I'm so sick of these weak women who are willing to do whatever a man says just to keep him from leaving. I thought Blaire was better than that. She's always appeared strong. Confident. Focused on making it to the top.

But today she was weak. Unsure of herself. And just plain ignorant, acting as though she didn't realize that what she's been doing all these years was wrong. Would she have been okay with someone else in the office blackmailing the boss? Getting special favors from his wife? No, she would not. She'd be furious and trying to get the person fired.

I have done so much for that girl. Can she not see that I've been on her side this entire time? Helping her rise in her career? Boosting her social standing? She was a mess when I met her. She didn't even know the proper fork to use or how a suit should properly fit. I groomed her, taught her how to behave, how to speak. I made her who she is today. So how could she be so ungrateful?

My phone rings. It's Addison calling again. The poor girl has no ability to make a decision. I hired a wedding planner so she wouldn't have to decide anything and she still calls me at least once a day to get my opinion.

"Hello, dear," I say, trying not to sound annoyed. It's not that I don't enjoy talking with her, just not about the wedding. We've talked about it to death and I really can't take any more.

"Mom, the caterers are asking if we should have the Jordan almonds in little bowls on the tables or wrapped in tulle for each place setting. What do you think?"

Where did I go wrong with this child? I can't for the life of me understand how she can be so confident and capable in her professional life but when it comes to personal matters, she's unable to make the simplest of decisions. My other daughter isn't much better. This is why I took Blaire under my wing. She's the strong, dominant, take-charge type of girl I wanted for a daughter, or she was until just recently.

"Addison, you have a wedding planner. Let her make the decision. That's what she's there for. To make these decisions so you don't have to."

"Yeah, okay. I'll let her decide."

"How is everything else going? Besides the wedding."

"Great! I met grandfather for dinner last night."

"Wonderful," I say in a fake cheerful tone. Both my girls love their grandfather, but it's because they don't know him like I do. The man was a horrible father. Growing up, he told me what to do and when. I had no freedom. Marrying Marcus was the first decision I made for myself, and I only did it to rebel against my father. He'd already chosen someone for me to marry. The man was ten years older than me and came from a family who owned a large commercial development company. My father explained that marrying into this family would benefit the Rockingham Group. He was looking to increase his fortune. He didn't care if I'd be happy with the man.

My father was livid when I told him I was marrying Marcus. That's how I knew he was the right man. I didn't love Marcus, but I liked him. He was different than other men I'd dated. He was easy-going and did silly things that I thought were rather humorous. I later found those traits to be annoying and immature. I was hoping he'd grow out of them and become more serious and driven, but sadly, that didn't happen.

"Grandfather talked about you," Addison says.

"Is that so?" I'm surprised because my father likes to pretend I don't exist. He devotes his time and attention to my brothers and their families. They were all given homes in Manhattan while I — as the black sheep of the family — was banished to Connecticut. "And what did he say?"

"Something about a mansion you sold up there. Is it the one that looks like a haunted house?"

"I wouldn't describe it that way, but yes, you and your sister used to think it was haunted."

"He said you got the owner to finally sell it. He made it sound like a big deal."

"I didn't sell it. One of our agents did. I don't get involved in those things."

"Grandfather said you must have been involved or it wouldn't have sold."

That's interesting. Perhaps my father has finally realized that I'm the one behind the success of our Connecticut office. He'd never admit that to me, but making that comment to my daughter, he had to have known she would tell me. I smile at that, pleased with myself.

"He said he taught you how to close a deal," Addison says.

Of course he would say that. I should've known my father's comment wasn't meant to praise me but to compliment himself. He takes credit for all my accomplishments. He loves to remind me, and everyone else, that he taught me everything I know. And if I do something he doesn't like, he blames it on my mother.

"Mom, I have to go. I'm on my way to meet up with a friend."

"Go ahead, dear. We'll talk later."

I end the call as another call comes in. I check the time, pleased that he's punctual. I was doubtful when Blaire hired this young man, but he's proven to be quite useful. He's willing to do most anything for money, which I suppose makes sense given his background. I was hoping Blaire would be just as easily coerced by money, but she's proving to be more difficult. Hopefully, after the little chat we had today, she'll get back in line.

"Hello, Troy," I say, easing back into my chair.

"Hey, Mrs. Rockingham. It's all set. I'm going there tomorrow. I'll go over in the morning, after her husband leaves."

"How did she seem when you were there? She didn't appear suspicious at all, did she?"

"No. She seemed relieved that I was going to take a look at it."

"What about her husband? Did she mention him?"

"Only to say he doesn't know anything about fixing stuff. Hey, if any of this comes back to me, you'll take care of it, right?"

"Of course. I can't have you getting locked up again." I smile. "I expect to have many more projects for you in the future."

"So when do I get my money?"

"Part of it will be delivered today. You'll receive the rest when the job is complete. And by complete, I mean she'll no longer be a problem."

"Yeah, got it."

"This will be our last discussion until I need your services again. Do you understand?"

"Yes, Mrs. Rockingham. I understand."

"Very good. Goodbye, Troy."

That's one problem solved. Blaire should thank me for this, but I'm not going to tell her. Now that she's suddenly found her morals, she'd try to talk me out of it. But I'm doing this for her own good. Alice is a meddling nuisance who's determined to get revenge on Blaire for being with Rob. She's already spreading rumors about Blaire so that potential home-owners won't want to work with her. Just last week at the country club, I overheard Alice saying that Blaire had offered her body to a married man if he agreed to buy a house that far exceeded the amount he wanted to pay. It was completely false. Blaire would never do something like that. She knows better, but if you say a rumor enough times, people start to believe it.

So, I really have no choice but to put an end to Alice. Her rumors would not only harm Blaire but the entire Rockingham Group. And really, will anyone miss having Alice around? All the woman does all day is eat, watch television, and spread gossip.

The day I overheard Alice at the country club, she was sit-ting next to Martha, a friend of mine from church. I stopped at Martha's table and told her a made-up story about a pipe bursting in my house and how much damage it had done. I told her my handyman said he'd seen a lot of that lately, something about faulty pipework in newer homes. I said it loud enough for Alice to hear, and being the nosy woman she is, she butted into the conversation, wanting to know what to do to prevent such a catastrophe. I told her to call a handyman and have him check it out, then gave her Troy's number.

Troy will show up at her house tomorrow to inspect the pipes, but he'll really be tampering with her furnace to cause carbon monoxide to leak out. It won't be immediate, but Alice will eventually be poisoned by the gas and die. I'm actually being quite kind. Alice may suffer with a headache, but other than that, it should be a rather painless death. And planning it the way I have, it will all look like an accident.

If Blaire only knew all that I've done for her, perhaps she'd be more grateful. I clearly have to work on her more or get rid of the people who are leading her astray, like that idiot husband of hers. Perhaps that's the answer. I need to get rid of Adam.

CHAPTER 35

Valerie

"He still hasn't done anything?" Alice asks as we wait for our skin to absorb the slimy green substance the esthetician slathered on our faces.

Alice and I are spending our afternoon at the spa. It's her treat, to thank me for my help in taking down Blaire. We both hate her but for different reasons.

For me, it's because I've spent years watching Marcus give Blaire every new construction project, along with all the listings that came in that he could've assigned to anyone. I could never prove it, but I assumed Marcus and Blaire were having an affair. Why else would he give her everything? Marcus isn't at all Blaire's type, but she'll do anything to get ahead, even sleep with an older, overweight man.

She'll also sleep with her neighbor's husband, which is Alice's reason for hating Blaire. When Alice told me Rob and Blaire were having an affair, I wasn't surprised. Blaire's lost all interest in Adam and I've seen how she looks at Rob. But, of course, Blaire claims the affair wasn't her fault. When she confided in me, telling me she'd slept with Rob, she made up this ridiculous story about not being able to remember doing it. It just shows she'll say anything to avoid having to take responsibility for her actions.

Poor Alice. I feel terrible for her. She's done so much for Rob, funding his business, supporting him as he built it into what it is now. But instead of thanking her, he sleeps with Blaire.

I'm sure Blaire initiated it. When she sees something she wants, she goes after it. She doesn't care who gets hurt. Everything's always about her. She uses people to get ahead. For years, I've tried to be her friend, but Blaire just wouldn't make time for me. I mean, sure, she's had me over for dinner and invited me to a few holidays, but that was only to keep me on her good side, in case I ever found out why she was getting such special treatment from Marcus.

I finally learned the truth, and it's all thanks to Alice. She called me about a month ago, asking if I'd like to meet for lunch. It'd been forever since I'd seen her. Alice and I grew up in the same neighborhood. Her house was two houses down from mine. She was several years older than me and always wore fancy clothes. She complained the clothes weren't her style and that her mother dressed her that way, but I thought she looked beautiful. We got to be friends, but it was only for a couple years, until she moved to a different neighborhood.

I'd honestly forgotten about her until she called me. When we met for lunch, she caught me up on her life, telling me all about Rob, their house, where they lived. When it was my turn to talk and I told her where I worked, she asked if I knew Blaire, who just happened to be Alice's next-door neighbor. I told her I'd known Blaire for years. Alice commented that she really didn't like Blaire, and I found myself agreeing with her. I normally wouldn't talk bad about a co-worker to someone outside the office, knowing it could reflect poorly on me, but Alice and I had been friends before so I felt I could tell her what I really thought of Blaire.

The more I told her, the more she told me. That's when I learned about Blaire's affair with Rob. I also found out Blaire had been meeting with Lydia, Marcus' wife. Alice had seen them go into the private dining room at the country club. She'd also seen Blaire's SUV going through the gate at the Rockingham mansion. The mansion is only used for family gatherings. Marcus and Lydia don't live there, so why was Blaire there? Was she meeting with Lydia behind Marcus' back?

I had to know what was going on. I knew Blaire wouldn't tell me, so I tried to listen in whenever Marcus and Blaire were together. Waiting outside Marcus' office would be too obvious so I would wait until Marcus went to Blaire's office, which is directly across from mine. One day, when he was in her office with the door closed, I stood outside it and heard Marcus telling Blaire something about a secret. As they talked, I found out the secret was something related to Marcus. Blaire apparently knew about it and was using it to get Marcus to give her all the new listings that came in. I wasn't sure how, or if, this was connected to Blaire meeting with Lydia, but clearly her involvement with the Rockinghams was the reason why she was so much more successful than the rest of us.

Even though I suspected something was going on, I was furious to find out it was true. No wonder nobody else could get ahead. Blaire owned Marcus. He had to do whatever she said, or she'd tell his secret. I still don't know what the secret is, but it doesn't matter. What matters is that she's blackmailing him and it's hurting the careers of everyone else in the office.

"He took her off the condo project," I say to Alice.

"You already told me that."

"Yes, but I thought she might convince him to give it back to her. As far as I know, he hasn't."

"He should've put you in charge of it, not that other woman."

"I agree, but I'd still rather have Karen in charge than Blaire."

"Did you send Marcus any more messages?"

"Not today. I sent one yesterday."

I've been using a burner phone to text Marcus. I pretend to be Blaire and threaten that I'm going to tell his secret. I was hoping the threats would lead to him firing her or giving her projects to someone else, but weeks went by and nothing happened. Then Blaire told me Marcus gave her that condo project, which was the exact opposite of what I wanted him to do. I told Alice and she suggested I spread a rumor about Marcus and Blaire having an affair. It was perfect because I knew people would believe it. Blaire is always in Marcus' office and the affair would explain why Marcus does so much for Blaire, like planning that huge birthday party for her. The plan worked, and finally, Marcus took action and gave Blaire's condo project to Karen and me.

"The messages don't seem to be working," I say.

"Maybe they are and you just haven't been around to see it. Has Blaire seemed stressed lately? Or has she been acting differently?"

"Yes, but that's because her marriage is falling apart and she thinks someone's trying to kill her."

"Kill her?" Alice laughs. "Are you joking?"

"No. Blaire thinks someone's trying to kill her." I take the cucumber slices off my eyes and see Alice has removed hers as well and is looking at me. "I'm not supposed to tell anyone this, but like I'm really going to listen to Blaire?" I roll my eyes.

"So, what happened? Why does she think someone's trying to kill her?"

"She thinks the night of her party someone pushed her down the stairs." I smile. "She thinks you might've done it."

Alice laughs so hard she starts to cough. She picks up her water bottle and takes a drink. "Blaire really thinks I tried to kill her? She said that?"

"Yes, but she also thinks Adam might've done it. Or the man we hire to do repairs."

"Was it you?" Alice asks with a devilish grin. "Did you push her?"

"No!" I swat at Alice's arm.

Alice shrugs. "I had to ask. You do hate her, after all."

"So do you."

"A lot of people hate her. It could've been anyone."

"Assuming it's even true. With her brain injury, the doctor said any memories she gets back may not be real."

"If someone really wanted to kill her, maybe they'll try again." Alice leans back on the lounger and puts the cucumbers back over her eyes. "Then we'll finally be rid of that bitch."

"That's a little harsh. I mean, I hate her, but I don't want her dead."

"You do. You just don't want to admit it."

Looking over at Alice, I see the grin on her face as she imagines Blaire dead. Sometimes Alice concerns me. I'm not sure she's mentally stable. When we were younger, she'd say some rather disturbing things, like how she wished a girl who bullied her would fall and break her neck. Or one time, when her mother grounded her for coming home drunk, Alice talked about poisoning her mother's coffee. She never did, and I told myself she was just making a joke, but part of me wondered if she was serious. Alice has a dark side to her. I wouldn't be surprised if she pushed Blaire down the stairs, but I know she didn't. She'd tell me if she did.

"Oh, I can't meet for lunch tomorrow," I say, looking at my phone. "I scheduled a showing for noon. It's the only time the couple can see the house."

"That's fine," Alice says. "I've got a repair guy coming over in the morning. He might be there for a few hours. I probably would've had to cancel anyway. What about tonight? You want to meet for drinks later?"

"I can't. I need to catch up on some paperwork at the office. And then I want to swing by the house where we had Blaire's party and take some photos. The house isn't listed for sale yet so we're not supposed to show it, but clients keep asking about it and I thought, what's the harm in showing them photos?"

"I'm guessing Blaire's the listing agent on that one too?" Alice says, sounding annoyed.

"Of course. Who else would Marcus give it to?"

"That woman needs to go. It's the only way you'll get ahead at that place."

She's right, but Blaire's never going to leave the Rockingham Group. She'd have to be forced out, which Marcus would never do.

The only way I'll ever be rid of her is if she's dead, but that's never going to happen. I'm sure that memory she had wasn't real. No one would try to kill Blaire.

CHAPTER 36

Marcus

"Hello, darling," I say as I come into the house.

Lydia is sitting on the sofa, flipping through a fashion magazine. She criticizes me for not doing enough at the office and yet she spends her days shopping, getting facials, and lounging around the house, reading magazines. I'm sick of her hypocrisy. Whatever rules she makes for me somehow don't apply to her.

"You're late," she says, not looking up from the magazine.

"There were issues I had to address at work." I take my coat off and set it on the chair.

"You could've called," she snaps. "Dinner was an hour ago. Terrance needed to go home so he wrapped everything up and put it in the fridge."

Terrance is our chef, but he only takes orders from Lydia. She decides the menu for every meal, along with the timing. Dinner is always precisely at five-thirty, which is much earlier than I'd like, but Lydia insists that eating later than that interferes with her sleep.

"I'm sorry I'm late, dear." I lean down and kiss her cheek, nearly gagging on her perfume. It's too strong and doesn't mix well with her skin, but it's the only one she wears, even though I've given her a dozen other perfumes as gifts, hoping she'd at least try them. She didn't, of course, and I'm certain it's because she knows her perfume makes me ill and she wants me to suffer.

The woman hates me. I feel the same way about her. I used to love my wife, but that was years ago, when I thought she felt the same way about me. But soon after our wedding, I realized she only married me to anger her father. He'd already chosen a man for her, but she went against her father's wishes and married me instead. She used me, and is still using me. Controlling me. Making my life miserable.

I can't do it anymore. I can't spend the latter half of my life being controlled by this woman. I need my freedom. I need to finally do what I want and make my own decisions. My daughters will be upset when she's gone, but they'll get over it. They were never that close to her anyway. Neither one of them is like Lydia. They're not controlling and they don't get pleasure from making others miserable. I'd like to think they're more like me, but the younger me, not the person I am now. Spending all these years shackled to my angry, vengeful, unhappy wife has made me hopeless, depressed, and always on edge, worried about what Lydia will do next. If I don't get rid of her, I may never be able to return to the man I was before I met her. The easy-going man who had joy in his life and hope for the future.

"I assume you ate without me?" I say.

"Of course." Lydia tosses her magazine on the couch. "You know I can't eat past six. I wouldn't get a good night's rest."

"I'm terribly sorry, dear. The time got away from me."

Lydia sniffs the air. "Go change your shirt. You smell like the office."

"I wasn't aware the office had a smell."

"It's the smell of paper," she says, scrunching her nose. "Like the children's backpacks when they'd come home from school. It's not at all pleasant."

"I'll go up and change." I'm heading to the staircase when I hear her talking again.

"Wear the white shirt with the navy blazer," she says. "And the gray pants. The light gray, not the dark."

"Yes, dear," I mutter through gritted teeth.

I'm a grown man and not even allowed to pick out my own clothes. Lydia buys them for me and tells me what to wear, even if we're just sitting around the house. It's infuriating, and there's nothing I can do about it. I've tried standing up to her, but it only made her more determined to control me. So I gave up. Gave in. Let her have her way. It was either that or divorce her, but divorcing her would mean losing everything. Lydia would take it all and leave me with nothing. She'd use her influence and connections to destroy me.

That's why I have to do this. It's my only option. I wish there was another way, but there's not. Lydia's given me no choice but to take drastic measures to end this. It's a wonder I've made it this many years. I only did because of the one area where Lydia doesn't control me. The secret I've kept from her for our entire marriage. I'm always worried she'll find out, which is both good and bad. Fearing what she'd do to me if she found out is bad, but having this part of my life she doesn't know about is wickedly good. It's thrilling in a way I can't even describe. The feeling has become an addiction. Every time I go to the club, I feel like I'm getting away with something. Every time I lie to Lydia about where I've been, I feel like I'm getting revenge against her for putting me in this prison.

When Blaire found out my secret, I felt completely deflated, like all the air had been let out of the balloon and the fun was over. I was certain she'd tell Lydia, but instead, Blaire sat down with me in my office and said she wasn't going to tell my wife, or anyone else. I assumed she'd want something for her silence, but she told me she didn't. She said she didn't want to cheat her way to the top. She wanted to earn her way there.

I didn't believe her, but weeks went by and Blaire kept quiet. Months passed, and Blaire still didn't tell Lydia my secret, but I kept worrying she would. So, just to be safe, I gave Blaire all the new business that came in. Whatever wasn't already assigned to someone else went to Blaire. I told her it was because she was such an excellent agent, which she was, but we both knew the real reason I sent so much business her way.

All these years, Blaire has never threatened to tell on me, until just recently, when she began sending me threatening text messages. The first one said, *I'm going to tell your secret. Soon everyone will know.* Similar messages followed, but none of them said why she was doing this or when she was going to tell on me.

What I did next is something I didn't want to do, but just like with Lydia, Blaire didn't give me a choice. She made me do it.

The night it happened, I thought it was over, but no. As usual, Blaire came out ahead.

I took it as a sign to give her another chance. I tried talking to her. I told her to stop sending those messages. I asked her why she was doing it. Was she really going to tell Lydia that I liked playing dress-up and doing things with men? Or was this some kind of game Blaire was playing to get me to do even more for her?

When the threatening texts continued, I decided it was time to show Blaire what it's like to live in a constant state of fear and uncertainty. I hired a man to follow her and give her a threatening note. It was a warning. Her last one. But she didn't seem to care. Nothing changed. The threatening texts kept coming.

By that point, I was done. There would be no more special treatment. No more rewards. I took away her condo project and made a new plan.

This time, she wouldn't be so lucky. I'd make sure of it.

"Marcus!" Lydia shouts as I'm coming downstairs. "What is taking so long?"

"I'm right here, dear." I walk up to her as she stands in the hallway.

She looks me up and down while I wait to see if I pass her inspection.

"That shirt looks tight on you. Have you gained weight?"

"I don't believe so, but I'll be sure to weigh myself in the morning and adjust my diet accordingly."

"Good." She smiles. "It's always best to take action before a problem gets worse."

I couldn't agree more, which is why I'm taking action on the problem in front of me.

Things will never get better with Lydia. They'll only get worse. So I'm doing as she said and taking action.

CHAPTER 37

Marcus

"What would you like tonight, dear?" I ask, referring to Lydia's nightly cocktail. She always has one after dinner. "Perhaps an old-fashioned?"

"No. I'm not in the mood for that. I'll have a glass of wine."

Good. It'll mix better with wine, although it'd be more lethal with hard liquor.

We go into the drawing room. It's actually the formal living room, but Lydia insists we call it the drawing room. If I don't, she corrects me.

"What kind of wine?" I ask, going over to the bar while Lydia sits down on one of the leather chairs that flank the fireplace. "Red or white?"

"Red. A cabernet."

I take one from the wine cabinet and bring it over to her. "Will this do?"

She takes the bottle and inspects it. "Yes, and be sure to use the proper glass."

After all these years, she still feels the need to remind me of this, as if I don't know what glass to use. I'm not an idiot.

Does she think I'm going to serve her red wine in a martini glass?

As I'm opening the wine, I look back and see her watching me. How am I going to do this? The crushed pills are in my pocket. I need to take out the bag, pour the powder in the wine, and mix it up, all without her noticing.

"Was that the door?" I ask, turning back to Lydia.

"Stop talking nonsense and pour my wine."

"Darling, I'm certain I heard someone ring the door. Perhaps you should go check."

"No one is at the door. They'd have to get through the gate before they got to the door."

"You're right," I say with a nervous laugh. "I don't know what I was thinking."

That was a careless thing to say. I can't have Lydia suspecting something's up. I need to focus, but I'm terrified this won't work, which is making me not think straight.

"Here you go, dear." I hand her the glass of wine. I'll have to find another way to get the pills in her. Maybe in the next glass.

"Aren't you having some?" she asks.

"I believe I'll have a scotch," I say.

"We've already opened the wine," she says, implying that's what I should have.

I feel like challenging her and just having the scotch, but that could make her suspicious and ruin my plan.

"It's quite dry," she says, taking a sip of the wine.

"Do you not like it?" I ask, sitting down with the wine I didn't want.

"It's acceptable." She takes another sip. "I spoke with Addison today."

"And? How is she?"

"She was fretting about the wedding details. She wanted my input."

I feel guilt rising inside me, knowing I'll be taking my daughters' mother from them. But it has to be done. If my girls knew how miserable I was with their mother, they'd understand.

"Did you assist her?" I ask.

"I told her to ask the wedding planner for input. That's what we're paying her for, after all."

I'm surprised Lydia's been so hands off with our daughter's wedding plans. I thought she'd want to decide every little detail, but the only part of it she's been involved in is Addison's wedding dress and the bridesmaids' gowns. When it comes to our girls, Lydia seems to pick and choose what to control in their lives. With me, she controls everything. I've never understood that.

"I assume you paid the bill from the caterer," Lydia says, swirling the wine in her glass.

"What bill?"

"The money we owe to reserve the caterer. I put the bill in your office."

"I don't recall seeing it. Where did you leave it?"

She sets her wine glass on the table and gets up. "Honestly, Marcus, I don't know how you can be your age and still be this irresponsible." She walks out of the room.

She's gone. This is my chance!

Reaching into my pocket, I pull out the bag of crushed pills, keeping watch on the door. I pour the powder into Lydia's wine and mix it in with my finger. I lick the wine off my finger and shove the empty bag in my pocket just as Lydia returns.

"Here." She shoves the bill at me. "Pay it first thing tomorrow and make sure you apply a stamp and put it in a mailbox."

I hate the way she describes in detail how to do the most basic things. She does it all the time, to make sure I know what she thinks of me. She even does it when we're in public, just to humiliate me.

As she drinks her wine, I try not to smile. I try to hide the giddiness I feel as I anticipate the taste of freedom. I've been controlled for so long that it'll take me a while to believe I'm actually free. I'll probably spend the next year looking over my shoulder to see if Lydia's there, waiting to tell me what I did wrong and what I should be doing instead.

"Would you like another glass?" I ask as Lydia finishes her wine.

"Yes. One more."

I pour her another glass, wondering how long it'll be before she's dead. She'll fall asleep first, which should be soon given how many pills I gave her. They're Lydia's prescription sleeping pills and are quite strong. Taking too many can be deadly. Taking them with alcohol makes them even more deadly.

If she's not dead tonight, she'll definitely be dead by the morning. I'll call for an ambulance, but it'll be too late. An autopsy will be done, which will find the pills combined with the wine caused her death. It'll be ruled an accidental overdose or perhaps a suicide. They won't consider I did it, because I wasn't here. I forgot something at the office and had to go back. When I got home later, Lydia was asleep in bed. In the morning, I woke up and found she wasn't breathing. That's the story I'll tell if I'm asked.

"Lydia?" I say it loud to see if she'll hear me.

She doesn't respond. Her head is hung forward and her eyes are shut.

It's started. The pills are working.

"Lydia." I reach over and poke her arm. "Did you fall asleep, dear?"

She's out cold. I dump my wine and clean out the glass, then go over to Lydia and pick her up.

"You must be tired," I say. "Let me help you to bed."

I bring her upstairs to our room and put her into our bed.

"Goodnight, darling." I smile as I say it, knowing it's the last time I will say those words.

Going back downstairs, I grab my keys and go out to my car. As I'm driving away from the house, I call Blaire.

"Hello, Marcus," she answers.

"Blaire, I'm sorry to call this late, but an issue came up with the house on Lyndale. The builder called and said he wants your opinion on where the cabinets should go for the basement bar. The guys are installing them tomorrow, so he needs to know tonight."

"I thought they'd already decided where the cabinets would go. It's in the mocked-up plans."

"There was an error in the plans. The measurements were off, so now the cabinets have to go on another wall or they'll have to come up with a whole new design for the bar. I know it's a lot to ask, but would it be possible for you to go over there?"

"I suppose I could. I was on my way home, but I can turn around."

"Thank you, Blaire. I really appreciate this."

"Sure. I'll call Nick when I'm done and let him know my thoughts."

"Call me instead. I don't want you calling Nick this late."

"It's not late," she says with a laugh. "It's just after seven. And you just told me he had to know tonight."

"I meant before his workers get there tomorrow. Nick's out with his wife tonight, and I hate to bother him. One of us can talk to him first thing in the morning."

"Um, okay. I should be there in about twenty minutes. I'll let you know what I think."

"Great. Thanks, Blaire." I end the call.

Twenty minutes is perfect. It gives me time to get over there and get ready for her arrival.

I didn't want to do this, Blaire, but you gave me no choice. I want my freedom, not just from my wife but from you as well. But you won't let me have it. You keep threatening me, holding this secret over me. Even with Lydia gone, you'll still threaten to expose me, knowing something like that would ruin my reputation and my career.

You had a second chance, Blaire, but you blew it. So I'm forced to try again.

And this time, I'll make sure you're dead.

CHAPTER 38

Blaire

Something about this doesn't seem right. How could the measurements for the cabinets be off? The design software doesn't make mistakes like that, and Nick always double-checks the measurements before he orders the supplies.

"Hey, babe," Adam says, answering my call.

"Hey, I'm going to be late getting home."

"I thought you were almost here."

"I was, but Marcus needs me to check something at the house where we had my party. There's an issue with the cabinets for the basement bar."

"You want me to meet you over there? I don't like the idea of you going there alone after what happened."

"That's sweet of you to offer, but I'll be fine. I won't be there long. Probably not more than ten minutes, then I'll head home."

"Caitlyn, turn down the heat for the sauce," Adam says to her. "Your mom's going to be late."

"You guys don't have to wait for me. Just go ahead and have dinner."

243

"Hold on," he says. "Caitlyn, I'll be right back."

"Where are you going?" she says, but her voice is distant, like Adam left the room.

"Blaire, we had a deal," Adam says, lowering his voice. "We do stuff as a family now. We agreed we'd have dinner together, all three of us."

"I know, but it's just this once."

"That's how it starts, and before you know it, it's every night. We can't do this again. We agreed we wouldn't let ourselves go back to that."

"You're right," I say, loving that he's so committed to this. He really wants our marriage to work, and so do I. "We'll eat when I get home."

Adam and I have been talking a lot since that night I told him what happened to me at the party. I feel like we're finally going back to how we used to be. We're opening up to each other, trusting each other, and feeling the love for each other that we thought was gone.

"Call when you're heading home," Adam says, "so I can get everything heated up."

"I will. What are you two making?"

"Spaghetti and meatballs. Real meatballs, not those frozen ones. Caitlyn found a recipe online."

"Sounds wonderful." I smile as I imagine the two of them cooking together.

When Adam and I were talking the other night, I told him he needs to be more involved with Caitlyn. She needs her dad, although she'd never admit that. She needs her mom too, which is one of the reasons I wanted to leave here and get a fresh start somewhere else.

But Lydia won't let me. She's determined to hold me hostage here. If I tried to move away, just took off without telling anyone, she'd find me. I know she would. She has that kind of power.

I used to respect Lydia and look up to her, but that was before I knew what she was really like. Marcus used to tell me how horrible she was and how she had to control everything, but I thought he was exaggerating or that he just perceived her to be that way because they had a bad marriage.

Lydia was never cruel or controlling with me. She was always kind and supportive, cheering me on in my career. Now I see that was all an act. She's just as horrible as Marcus described, maybe even worse. She wants to take control of every part of my life, including my personal life. I'm worried she's going to try to coerce me into divorcing Adam. I'd tell her no, of course, but Lydia doesn't take no for an answer. She always gets her way. But what does that mean? Would she do something to Adam to get him out of my life?

I don't think she'd go to that extreme, but maybe she would. She's already gone too far by ordering me to stay here. I need to talk to Adam about that, but I already know what he'll say. He'll call Lydia crazy and say we're still going to leave and not to worry about her. He doesn't understand that it's more complicated than that. When Lydia orders you to stay, you don't have a choice in the matter. She won't allow you to leave.

Maybe Marcus could help me. He knows Lydia better than anyone. He'd have some advice for me, although it probably wouldn't work given that he can't even help himself. He's still chained to her and probably always will be. He desperately wants out of his marriage but is scared to death to leave her. I used to think he was weak and a coward for that, but now I get it. The woman is frightening.

When I get to the house, I see Marcus' car in the driveway. What is he doing here? He didn't say he was stopping over. Maybe he wants to see the cabinet issue for himself before he talks to Nick tomorrow.

"Marcus?" I say, going into the house. It's dark except for the light coming from the kitchen. I flip on the recessed lights in the living room. "Marcus, where are you?"

"Right here." He comes out from the kitchen, a big grin on his face. "I thought I'd stop by so we could go over the cabinet issue together."

"Sure." I smile. "You seem to be in a good mood. Any reason why?"

He clears his throat. "I talked to Addison on the way over. She's getting quite excited about the wedding. I love hearing how happy she is. It puts me in a good mood."

"That's wonderful! She'll make a beautiful bride." I walk toward him. "Is Lydia planning a trip to New York to help with the wedding plans?"

"No." He coughs and looks behind him. "She's letting the wedding planner handle it."

"Is something wrong?" I ask, noticing he's suddenly acting strange, almost nervous.

"I just had something in my throat." He rubs the front of his neck. "Should we head down there? Check out the basement?"

"In a minute. I wanted to talk to you first."

"About what?"

I walk past Marcus to the kitchen as he follows behind. I stop next to the center island and set my purse down.

"Are you feeling okay?" I ask Marcus, noticing sweat beading up on his forehead.

"I feel fine. What did you want to talk about?"

He glances behind him at the door that goes to the basement. His hands are at his sides, but he keeps clenching them into fists, then relaxing them. He's acting very agitated and fidgety. Just a minute ago, he seemed fine. Happy. Almost giddy. And then he suddenly changed. It happened right after I asked him about Lydia. Maybe she did something to upset him and when I mentioned her name, it reminded him of it.

"We can talk later," I say, deciding this isn't a good time. Marcus seems distracted. I need to talk to him about Lydia when he's alert and focused, maybe tomorrow morning.

"Should we go downstairs?" He grins and motions to the door to the basement. "Ladies first."

Something doesn't feel right. I can't figure out what, but my gut's telling me not to go down there.

"What are you waiting for?" Marcus asks. "Don't you want to hurry this up so you can get home?"

"You go ahead." I get out my phone. "I need to check something."

A text alert chimes on Marcus' phone. He looks at it, his expression turning grim. "You're doing this *now*? When you're right in front of me?"

I glance up from my phone. "Doing what?"

He shoves his phone in my face and I see a text that reads:

Time's running out. I'm telling your secret.

"I didn't send that," I tell him. "How could I? I'm standing right here."

"Holding a phone." He grabs it from me and tosses it on the floor.

"Marcus! What are you doing?" I reach for my phone, but he gets in front of me.

"Why are you doing this, Blaire?" He steps forward, forcing me back against the counter. "I've given you everything. What else could you possibly want?"

"Marcus, I promise you I didn't send that." My pulse races as I see the rage on his face, the darkness in his eyes. "That wasn't sent from my number. It was from someone else."

"Someone you hired," he spits out. "Or maybe it's your husband. You two are probably in on this together. Guess I'll be taking care of him next."

"Taking care of him?" I take a shaky breath. "Marcus, what is going on?"

"It's over, Blaire. I'm done being controlled. By you. By my wife. I can't do it anymore. I'm taking back my freedom. Even with Lydia gone, this will never end. You'll threaten to expose me if I don't give you money and whatever else you want." He plants his hands on the counter on either side of me, caging me in as he leans down to my face. "It'll never be

247

enough. You'll always want more. You'll never be satisfied. You'll just keep wanting more and more."

"What do you mean . . . with Lydia gone?"

"She's gone." He laughs a little. "She fell asleep and won't be waking up."

He killed her. Marcus killed her! I didn't think he was capable of it, but he did it. He really did it!

I have to get out of here. I have to get away from him. But how? Marcus has me backed against the counter.

His eyes lock on mine. "I did everything for you. Gave you everything you wanted. And still, you wouldn't let it go. You keep threatening to tell."

"That wasn't me. I promise you, I didn't send those texts."

"You can stop denying it. It doesn't matter now. Because this is ending. It ends tonight."

"What . . . what do you mean?"

"I gave you so many chances, Blaire. After you survived the first time, I was going to let you live. I thought after almost dying, you'd realize the danger you were putting yourself in by continuing to threaten me. But the threats didn't stop. They just kept coming. You wouldn't give up, even when I had you followed. I thought that would scare you into keeping quiet but it didn't. You left me with no options, Blaire. There's only one way to end this."

It was Marcus. He's the one who pushed me down the stairs. He wanted me dead. He planned that party for me, knowing that was the night he was going to do it. He made sure everything was outside — the food, the drinks, the music — so my guests would be out there and not inside. Then he waited until I was alone in the house and shoved me down the stairs.

This whole time, I never suspected it was Marcus. But it was him all along.

Marcus pushed me down the stairs.

He tried to kill me.

And now he's going to try again.

248

CHAPTER 39

Blaire

"You don't have to do this," I say to Marcus, my voice shaking. "I'll leave town. I'll go far away. I'll never—"

"Stop talking!" he yells. "This isn't a negotiation!"

He's breathing hard and his neck is turning red.

I look him in the eye. "I have a daughter. She's only fifteen. She needs me."

His expression softens and he sighs. "I didn't want to do this. You know this isn't me. I just . . . I can't do this anymore." He takes his hands off the counter and leans back, lifting his arm to wipe the sweat off his forehead.

I take the opportunity to sneak past him and run to the sliding glass door.

"Blaire!" Marcus tries to grab me but misses.

I make it outside and run to the fence door. Swinging it open, I race to the driveway, straight to my SUV.

The door is locked. And I don't have my keys! They're in the house.

"Where could Blaire be?" Marcus yells in a tone that sounds like we're playing hide-and-seek. "Where oh where could she be?"

What do I do? I could try running down the road, but I'd be running for miles. There's nothing out here but this house. Someday this will all be a neighborhood, but right now it's just this house on a dead-end street, surrounded by woods.

"I'm coming for you, Blaire!" Marcus yells. He's getting closer. I hear him walking around the side of the house.

Running back inside, I close the door behind me.

I hear Marcus talking. "Are you out here, Blaire? There's no use hiding. You know I'll find you."

The man is crazy. He's completely lost it. Or maybe he's always been crazy and I just didn't know it.

"Blaire!" Marcus yells as he opens the door.

Why didn't I lock it? I could've locked him out!

As he comes into the house, I race to the basement door and fling it open and flick on the light above the stairway. Then I dart into the pantry that's just off the kitchen, directly across from the basement door. It's a long, narrow room with shelving and cupboards. I hide in one of the bottom cupboards as I hear Marcus' footsteps getting closer.

"I know you're in here, Blaire. Hiding from me is pointless. You know I'm going to find you."

He's in the kitchen now, his shoes making a loud, clicking noise as he walks around the wood floor.

My heart's beating so fast I feel like it's in my throat. I try to think of anything I could use as a weapon. I might have something in my purse, but my purse is on the kitchen counter.

If only I could get to my purse, I'd have my keys. I could leave.

I'll wait for Marcus to go upstairs. Then I'll grab my purse and get the hell out of here.

The pantry door opens and I hear Marcus walking in.

Oh, God, he's here! He's going to find me! He's going to open this cabinet and find me!

I hold my breath and try not to make a sound.

"I don't have time for this, Blaire. Just come out so we can end this."

The room goes silent, then I hear his footsteps leaving the pantry.

He's gone. He didn't find me. Maybe he'll look upstairs now.

I slowly open the cabinet and quietly crawl out of it. I take off my shoes and tiptoe to the pantry door. As I'm about to open it, I hear Marcus again.

"That's clever, Blaire. Turning on the light? Making it look like you're down there?"

Opening the pantry door just a crack, I see Marcus staring down at the basement, his back to me.

This is my chance. I don't know if it'll work, but I have to try.

Whipping open the pantry door, I run up behind Marcus and shove him as hard as I can.

He stumbles forward, reaching for the railing but missing it. I watch as he falls head first down the stairs, his skull banging against the wood, his heavy body hurling forward, over and over, until finally landing on the concrete floor with a thud.

I stand at the top of the stairs, staring down at Marcus. His eyes are closed and his neck is twisted to the side, far more than it should be. The fall must've snapped his neck, which could very well mean that he's dead.

I'm tempted to go down there and check, but I can't make myself do it. What if he's not dead? What if he suddenly wakes up and grabs me, like what always happens in horror movies?

I can't go down there. It's too risky. So I do what he did to me. I shut off the light and close the door.

Going back to the kitchen, I grab my purse and my phone, then put on my shoes and leave the house, locking the door behind me.

When I'm safely in my SUV, I speed down the deserted road, wanting to get as far away as possible from that house. If Marcus isn't dead already, he will be by tomorrow when the work crew arrives.

I just killed someone. A man I've known for years and used to consider a friend. But it was him or me. He wasn't going to let me leave there alive.

This didn't have to happen. If Lydia is truly dead, Marcus didn't need to do this. I would've been free to move away. Marcus wouldn't have had to worry about me knowing his secret because I'd be gone.

Maybe that wouldn't have mattered to him. Maybe he'd think my moving away wouldn't change anything. That I'd come back, asking for money, and this would never be over. I'll never know because he never gave me a chance to tell him I was leaving.

When I get home, Caitlyn and Adam are in the living room watching TV.

"You're home," Adam says, getting up to greet me. He gives me a kiss. "I thought you were going to call on the way."

"Yes, sorry, I forgot."

"So can we eat now?" Caitlyn says. "I'm starving."

"Yeah, go see if the sauce is still hot," Adam tells her.

She runs off to the kitchen.

"You okay?" Adam says, putting his hand on my shoulder as I set my purse down. "You look kind of . . . sick. Did something happen when you were at that house? Did you have more flashbacks?"

"Actually, I didn't go." I force out a smile. "Marcus said he'd go over there instead. But since I was already out that way, I ran some errands I've been meaning to do on that side of town. I should've called to let you know, but I didn't think it'd take that long."

"Don't worry about it. I'm just glad you're home."

"It's ready!" Caitlyn yells from the kitchen.

The three of us have dinner in the dining room. The homemade meatballs and sauce are delicious, but I'm having a hard time eating after what just happened. I decided it's best if Adam doesn't know. That's why I told him I wasn't there.

As we're cleaning up dinner, my phone rings from the counter.

Caitlyn glances at the screen. "It's Val. Can I answer it?"

"No, we're not talking to her."

"Mom, c'mon. Just because you two are fighting doesn't mean I can't talk to her."

"She said no," Adam says. "Go get the rest of the dishes."

My phone goes to voicemail, then starts ringing again.

"It's Val again," I say, picking up my phone. "She doesn't usually call this late. I wonder what she wants."

"Are you going to answer it?"

I nod, answering her call as I walk to the living room.

"What is it, Val?"

"Blaire! Thank God you picked up! I need help! I don't know what to do!" Her voice is higher than normal and she's talking really fast.

"Where are you?"

"At the house. The one where we had your party. I came to take some pictures and . . ." She breaks down crying. "He's dead! Marcus is dead!"

"Wait. Slow down. Tell me exactly what happened."

"When I got here, I saw Marcus' car in the driveway so I went inside and looked all over for him but couldn't find him." She sniffles. "Then I opened the door to the basement and there he was. Dead! At the bottom of the stairs!"

"Are you sure he's dead?"

"Yes. I checked for a pulse. He's definitely dead. What do I do?"

"Call the police."

"What if they think I did it? I'm the only one here."

"That doesn't mean you killed him. It was an accident. He must've fallen down the stairs."

"What if the police think I was involved? You said someone pushed you. What if the police think I pushed Marcus?"

"They wouldn't. You have no reason to."

"The police might think I did, if they found out about the messages. They could use that as a motive."

"What messages?"

She sniffles. "I was sending him texts. It was stupid. I shouldn't have done it. It didn't even make a difference."

Valerie was the one sending those texts to Marcus. She must've overheard us talking and found out I knew a secret about him.

"What did the texts say?" I ask.

"It doesn't matter. He's dead! Marcus is dead! What do I do? Should I just leave and let someone else find him?"

"No. Call the police. Nothing's going to happen to you. You didn't do anything wrong."

"Yes. Okay. I'll call them. I'll call right now."

I look at my phone and see she ended the call.

"What's going on?" Adam says, coming up behind me. "That sounded pretty serious."

"Valerie's at the house where I had my party." I turn to Adam. "She found Marcus there. Dead."

"Holy shit, are you serious?"

"Apparently, he fell down the stairs."

"Just like you," Adam says in a suspicious tone. "Or I guess you didn't fall."

"I did," I say, deciding to go with the original story rather than the truth. Adam doesn't need to know what really happened. It's over now. Marcus is no longer a threat to me, and I'd rather have Adam think I fell than have to explain why Marcus tried to harm me.

"You said you were pushed," he says.

"Yes, well, after thinking about it, I realized that didn't actually happen. It was just a false memory like we originally suspected."

"So, it was just an accident? And now the same thing happened to Marcus?"

"Yes. What an odd coincidence."

"Really odd," Adam says, again in that suspicious tone.

254

"I kept telling Marcus those stairs were dangerous. He didn't believe me. Anyway, Valerie wasn't sure what to do. I told her to call the police and wait there until they arrive."

"Why did Val call *you* about this? You two aren't even friends anymore."

"She values my advice. She always has. We should finish cleaning up." I walk past him to the kitchen.

"You don't seem that upset about this," Adam says, joining me by the sink. "You worked with the guy for twenty years."

"Yes, but we weren't close." I glance at Adam as I rinse the dishes. "What would you like me to do? Start sobbing? You know I'm not a crier, Adam." I turn the faucet off and dry my hands. "How about we have some dessert? Did you and Caitlyn make anything?"

"No, but there's ice cream in the freezer."

"Dish some out for us. Ice cream sounds wonderful."

Adam's still looking at me in a suspicious way. He knows something's up, but I'm hoping he's smart enough to know not to ask questions.

We have the ice cream, along with some cookies Adam found in the cabinet.

Now that I know Marcus is dead, my appetite has returned.

I'm free. Free of Marcus. Free from his secret. Free from Lydia.

I can get away from this place and start over.

CHAPTER 40

A Month Later
Blaire

"It's a beautiful house," I say to Mark and Alexis as we stand in the driveway. "I'm sure your family will be very happy here."

"We definitely will," Alexis says, smiling up at her husband. "I could feel this house was right for us the second we walked in. Don't you agree, honey?"

"Um, sure," he says, not sounding the least bit sure.

Alexis turns to me. "You know when you feel like something just has a good energy to it?" She laughs. "Mark doesn't get it, but I'm very sensitive to those things, and this house . . ." She gazes at it. "It has a really good energy to it."

She wouldn't think that if she knew a man was killed here. But that's something she'll never know. Nobody will. Only I know what really happened to Marcus.

When the police showed up here the night Marcus died, they assumed it was an accident. But the next morning, when they found Lydia dead in her bedroom, they got suspicious. An investigation was started but ended a week later, with Lydia's death being ruled a suicide and Marcus' death an accident.

I found it rather convenient that the investigation ended soon after Artis Rockingham arrived in town. Artis is Lydia's father and the president and CEO of the Rockingham Group. He was here for just a couple days, but in that short time, the investigation into Lydia's and Marcus' deaths came to a sudden halt. I don't know if the police just decided that the original causes of death were correct or if Artis made some kind of deal with them to end the investigation. Given Artis Rockingham's vast wealth and power, I'm guessing a deal was made, one that came with a large sum of money.

I was relieved when the investigation was dropped. While it was going on I was a nervous wreck, worried the police would somehow link Marcus' death back to me, but they never even considered me. The police interviewed Valerie, not as a suspect but to ask her questions about the night she found him. She was so afraid they'd arrest her after the interview, she took several days off from work to recover from all the stress. When she returned to the office, I told her to get her things and leave. It was my first official act as Marcus' replacement.

The position is only temporary. I'm not a broker, so I can't actually replace Marcus, and I have no desire to. If I'd been able to, I would've resigned weeks ago and spent that time packing to leave town. But that would've looked suspicious. Plus, it's not that easy to pick up and leave when I have a house full of belongings and a child in school. Adam and I are still committed to moving, but we haven't decided where to go. I'm in more of a hurry to leave than he is, which is surprising since he was always the one wanting to get away from here. But I think that was more because of what living here did to our marriage. Now that it's back on track and we're becoming closer as a couple, Adam isn't in such a rush to go. But Adam doesn't know the truth about Lydia and Marcus. He doesn't know about the Rockinghams and the power they have to control people.

With Lydia and Marcus gone, I thought I'd be free to leave. But then Artis showed up. He came into the office not seeming the least bit sad that his daughter and son-in-law had died. He introduced himself to me, then told me I'd be managing the office until a replacement was found. I wanted to tell him no, but I knew he wouldn't accept no for an answer.

So here I am, running the office and counting the days until I can leave. I told Artis I wouldn't be staying. He didn't respond when I told him. He just gave me a slight smile that eerily reminded me of Lydia's smile.

Mark looks over at me. "So, about the price. Is there any room to negotiate?"

"I'm afraid not. Given how many people are interested in this house, I wouldn't be surprised if we get some offers that are above the asking price. If you really want it, I'd get the offer in today so you don't lose it or end up in a bidding war."

Mark rubs his jaw as he gazes at the house. "It's a lot more than I wanted to pay."

"But, honey, it's perfect for us," Alexis says.

"As for the price," I say to Mark. "You should consider it an investment. You'll have the first home in a new development. The prices will only go up from here. Being the first, you're getting a bargain. If and when you decide to sell, this house will be worth far more than it costs now."

He lets out a long sigh. "Okay, let's do it."

"Great!" I give them both a big smile. "Let's meet back at my office and we'll get the paperwork started."

"I'm so excited!" Alexis squeals as she looks at the house. "I love it! I absolutely love it!"

I'm glad they decided to buy it, not just because I wanted it sold but because I think they truly will be happy here. They'll fill it with good memories to wipe out all the bad. I doubt they'll ever know what happened here. Very few people do. The Rockingham family used their power and money to cover it up and keep it out of the press. I'm certain that's why Artis shut down the investigation, assuming that's what happened.

On my drive back to the office, Rob calls.

"Good morning, Rob," I say, answering the call.

"Blaire, hi. I'm calling to see if there's been any interest in the house."

"I got a call from a few agents who plan to show it today and there were two over there yesterday."

"That's good, right?"

"It's pretty typical for a new listing. There's a lot of traffic the first week."

Rob moved out of his house the day his wife was found dead in it. He didn't want to be in it after that. He stayed in a hotel, which is where he's still living, but he's moving to Florida this week. After all that's happened, he wanted to get away from here.

When I found out Alice had died, I honestly didn't believe it. Adam had gone home for lunch that day and called me at work, saying the police were next door and that Alice was dead. I thought he must be mistaken, that maybe the police were there for some other reason. But he said he heard the neighbors talking, saying Alice was found dead inside her house and that the cause was believed to be carbon monoxide poisoning.

It's been a month since she died and I still can't believe she's gone. Every time I walk by her house, I think she's going to come out and make some comment about what I'm wearing and how it's not appropriate.

"When do you think we'll get an offer?" Rob asks.

"I can't say for sure, but I'm guessing by next week. Houses in that area tend to sell fast."

"When are you putting yours up for sale?"

"Probably not for another month or two. Adam and I need to decide where we're going first."

"I'm really going to miss you, Blaire."

Rob still has feelings for me, but I have no feelings for him. I never did. What I felt for him was purely attraction. I was bored and frustrated with my marriage and looking outside it for something better. But even when I was spending time with Rob, my heart was still with Adam. He isn't perfect — not by a long shot — but he's perfect for me.

"I'm sure you'll make plenty of new friends in Florida," I tell him. "You're leaving this week?"

"Yeah, but I'll be back to check on my gyms and make sure everything's running okay."

He still owns a few gyms in the area, but now that he's moving away, he's considering selling them.

"I'm almost at the office so I need to go," I tell him. "But I'll let you know if any offers come in."

"Sounds good. Thanks, Blaire."

I end the call and pull into the office parking lot to my reserved spot that still has Marcus' name on it.

"Hey, Blaire," someone says as I step out of my SUV.

"Troy," I say as he walks up to me. "This is a surprise. I don't usually see you at the office."

"I work here now." He has a big grin on his face. "Well, not at the office. I'm just here to sign some paperwork. They hired me full-time. No more of that contract stuff. I got an actual job, with benefits and shit."

Who gave Troy a job? And why didn't anyone tell me? I'm in charge of this office, which means I'm supposed to approve all new hires.

"What do you think?" he says, still grinning. "Cool, huh?"

"It's wonderful. Congratulations!" I glance at the office, then back at Troy. "So, um, who was it that hired you?"

"That old guy. The one who was here a few weeks ago. The one who owns the place."

"Artis? Artis Rockingham?"

"Yeah, that's him. I couldn't remember his name. What kind of name is Artis? I've never heard that before."

"Artis called you? And offered you a job?"

"Yeah. He said he heard I do good work."

"I don't understand. Who told Artis about you?"

"I'm guessing his daughter. That old lady? The one who died? I did some jobs for her. I guess she must've liked my work if she told her dad."

"You worked for Lydia?" I ask, trying to make sense of this because this whole thing is very odd.

Troy is not the type of person Lydia or Artis would want anywhere near them, so why on earth would they hire him? I had to practically beg Marcus to hire Troy for just a few hours a week. He didn't like Troy because of his criminal record. I would think Artis would be concerned about that as well, but apparently not.

"What kind of work were you doing for Lydia?" I ask.

He laughs a little. "I took care of things for her. Let's just leave it at that."

I'm taking that to mean he wasn't doing home repairs.

"You sure you want to do this?" I say, lowering my voice.

"Why wouldn't I? I'm gonna make a ton of money."

"Yes, but once you're involved with these people, it's hard to get out. You should think about this more before signing the paperwork."

He shrugs. "I'm good. I know what I'm getting into." He steps closer to me and whispers, "You don't even want to know the shit I've already done for them. I figure if I was okay doing that, I'll be okay doing whatever else they make me do." He smiles. "As long as they pay me well." He steps back. "I gotta get going. See ya, Blaire."

As he walks to the office, I'm wondering what he meant. What he's done. I know it was something bad, but how bad?

I need to get out of this place, away from the Rockinghams. And I need to do it soon.

CHAPTER 41

Six Months Later
Blaire

"I'll have the paperwork done tomorrow," I say as I'm walking into my office. "I'll call when it's ready. Talk to you soon, Mr. Wilkins."

I end the call and smile when I see Adam behind my desk.

"What are you doing here?"

"Taking you to lunch." He gets up and comes over to give me a kiss. "And don't tell me you don't have time."

"I wasn't going to." I put my arms around him. "I always make time for you."

It wasn't true before, but it is now. Now that I'm finally away from the Rockingham Group and the life I had when I was working there.

Adam, Caitlyn, and I moved to a town just outside of Philadelphia. It's a wealthy community that reminds me a little of the one we left behind. I got my broker's license and opened my own real estate company. I only have one agent working under me, along with an office assistant, but that's enough for now. I'm confident I can grow the company quickly. Just as I did when I moved to Connecticut, I'm getting my name out there, going to social events, meeting people. I'm just as driven as I was before, but this time I'm not going to forget I have a family waiting for me at home. Even when I work nights, I make sure to at least be home for dinner.

"Where are you taking me?" I ask as Adam and I walk hand in hand to the parking lot.

"To that place you keep talking about. The one with the food I can't pronounce? I looked it up and they're open for lunch."

"Adam, we don't have to go there. You're not going to like anything on the menu."

"I'll find something." He opens the car door for me.

Adam never used to do that. He didn't open the car door for me, wouldn't go to restaurants he didn't like. But all that changed when we decided to try to save our marriage. We've both been putting in more effort, doing things for each other we didn't do before, to show that we're committed to making this work.

"My parents called this morning," Adam says as we're driving to the restaurant. "They want to come here in a few weeks."

"That'd be nice," I say. "Did you tell them they could stay with us?"

"Not yet. I wanted to make sure you were good with it."

"Adam, of course they can stay with us. They're family."

"Yeah, but you and my dad—"

"We'll be fine."

I don't like Adam's father. I never have. He makes horrible comments about women and doesn't treat Adam's mother well. But he's an old man in poor health and probably won't be around much longer, so it's important that Adam spend time with him.

"Maybe your parents could come too," Adam says. "I mean, not when my parents are here, but later."

"They can't. Not with my dad's eyesight failing and my mom's fear of driving on the highway."

"I could drive there and get them."

I look at Adam. "You'd really do that?"

"Sure. You think they'd be up for it?"

"They'd love it. And it'd be nice to have them here. They could see the new house and it'd give Caitlyn a chance to spend time with her grandparents."

"Call them tonight. See when they want to come."

"Okay." I smile at my husband, noticing how much happier he is now than when we lived in Connecticut. He hated selling cars, and yet he did it for all those years because of me, because I made him. I feel terrible about that, knowing he was so unhappy.

Now Adam is working as a mechanic, which is what he always wanted to do. He works at a small garage owned by a man and his son. Adam loves it there. He grew up fixing cars, but a lot's changed since then so he's taking auto-repair classes at the community college.

"What do you think about us getting Caitlyn a car?" Adam asks.

Caitlyn's sixteen now and just got her driver's license. She won't admit it, but I think she's happy here. She threw a fit when I told her we were moving, but soon after we got here, she met a boy she likes and suddenly this place wasn't so bad.

"I thought we were going to wait," I say.

"We can, but this guy came into the shop yesterday and is thinking of selling his car. It's small and a few years old, but it's in really good shape. It'd be a good first car for her."

"Could I see it? Is it at the shop?"

"Yeah, we're just doing some maintenance on it. We could go there tonight and look at it."

"We can, but if we get it for her, are you going to take her driving? She needs more practice before I'll feel okay with her driving alone."

"Yeah, I'll take her out." He smiles. "She loves hanging out with her dad."

He says it jokingly, but Caitlyn really does like being with him.

My phone rings as Adam parks in front of the restaurant.

"You need to get that?" he asks.

I look at my phone, my heart racing when I see the name on the screen. Why is he calling me? There's no reason to. I don't work for him anymore.

"Um, no," I say, putting my phone away. "They can leave a message."

As we're walking to the restaurant, my phone rings again. I take it from my purse and see he's calling again.

"You sure you don't want to answer it?" Adam says. "I can go wait in the restaurant."

My heart pounds harder as I consider what to do. "Um, yes, go ahead. I'll meet you in there."

Adam goes into the restaurant as I answer the call.

"Hello, Mr. Rockingham."

"Blaire," he says. "I was starting to wonder if you were ignoring me. But I know you wouldn't do such a thing."

I can ignore him if I want. I'm no longer his employee. So why did I answer his call?

"Mr. Rockingham, I'm on my way to a meeting," I lie, "so if you could just tell me why you're calling . . ."

"You'd like me to get to the point. I'm the same way. I despise idle chit-chat. The reason I was calling was that I'm considering opening an office there. In Philadelphia. I'd never considered it before, but when you mentioned you were moving there, it got me thinking that perhaps I'd be wise to consider it. We've been wanting to expand out of New York, and given how profitable our Connecticut office is, I'm certain we could do just as well elsewhere."

"I don't know about that," I say, noticing my hand shaking as I hold the phone. "This is a completely different market than Connecticut. The office there caters to people who work in Manhattan. They have much higher incomes. They move a lot for their jobs. It's a much more active and profitable market than here."

"Are you implying I haven't done my research? Because I can assure you I have, and if I decide to go forward with this, I'd like you to be in charge. Congratulations, by the way, on getting your broker's license."

"Thank you, Mr. Rockingham, and I appreciate the offer, but I'm working for myself now and doing quite well."

"Yes, well, just think about it. Nothing's definite yet, but if and when it is, perhaps you'll reconsider."

"I'm committed to growing the business I just started, but I'm sure I could help you find someone who's qualified and would do an excellent job."

"I'm sure you could, but I'd prefer to hire someone I know. Someone who can be discreet." He pauses. "Lydia always admired your ability to keep quiet about certain things. She valued your silence and rewarded you because of it. Isn't that right, Blaire?"

How does he know that? Marcus said Lydia never spoke to her father.

"I'm not sure what you mean," I tell him, my hand shaking even more.

"It's such a shame what happened to her. I told her not to marry Marcus. If only she'd listened to me, she wouldn't be dead right now. But at least you finished him off, saving me the trouble. And for that, I feel I should reward you by giving you leadership over the new office, assuming it comes to fruition, of course."

He knows I killed Marcus? And that Marcus killed Lydia? How in the world does he know this? How is it even possible?

"I'll let you run along to your meeting," he says. "Or was it lunch with your husband?"

I look around the parking lot. Where is he? He has to be here. Why else would he say that? I never told him I was having lunch with Adam.

"It was lovely speaking with you, Blaire. Have a wonderful day."

"Blaire." I feel a hand on my back.

I whip around. "Adam! What are you doing out here?"

"I came to see what was taking so long." He puts his hand on my shoulder. "Babe, what's wrong? You're really pale." He glances down at my body. "And you're shaking. Do you need to sit down?"

"No." I swallow, then take a deep breath. "I'm fine. I just thought I might've made an error on a contract I did for one of my buyers, but I can look at it when I'm back at the office."

"Are you sure that's all it is? You seem really upset."

"I'm fine." I put on a smile. "Did you get us a table?"

"Yeah. You ready to go in?"

"Yes, let's go." I take his arm, using it to help me remain upright as we walk to the door. I'm feeling lightheaded after that call. I wish I could tell Adam about it, but I can't. I never want him knowing about my involvement with the Rockinghams. As far as he knows, I just sold houses for them and that was it.

I thought it was over. I thought I'd escaped.

But it appears it doesn't work that way. Moving away from them didn't help.

It's like I told Troy, when you get involved with the Rockinghams, it's hard to get out. I thought I'd found a way, but Artis is trying to pull me back in.

I won't let him. There is no way I'm taking that job. I don't care how much money Artis offers me, I'm not taking it. I like what I'm doing. My life now is better than I ever dreamed it could be and I'm not giving it up to work for Artis.

As I'm seated at the table, looking over the menu, my phone chimes as a text comes in. It's from a number I don't recognize. I unlock my phone and see the text. It's an image.

I enlarge it and see it's a photo of the staircase. The one that almost killed me. The one that killed Marcus.

Another text pops up. It's from the same number.
I nearly pass out when I read what it says.

Just something to look at while you consider my offer.

How does he know? How does Artis know what I did? Does he have proof? He must, or he wouldn't be using this to threaten me.

Was there a camera in the house that night? Does Artis have video of me pushing Marcus down the stairs? Leaving him there to die? If he does, my life is over. I'll spend the rest of it in prison.

"What is it?" Adam asks. "What are you looking at?"

"It's, um, a job offer."

"Job offer? You have your own business."

"Yes, but you never know."

"Never know *what*? You're actually considering taking a job after all the work you did to start your own company?"

"Maybe. I was planning to turn it down." I gaze at the photo of the stairs. "But thinking about it now, I think I'm going to take it."

THE END

THE JOFFE BOOKS STORY

We began in 2014 when Jasper agreed to publish his mum's much-rejected romance novel, and it became a bestseller.

Since then, we've grown into the largest independent publisher in the UK. We're extremely proud to publish some of the very best writers in the world, including Joy Ellis, Faith Martin, Caro Ramsay, Helen Forrester, Simon Brett and Robert Goddard. Everyone at Joffe Books loves reading, and we never forget that it all begins with the magic of an author telling a story.

We are proud to publish talented first-time authors, as well as established writers whose books we love introducing to a new generation of readers.

We won Trade Publisher of the Year at the Independent Publishing Awards in 2023 and Best Publisher Award in 2024 at the People's Book Prize. We have been shortlisted for Independent Publisher of the Year at the British Book Awards for the last five years, and we were shortlisted for the Diversity and Inclusivity Award at the 2022 Independent Publishing Awards. In 2023 we were shortlisted for Publisher of the Year at the RNA Industry Awards, and in 2024 we were shortlisted at the CWA Daggers for the Best Crime and Mystery Publisher.

We built this company with your help, and we love to hear from you, so please email us about absolutely anything bookish at feedback@joffebooks.com.

If you want to receive free books every Friday and hear about all our new releases, join our mailing list here: www.joffebooks.com/freebooks.

And when you tell your friends about us, just remember: it's pronounced Joffe as in coffee or toffee!

www.ingramcontent.com/pod-product-compliance
Lightning Source LLC
Chambersburg PA
CBHW011450170626
46816CB00009B/2610

* 9 7 8 1 8 0 5 7 3 1 5 6 6 *